BOOTLEGGER HEAVEN

The Shelton Gang Story

A Novel

"If history were taught in the form of stories, it would never be forgotten."
~ Rudyard Kipling

Kevin Corley

DEDICATION
For
Sloane Evelyn Corley

Also to:
Author Ruthie Shelton and all the
descendants of the Shelton clan

Special thanks to:
Historian Jon Musgrave

NOTE FROM THE AUTHOR:

As in my previous work, I have taken actual characters and events from Illinois history, imagined some dialogue, and transformed them into novels.

Whenever possible, I have used the actual words historians report were spoken by the characters.

If my interpretation of a person's character sways too far from what historian's report, I have changed the name to that of a fictional character.

Because my readers want to know which events are based on fact and which are fiction, I have, for my last two novels, included a chronology of true events at the end of the books.

For dramatic effect, I have, on occasion, changed the order and date of some events. The chronology at the end specifies the correct order and dates.

I hope this story inspires you to do more research on the subject and uncover the fascinating history that surrounds us.

Also special thanks to the following historians without whose research this book would not have been possible:

Paul M. Angle, *Bloody Williamson: A Chapter in American Lawlessness*, Prairie State Books, 1952.

Taylor Pensoneau. *Brothers Notorious,* Downstate Publications, 1998.

Taylor Pensoneau. *Dapper and Deadly: The True Story of Black Charlie Harris,* Downstate Publications, 2010.

Ralph Johnson and Jon Musgrave. *Secrets of the Herrin Gangs,* IllinoisHistory.com

Ruthie Shelton and Jon Musgrave. *Inside the Shelton Gang: One Daughter's Discovery,* Illinois History.com, 2014.

Daniel Waugh. *Egan Rats: The Untold Story of Prohibition-Era Gang That Rules St. Louis,* Cumberland House Publishing, Inc. 1977.

Daniel Waugh. *Gangs of St. Louis: Men of Respect*, The History Press, 2010.

William Helmer. *Al Capone and His American Boys: Memoirs of a Mobster Wife.* Indiana University Press. 2011.

William J. Helmer & Arthur Bilek. *The St. Valentine's Day Massacre: The Untold Story of the Gangland Bloodbath That Brought Down Al Capone,* Cumberland House, 2004.

Kenneth LaMaster. *Leavenworth Seven: The Deadly 1931 Prison Break*, The History Press, 2019.

Thomas E. Gaddis and James O. Long. *Panzram: A journal of Murder,* Amok Books, 2002.

INTRODUCTION

One of the hardest tasks for an author/historian is to capture a past period of time in all its dimensions. Kevin Corley's *Bootlegger Heaven: The Shelton Gang Story* is a testament to the many hours of extensive research and development it takes to get it right. Bringing to life actual characters and historical events while building a storyline around those events isn't easy. From the first page to the last page, Kevin places the reader in the story as a witness along for the ride in an era of lawlessness and desperation. While many know the stories of the infamous gangsters of the 1920s and 30s, Kevin digs beyond the history books to give life to Charlie Birger and the Shelton Brothers, shedding light on the crimes they committed and the wars they waged against each other while still showing them as multi-dimensional people. I tip my fedora and raise my flask of Kentucky's finest your way, Mr. Corley. You have done an outstanding job with this amazing work.

Leavenworth historian and author of *Leavenworth Seven,* **Kenneth M. LaMaster,** is a retired correctional professional, having worked at the United States Disciplinary Barracks at Fort Leavenworth, the Kansas State Penitentiary, and the United States Penitentiary, Leavenworth. His published works include three pictorial histories and numerous newspaper articles. As a guest speaker, he has appeared on CSPAN's Book TV, as well as given television and radio interviews. He has provided technical advisory work for television programs, documentaries and printed works by other authors. He currently resides in Leavenworth, Kansas.

MAJOR CHARACTERS

SHELTON GANG AND WIVES

Carl Shelton – 1888-1947   Margaret Shelton – 1890-1933
Pearl Vaughn – 1912-1997

Earl Shelton – 1890-1996   Earline McDaniel - 1911-1994
Bernie Shelton – 1899-1948   Carrie Stevenson -? -1961
Roy Shelton – 1885-1950   Lela Stella Shelton – 1886-1975
Ray Walker – UNKNOWN
Little Earl Shelton – 1919-1998
Lula Shelton – 1909-1980
Blondie - The Blond Bombshell UNKNOWN

BUSTER WORTMAN GANG
Also former Shelton Gang

Frank "Buster" Wortman – 1904-1968
Black Charlie Harris – 1896-1988
Blackie Armes – 1906-1944

CAPONE'S "AMERICAN BOYS"
formerly Egan Rats

Fred "Killer" Burke – 1893-1940
Gus Winkler – 1901-1933
Bob Carey – 1894-1932
Johnny Reid – 1890-1926

OTHERS

Al Capone – 1899-1947
Jake "Greasy Thumb" Guzik – 1886-1956
Carl Panzram – 1891-1930
Robert Stroud – 1890-1963
Frank Nash – 1887-1933

BOOTLEGGER HEAVEN

The Shelton Gang Story

BOOK ONE

1928-1935

Benton, Illinois
April 18, 1928

"Hey, you boys down there!" Charlie Birger shouted at a group of youngsters playing hangman outside his window. "Get off them gallows! They's mine!"

The frightened boys scampered down the thirteen steps.

"You seem mighty happy."

Birger knew that voice. It belonged to his longtime nemesis. Carl Shelton. He didn't flinch nor turn around when he heard it. He continued staring out the barred window with his head lowered and one hand on the wall. "I won't tolerate a wet goodbye. What you doin' here, Carl?"

Birger had donned a clean shirt after the newspaper reporters left him alone in his private jail cell. He wanted to look relaxed and proper before the arrival of the *St. Louis Post-Dispatch* reporter. That journalist had always given him fair press, so he'd been invited to spend his last night with him, though Birger wasn't sure he'd feel much like talking.

He slowly turned around. "You fixin' to kill me, Big Carl? Why, I'm already good as dead."

"Yes, I'd expect you've got twelve hours at the outside." Carl looked around the messy room. "There's enough dirt in this place to fill your grave."

The floor was littered with paper—as well as dirt from the feet of dozens of reporters who smoked constantly and used the cell floor as an ash tray.

"I gave my cleanin' lady the day off."

"Your boys gonna bust you out?"

"Those boys couldn't pour piss out of a boot if the instructions were written on the heel."

"If that's supposed to be funny, I'll try to laugh next time you say it."

Birger sat down on one of the two cots in the room and lit a cigarette. "Ol' Bernie would've got me that day last spring had he come prepared."

"Yes." Carl nodded slowly. "Bernie throws a long lasso but always forgets to hang onto his end of the rope. I just came here to tell you that Helen never meant anything to me. You didn't need to have her killed."

"You know, I'll be comin' for you boys." Birger's eyes were ablaze, but the name of the recently deceased Helen Holbrook wasn't the reason for the fire. "If'n I do get outta this fix."

"You won't be needing to make no more tomorrow plans." Carl turned to go. "That'd be a fact, fer sure."

"I'm going to enjoy ever minute of life," Birger said loudly to the back of his antagonist. "Whether it's one year or one day."

"Okay, well." Carl laughed over his shoulder. "You got one day. Start enjoyin'."

"Carl!" Birger had one more bit of unfinished business. The Shelton gang boss turned and looked at the condemned man. "We had a good go of it for a long time. My one bit of advice. Make sure you hang up your guns and enjoy life—before the bullet sends you to bootlegger heaven."

***

The next morning, the sheriff allowed Carl a private view of the proceedings from the window in Birger's jail cell. At one time or another the lawman had been on the payroll of both the Shelton and Birger gang.

The shutters were open but barely a sound could be heard from the five hundred spectators standing shoulder-to-shoulder in the big courtyard surrounded by a high wooden fence.

Outside the grounds were thousands more— men, women, and children. They were on top of every building, in every window, hanging from trees as high as the branches would hold their weight. Most had no view of the public hanging at all. They just wanted the bragging rights—to be able to someday tell their grandchildren they had been there for the hanging of Charlie Birger, the most notorious outlaw of the 1920s.

Birger strode to the gallows as if he were a politician walking onto a platform to deliver a speech. He waved, smiled, and shook hands as best he could with his wrists shackled.

Carl looked at the faces in the crowd, almost wishing that members of the Birger gang would make a last-ditch rescue attempt to save their bootlegger boss. There were many things he was going to miss about Birger. Theirs had been a tempestuous like-hate relationship. They had fought side-by-side to rid southern Illinois of the Ku Klux Klan. Then, after the two-mile-wide tornado ripped through Missouri, Illinois, and Indiana, killing nearly a thousand people, they had banded again to help rebuild the communities.

Soon after that, their relationship went sour. Their mutual attraction for beautiful Helen Holbrook had only been a small part of it. The fact was, there could only be one real ruler of the Little Egypt bootlegging, gambling, and prostitution empire. Neither the Shelton nor Birger gangs were willing to concede any of the millions of dollars that were to be made from these criminal enterprises.

Carl lowered his eyes when the hangman, Phil Hanna, placed the black hood over Birger's head. It could've been any one of the three Shelton brothers instead.

"It is a beautiful world."

The tiny hairs on the back of Carl's neck stood at attention. Charlie Birger's last words mystified him more than any utterances he'd ever heard from the mouth of his rival in the bootlegging industry. There were people who only operated in extremes—and Birger had always lived his life in extremes. Even in the moment before his final breath, his life ended in mystery. What had he seen or thought that made him say those five words?

The sound of the trap door opening wasn't as loud as the sickening snap of Birger's neck. Carl raised his eyes as he heard the screams of horror from those in the crowd. Women fainted into their husband's arms—or collapsed to the ground if their men were too shocked to catch them.

From his angle, Carl couldn't see directly beneath the gallows. But the weight of Birger's limp form dangling from the long rope allowed for one wide swing, bringing the notorious gangster's body into his sight for a final moment.

"Goodbye, Charlie," Carl whispered.

2

Four years before

Heads didn't often turn when a Cadillac touring car puttered down the main street of Kincaid, Illinois. After all, there were plenty of coal company officials who could afford such luxuries. But on September 27, 1924, the big, green vehicle with the dark side curtains caused whispers among the shopkeeps setting up for the morning business.

Inside the bank, cashier Ira Aull counted money onto his desk. Hearing the car's big engine, he glanced through the window just as three tall men dressed in business suits exited the back doors of the Cadillac. The two female tellers on either side of him showed no interest in the sound of the well-oiled machine.

The door burst open and three men waving revolvers ran in.

Aull and the women screamed and fell to the floor.

"Put 'em up!" the tallest of the bank robbers shouted.

The president of the bank, Bruce Shaw, emerged from the vault. He'd been preparing for this moment for years and had a fleeting dream of being hailed a hero in the sleepy little town where nothing exciting ever happened. The trouble was, he'd always imagined the bank robbers would be dumb kids who'd scare away at the first sign of resistance. Therefore, when he pulled the revolver he kept under papers on his desk and fired a half dozen shots into the wall and ceiling, he thought fame was finally his.

Instead, a hail of return fire ricocheted off the bank vault. He leapt like a ballerina and dove head first behind the iron door. Finding his foot close to the alarm button on the wall, he tapped it with his foot. As the bell sounded, he kicked the heavy door shut, then leaned forward and gave the combination dials a fast spin. That was when he noticed blood oozing down his fingers, the result of a bullet nicking his gun hand.

"Hold your fire, men!" the tall bank robber screamed over the blare of the bank alarm.

At their leaders command, the gangsters ceased shooting. Shaking violently, Shaw glanced up into the criminal's eyes. The slightly shorter, bespectacled robber calmly reloaded his revolver. Another bandit watched the street through the big glass window, while the tall man strode over to Ira Aull, lifted him by the hair, and slammed his face hard against the wall.

Aull raised his hands so straight above his head, his fingers were inches from the ceiling. The gangster stuck the barrel of his revolver into his ear.

The bespectacled bandit stepped forward and kicked Shaw hard in the ribs. "Open the vault!" he shouted.

"We can't!" Shaw squealed, his voice so shrill even he didn't recognize it. "It's on a time lock and can't be opened again until tomorrow morning."

The robber shouted an obscenity and pistol-whipped Shaw's head several times until the man lay sprawled and bleeding on the wooden floor.

"Fill this satchel with all the money on the counter," the tall leader demanded. He threw a valise at the two women cowering on the floor.

Their entire bodies shaking, they rose quickly to their feet and filled it with money they had just laid out for the day's business.

Gunshots erupted from the street. The man guarding the window raised his rifle and fired through the glass at a beautiful woman who was shooting at the getaway car from a hardware store boardwalk. Her feet were spread apart in a firing position that indicated she was well practiced.

The tall bandit grabbed Aull and jerked him to his feet. Shoving him in front, he used Aull as a body shield. The other two bank robbers also crouched behind Aull. Pushing him ahead of them and out of the building, they raced toward a parked getaway car.

A fourth bandit behind the wheel of the Cadillac, and a fifth man standing on the running board, fired with pump-action shotguns at anyone who showed themselves on the street.

The tall robber behind Aull used the money satchel to urge him forward while shooting with his pistol in his right hand. "Get out of here, you son-of-a-bitch," he shouted at a man on the boardwalk who wore an apron with blood stains all over it.

Albert Matozzo was bloody from cutting meat in his butcher shop since four o'clock. The grocer had been getting ready to change aprons when the shooting started, followed immediately by the bank alarm. Motozzo didn't abide bad behavior in his community. He'd paddled the britches of many youngsters for trying to steal from his grocery store, so it wasn't surprising to anyone except the bank robbers that the revolver behind his counter was loaded and ready.

Having experienced the trenches of the Argonne Forest during the recent Great War, Matozzo moved immediately to a doorway that offered adequate cover. His training took over. *Take aim, shoot, and quickly duck. Then move to a different position and repeat.*

The tall bank robber carrying the satchel lowered his gun to push Aull into the car. Matozzo stepped clear of the doorway, placed his feet firmly in the firing stance, took careful aim and squeezed off a shot that knocked the right leg out from under the bandit. The satchel skidded on the hard road just as the getaway car began rolling forward. With his good knee on the running board the wounded man reached back for the money.

"Come on, goddamn it!" a voice in the Cadillac yelled. "To hell with the money!"

Hands reached out, grabbed the wounded man by his coat and dragged him inside the vehicle.

Matozzo ran into the street to chase the getaway car. A man stuck a sawed-off shotgun out the window to fire back at the grocer. Matozzo got into a crouched position. Resting his gun hand on his forearm, he took one more careful aim. His bullet hit the robber in the wrist, causing him to drop the shotgun.

The car sped out of town with a hostage, but minus the bank money as well as one very nice sawed-off shotgun.

***

Christian County Courthouse
Taylorville, Illinois
1928

"And that's the way it happened," Ira Aull told the jury. "They made me duck down on the backseat floorboard with my head between my knees. The man beside me's leg was bleeding. Thinking that if I was nice, they wouldn't hurt me, I handed him my handkerchief.

"When they got a few miles from town, they stopped the car and told me to get out and cross a fence into a field, then lay down. I lay there for what seemed like an eternity, just waiting for a bullet in the back of my head." Aull pulled a kerchief from his breast pocket and wiped his nose.

"Can you identify the man with the leg wound you gave your handkerchief to?" the prosecuting attorney asked.

Carl Shelton sat at the defendant's table, his posture and mannerisms that of a proper businessman doing his end-of-the-day figures on a pad of paper. Despite pushing forty, the youthfully handsome man with only a hint of graying around the temples sat tall.

His younger brother Earl sat next to him. Whenever the opportunity arose, he smiled amiably at visitors in the gallery.

Their bespectacled youngest brother Bernie was twenty-eight, but could be mistaken for a delinquent teenager, mainly because of his behavior. He couldn't sit without slouching, and even put his feet on an empty chair. He smiled at his friends and scowled at people he didn't take a liking to, which was almost everyone.

Aull looked hard at the three defendants, especially the dark scowl of Bernie Shelton.

"Mr. Aull," the attorney said firmly, "are the men who took you hostage sitting in this courtroom?"

"I-I can't do it," Aull finally said, his hands shaking. "I was sitting with my face downward."

It was the prosecutor's turn to scowl—an unflattering look that would appear on his face many times over the next several days as witness after witness failed to identify the three brothers as the bank robbers.

Despite the lack of evidence, the twelve men on the Christian County jury gave the defendants stares as hard as those of Bernie. The only time they cracked a smile was when Carl Shelton was questioned on the stand.

"Do you run a saloon?" the prosecuting attorney asked.

"No, sir," Carl replied, his legs crossed and hands in lap. "I run a soft drink parlor."

***

Few restaurants had all the characteristics necessary for members of the crime world to use as a meeting place. The Parkway Tavern in Peoria, Illinois, was one of the good spots. Its back parking lot lay just below a heavily wooded, steep hill—a great escape route in case of a police raid. During underworld rendezvous' like this one, the Shelton brothers kept a car and driver ready in the graveyard at the top of the hill. A man waited there now, holding a Thompson machine gun in his lap as he chain-smoked cigarettes.

In the private dining area of the restaurant, Carl didn't take his eyes off the man sitting across the table from him, despite the room being full of burly thugs. Both men had brought their heavies. Earl and Bernie stood on either side of Carl. They stared at the three bodyguards behind the stocky man. The bodyguards stared back. Bowls of pasta, linguini, and tall bottles of red wine filled the table. The atmosphere in the room was not of hate or even fear, but rather caution and distrust.

"So, da Sheltons are doing pretty good for theyselves down south," the round-faced man commented.

"We have no complaints," Carl said.

"I saw you beat the rap on that Kincaid bank robbery." The man looked at Carl with a hint of respect. "Any plans to bring youse operations north of Peoria?"

"Nope."

"That's very wise of ya, Mr. Shelton. Youse boys keep your business between Peoria and Cairo, and we'll get along fine."

"Sounds reasonable." Carl raised his glass. "I hear you enjoy bird hunting. I hope you can come down south one day and join me and my brothers. Little Egypt has some of the fattest pheasant you ever saw."

"I'd like dat."

"Here's to both our successes, Mr. Capone."

3

The freight train traveling through Fairfield, Illinois, didn't stop or even slow. That didn't prevent two hobos from tumbling out of an open boxcar as soon as the train returned to the countryside. They rolled to a stop at the bottom of a ravine. Several hoots of delight came from other wayward men hitching free rides in, on top of, and even below the railcars.

While the train rumbled into the distance, the two rose, patted dust from their dirty jeans, and walked in the direction of a nearby house. Snow clouds hovered low in the northwest sky, and a cold wind blew dust across barren fields.

Lula Shelton hurried to take down sheets from the clothesline when she spotted the two coming along a path, each sporting a walking stick across one shoulder with a small roll of clothes tied together at the end. Barely out of her teens, Lula couldn't understand why her ma insisted on giving up the money her brothers had worked so hard to filch. Her brother Carl was even worse. He gave a ride to every tramp with a thumb out, and then handed over a wad of bills like he'd just plucked them off a money tree.

Lula wished her ma and Carl could be more like her youngest brother. Bernie would shoot at a vagrant for target practice, and then go buy a round of drinks for those who were more deserving.

"Ma! You got two more freeloaders," Lula called with indifference. "Looks like one of 'em might be a gal. It's hard to tell through all that dirt."

By the time the hobos arrived at the back porch, Ma Shelton was setting plates full of beans and cornbread on the top step.

"Thank you very kindly, ma'am," the taller of the two said. "God bless you."

"Don't bother with the blessin's unless you're truly saved," Ma said. "I'll not have the Lord's blessing from anyone just tryin' to beg a free meal."

"Oh, I have a nickel. I'd like to pay you for your kindness. My name is Malachi, by the way."

"A good Bible name, that's for sure. Keep your nickel."

"A penny saved is a penny earned," Malachi preached, returning the coin to his pocket.

"Yes, and a penny earned ain't worth very much," Ma retorted. The storm door to the kitchen clapped twice as a cold burst of wind blew it closed behind her.

"Your wife looks like maybe she used to be pretty," Black Charlie Harris observed. He'd just come around the side of the house along with Bernie Shelton and three surly-looking bootleggers. They were all startled to find two hobos on the porch eating.

The girl's nose was so flat it made her eyes appear wide apart. Scars ran down both cheeks to her neck, leaving a large part of her upper lip missing.

Charlie had just returned from his latest stint in prison, where mutated faces were common. Being a man of slight height and build, he preferred to maintain a dapper image, his clothes denoting a businessman and his demeanor a minister.

"Her face will cure hiccups," Lula scoffed. "That's for sure." She turned to join Ma in the kitchen.

"Did you do that?" Charlie asked, scowling at Malachi.

"I'm guilty of murder, mischief, and mayhem," Malachi said, "but I ain't never beat on a woman."

"Someone didn't leave her much of a face." Having grown up with an abusive father, Charlie was suspicious.

"That there's a fact." Malachi nodded. "She sure enough looks a lot better walking away than she does coming toward you. Show 'em, gal."

The girl wiped food from what was left of her lips and walked toward the icehouse, putting extra effort into the swing of her hips.

"The beatin' also left her a might addled, I'd 'spect," Malachi said. "You keep her head to the wind though, and she still makes a fine mount."

"A good whack on the head certainly has the potential to make a person feeble-minded." Being the youngest of twenty children, Charlie had seen plenty of times when it would take several months or even a year for one of his siblings to recover from one of their father's beatings.

"Go on in the wash house and clean up." A tough thug from St. Louis named Fred Burke pointed toward a small shed attached to the side of the barn. "There's soap and towels in the tack room. I'll see you directly."

"Clean your insides extra special," added Malachi. "You hear me, gal?"

"Abusing a woman simply doesn't sit right with me," Charlie said.

"Listen to you talk," Burke scoffed. "What about that bank teller you kilt. You ever think about his family?"

"Well, that's true." Charlie shrugged. "I suppose that when we associate with outlaws long enough, we tend to forget about the other side. But in my defense, I did shoot him in the leg to prevent his attack. Unfortunately, he bled to death."

Carl Shelton strutted out of the house in time to catch a glimpse of the girl and hear Charlie's words. He didn't like such talk. He yearned for social respectability—a hard sell for a crime boss. The Chicago mobster, Al Capone, had achieved such prominence, rubbing elbows with the Windy City's finest.

Southern Illinois gentry, though, weren't as accepting of crime and corruption as Chicago citizens. The Shelton brothers were feared enough to get invitations to proper events throughout Little Egypt, but scorned enough to receive little more acknowledgement than nervous smiles and unenthusiastic handshakes.

In fact, Carl was still steaming from being turned down by a beautiful and socially prominent lady the evening before. That made the well-endowed, adle-brained hobo woman with the disfigured face all the more enticing. He needed satisfaction as well as distraction from all his woes.

Just then one of the hobo woman's bare legs emerged from the wash room. The heel of her foot ran slowly and seductively up the door frame. A bare arm came next, the index finger of her hand motioning to come to her.

Fred Burke thought he had first dibs. He was stepping forward when the eldest Shelton removed his work gloves and walked boldly toward the shed. Burke extended a hand in front of Carl, who stopped and glared at him.

Carl's brother Bernie quickly retrieved a Tommy gun from behind a chair and stared coldly at the St. Louis gangster. Burke had run with Charlie Birger's gang for a while, so he still wasn't fully trusted by the Sheltons.

"Give me that weapon, Bernie," Carl ordered.

Bernie tossed the gun to his big brother and grinned a goodbye to Burke. His smile turned to dismay when Carl flipped the gun. Holding it by the barrel he offered it to Fred Burke. Bernie just shook his head and went through the kitchen door into the house.

"This thing work?" Burke accepted the gat and checked it for balance. "I've heard these weapons tend to jam."

"Occasionally, but they usually spout out enough chaos to make folks duck before they jam up. I've found it adequate time to draw and fire my side arm."

Burke caressed the weapon. He nodded to Carl, who took that as consent they had a deal. Flipping a suspender from his shoulder, he continued on toward the shed and entered.

From inside the washroom a moment later, Earl's dog yelped and came running out into the yard, where he lay down and licked the fur on his bottom back into place.

Black Charlie looked at the hobo man and gave a disgusted spit at his feet. The sound of skin slapping against skin and Carl's loud breaths filled the air. The rutting was noisy enough to bring Earl and Blackie Armes running from the carriage house.

"What's goin' on?" Earl asked as he passed Charlie. "Is Carl breeding the mare? I thought he was gonna wait 'til spring."

Charlie didn't answer. Instead, he returned to where other gang members were loading a telephone line repair vehicle in an effort to hide whiskey barrels.

"Why, that's big Carl's grunt," Blackie Armes said. "I haven't heard him that loud since Helen Holbrook was murdered. Why you suppose Black Charlie's mad? Was he wantin' to have the gal first?"

Blackie was devilishly handsome. He had little need to use a sporting gal for his pleasures. Still, he was debating whether or not to take his turn. If the price was right. It had been a dry spell of late. The Sheltons had kept him so busy transporting liquor, he'd had little time for frolicking.

"Don't be callin' him Black Charlie loud enough he can hear you," Earl shushed. "You don't mind being called Blackie, but Charlie Harris ain't partial to that nickname."

"Oh, yeah, I forgot."

"Carl gave him that handle, and he don't much like us Sheltons anyways. Plus, Bernie's the one who knocked Charlie's front tooth out when we was kids. He just got that gold tooth put in a few years ago. Anyway, Carl and me is about the only folks that can call him Black Charlie to his face and not get kilt." Earl turned and headed into the kitchen to see what Ma was cooking.

Bernie stood next to Ma while she iced a cake. He glared at Earl. "Black Charlie appears prison broke and branded."

"Yes, but he's fearless in a gunfight. He proved that during the Rochester heist." Earl reached for a swipe of icing from the cake and received a swat from Ma's wooden spoon.

"There's no fear when you have nothing to lose." Bernie liked to share profound quotes he saved for the right occasions.

Charlie Harris opened the outside door and lugged in a silver milk can.

Fearing Black Charlie's ears may have been burning, Bernie said, "I reckon I'll take a trot with that hobo filly." He rose and exited through the back door before it could swing shut.

"Charlie." Ma swung around and faced him. "Do you like your steak fallin' off the bone, or with a little fight left in it?"

"I suppose rare would be appropriate, since it's rare I get one." Black Charlie laughed at his own play on words, then glanced up.

Lula stared at his Navajo Indian belt buckle made of silver and turquoise—his only memento from his time in the Yuma lockup. A prisoner had died while curled up in a corner of the exercise yard. Charlie grabbed the belt buckle. By the time the screws found the corpse, it had also been stripped of its boots.

Charlie cocked an eyebrow at her, hoping young Lula might also notice the bulge rapidly growing in his jeans.

"I declare, Lula! You got any git in that gitty up?" Ma grumbled. "I'm 'bout ready to start the noodles, and you're still shuckin corn. Quit tryin' to take ever piece of silk off and get to tossin' 'em in the pan."

Lula shook her head hard, as if getting something out of her hair.

Ma jumped over and flicked her ear with an index finger.

"Ow!"

Ma then grabbed a fly swatter and slapped the spider racing toward her husband.

"Egad, woman!" Pa grumbled. "Don't disturb me."

"You're about as disturbed as they get." Ma retorted. She used the back of her hand to brush the smashed spider off the table. "Why don't you ever say nothin'? A person wouldn't even know you was here—except for your occasional farts."

"I'm about said out." Pa wadded his newspaper, stood slowly until his knees had loosened enough to hold his weight, then wobbled from the room. He found a corner spot beneath the stairwell where he wouldn't be disturbed by the coming and goings of a half dozen bootlegging gangsters.

All their talk of gunfights and robbing banks irked him to no end. How could their mother just ignore it and keep on pretending their sons were upstanding citizens?

An old, wooden box waited next to his chair. Pa opened it and extracted an expensive Cuban cigar. He refused to let his wealthy racketeering sons buy him a new home, a car, or clothes, but he didn't object when they kept his cigar box filled with fine tobacco from the Caribbean islands.

"Them boys is no good," Pa said in a low breath. He wet the tobacco leaves with his tongue, lit up, and then sat back to enjoy the fine aroma. "No good a-t'all."

***

On the side of the house, Charlie lit a cigarette and watched Ray Walker finish loading the truck. Despite the cold air coming in, Ray wore a sleeveless BVD that showed off his muscles. Like Blackie Armes, he considered himself a lady's man. Since the day he hooked up with the Shelton brothers, women were a dime a dozen. And Ray spent all the dimes he could get his hands on.

Following rank that was mostly determined by age, the gangsters took their turns visiting the hobo girl. Malachi sat guzzling from a jug and collected the coins from the customers before they partook of the young ladies' endowments.

When the telephone truck was loaded and disappeared through the trees, Carl squatted beside Black Charlie and offered him a Helmar Turkish cigarette. Snow fell thick and heavy.

"That's a mighty fine load of moonshine you're letting go of for a piddling price," Charlie said as he lit up. He'd known the Sheltons as long as he could remember, but that didn't mean he liked them. Though they often fought amongst themselves, the brothers were also clannish enough to successfully pool their resources and build a respectable sized bootlegging empire.

"Sometimes you have to take the bitter with the better." Carl spat to the side away from Charlie. "Battling court cases has left our cash flow strained a might, but now that Charlie Birger's dead, the whole of downstate vices is at our disposal. I'd 'spect we'll make out."

"I see you're planning on having some of the other boys become primary distributers," Charlie said. "You got anything left for me?"

"I'm glad you asked that. You still got connections in Detroit, don't ya? I need someone to run operations handling the hooch coming in from Canada. I tried to get Fred Burke to do it, but he and some of his Egan Rats boys are looking for their own action in Detroit. I'd expect you could still headquarter with them at Johnny Reid's place."

Charlie hung his head. Detroit was getting to be as rough a town as Chicago and New York. He would definitely need the St. Louis Egan Rats gang's muscle. There was one problem. He hated Fred Burke almost as much as he needed money.

"I'll take it."

"You'll take what, Charlie?" Bernie asked. Having just taken his turn with the hobo girl, he needed a cigarette, which Carl immediately offered. He tossed a heavy coat to his brother.

"Black Charlie's gonna be our man in Detroit." Carl put on the coat and buttoned it up.

"Well, that's fine, Charlie." Bernie lit up before continuing. "You wanna celebrate by going to The Pine with me tonight? I'm told a fine filly named Carrie Stevenson runs the joint. If she's as good lookin' as I hear, I might need a best man."

"Not tonight, Bernie." Charlie didn't care much for the night life. In fact, he didn't care much for being around large groups of people anywhere, especially if a Shelton was there. "Looks like a heavy snowstorm's coming in fast. If roads don't get too slippery, I'll be heading for Detroit first thing in the morning, I'd expect."

4

Carrie Strange Stevenson was having a love affair with the newspaper boys. They were as infatuated with her as she was with the cameras they carried.

Daughter of a rumrunner, Carrie owned and ran The Pine Steakhouse and Motel near Collinsville, Illinois. Since it was a hangout for everyone who was anyone in the St. Louis area, there were always plenty of cameras.

Bernie struggled to squeeze through the crowded room to get close enough to Carrie to have a good look at her. But first he had to push his way through the revelers on the dance floor. When he finally did manage to get near the bar, he removed his glasses and defogged them. Then he put them back on and squinted to get his eyes to refocus. His mouth dropped. Beautiful women were a dime a dozen. But this Carrie Strange Stevenson was no dime. She was the most exquisite and rare diamond he'd ever seen.

As if high cheek bones, a prominent jawline, and just a trace of dimples weren't enough, her eyes were marble gray and made even more cat-like by winged eyebrows and long, dark eyelashes. Shapely full lips begged to be kissed—and kissed often.

Carrie sauntered across the room in a tight, bare-shouldered dress that showcased her hour-glass figure. Bernie had never seen a waist so thin that it arched magnificently upwards to a perfectly shaped chest.

Bernie Shelton had not been denied any women he desired since he turned fourteen years old. He'd successfully seduced more females than he'd taken forcefully, and, in his mind, even those less enthusiastic had succumbed with little opposition.

With a bit of a wiggle, Carrie made her way to the grand piano. She arched her back as two men lifted her. Cheers from the crowd brought all else quiet. The dancers stopped dancing. The band stopped playing. The glasses stopped clinking.

Scores of customers—men dressed in their finest suits and women in their most elegant and revealing gowns—left their tables and gathered on the dance floor in front of her.

Then the band began a lively number and Miss Carrie Strange Stevenson erupted into a tap dance.

Bernie Shelton pushed his way through the crowd until he stood right in front of her. Then, in the middle of her Lindy hop, he jumped onto the piano bench and grabbed the beautiful vixen. She screamed and kicked, but he carried her outside and into one of the motel's quaint little cabins.

The curious patrons followed, emptying the restaurant so they could stand in evening attire in the snow and ice and listen to Carrie explode on Bernie with a torrent of expertly orchestrated swear words. The thundering slaps from inside the cabin caused a few of the more noble gentlemen to take a few steps forward before remembering it was a bloodthirsty gangster they'd face.

When the door opened a few minutes later, an unscathed Carrie Stevenson stepped outside. Adjusting her skirt, she glared at the crowd as if she were still standing on the piano after kicking a handsy drunk in the head.

"Sorry, folks. I was just practicin' for when I'm married!" Carrie shouted. "Drinks are on the house!"

Later that night, a very inebriated Carrie stumbled out the back door and walked to her nifty Pierce-Arrow sedan. Despite the cold, her thick Canadian mink stole was slung over one bare shoulder.

The Eads Bridge Road that crossed the Mississippi River was hazardous enough during summer months. A smashed blonde in a souped-up roadster on an ice-covered bridge was an accident waiting to happen. Carrie barely knew the spinning of the out-of-control car wasn't part of her intoxication. She shut her eyes so she wouldn't get sick. When she opened them, she was looking straight down into the icy, swirling foam of Ol' Man River.

"Carrie," a voice behind her car cried out, "don't move an inch!"

Movement was not an option. Vomiting was. The throw up on the windshield at least blocked her view of the raging river. Her head dropped onto the big steering wheel in an attempt to forget her plight and get some much-needed sleep.

"Hook that mule up to the car's fender!" Bernie Shelton hollered at a farmer who was riding his mule home from a night of boozing.

Carrie sensed her driver's side door opening and felt a strong arm wrap around her waist. She had the sensation of being pulled backwards, but when a wide-eyed mule skidded past her as it was being pulled off the bridge and into the water, she realized it was her car that had been moving. Hanging from her rescuers strong grip, she found herself still looking down into the water as her ten-thousand-dollar automobile and a fifty-dollar mule floated rapidly off toward New Orleans.

The next afternoon, Bernie showed up unannounced in Carrie's bedroom, followed by her elderly maid, who was hitting him with her broomstick.

The room was larger than most living rooms, with plush carpet and a big canopy bed adorned with beautiful white lace. An extremely large makeup table filled almost one entire side of the room. A vanity mirror with two more angled on either side were surrounded by a dozen round light bulbs. Bottles of perfume, powders, and two long jewelry boxes waited in rows on the table.

Bernie ended the battle with the maid by slamming the door in her face, then turning the skeleton key in the lock. Before Carrie could reach in her bedside drawer for her revolver, the gangster produced a locket on a gold chain and dangled it in front of her face. Carrie froze. The locket had diamonds shaped like a "C' on the front and a picture of him inside.

"You're my girl now."

"In your dreams." Carrie's head was still a little swimmy, but she'd enough experience with hangovers to function almost normally. Normal enough at least to accept the necklace after doing a quick count of the diamonds.

"The boys couldn't save your motor car," Bernie said, "but if you can get outta that bed, I'll take you to look for a new one."

The sunlight streaming through the open window forced Carrie to raise a hand and shade her eyes so she could better see her suitor.

"For a fella well over six feet tall, you don't cast much of a shadow."

"I might surprise you if you give me a chance." Bernie set on the edge of the bed. The fact that Carrie didn't kick him away gave him hope. "I'm headin' for Detroit next week to run a load of Canadian tonic to Little Egypt. You help me, and you can have the entire consignment. It will be enough to buy you a Rolls Royce."

5

Black Charlie Harris had never met an Egan Rat gang member he liked. The St. Louis thugs were dirty and uncouth—traits they seemed to take pride in.

The poker game in Detroit had been going on long enough that the apartment floor was wall-to-wall with cigarette butts, as well as whiskey and beer bottles. Egan Rats gangsters Fred Burke, Bob Carey and Johnny Reid tossed litter over their shoulders without regard for the fact that the other two players, James Ellis and Leroy "Doggy" Snyder, were paying for the room.

Black Charlie watched from his stool in the back of the room next to the bar. With legs crossed in the sophisticated style of a noblemen, he held a high ball in one hand and a cigarette in the other. He was already beginning to regret agreeing to Carl Shelton's request that he make a purchase of Canadian whiskey that Ellis and Snyder had smuggled in from Montreal. The only good thing about the evening was that

Burke told him they played five men at a time. Charlie didn't like gambling anyway, especially since the only money he had was what Carl had given him for the whiskey purchase.

It perturbed him to no end to be reliant on the Shelton boys. He didn't like playing second fiddle to anyone. That made his association with Johnny Reid and the Egan Rats all the more frustrating. He thought about talking to Ellis and Snyder about joining up with him to start their own operation. They were accomplished smugglers and Charlie was a good organizer when he had to be.

The game stayed friendly for the first few hours. Then, after several rounds of Scotch, the players began getting sloppy. All five men became so inebriated they started slurring their words and made reckless bets.

"I raise you two C's," Ellis said.

"You know I ain't got that kinda cash on me." Burke's face turned as flush as the five diamonds in his hand.

"How 'bout bettin' that gat you've been strokin' under the table all night?" Ellis suggested.

Burke raised the Thompson machine gun up on one knee. He'd been itching to use it since the day Carl Shelton gave it to him. It worked well enough when he practiced out in the country, but there was something about using it on a human that appealed to him. He looked back down at his jack-high flush.

"You're on," Burke said, placing the gun on the table, its muzzle pointed between Ellis and Snyder. "Call."

The minute Ellis laid four kings on the table, a wide-eyed Charlie jumped up, opened the door, and hopped into the hallway. Almost immediately, he heard the loud spitting of the gat as it raised the stakes in the game to a completely new level. He knew right away that he could forget starting up his own gang with the two smugglers.

The next morning, when the landlady opened the door to the room to change the towels, she saw the bodies of Ellis and Snyder, screamed, and called the police. The lawmen found a queen of spades in the shirt sleeve of James Ellis. As far as they were concerned, the killing was justifiable homicide.

That evening, Charlie laughed when he saw how little attention the card game murders were given in the newspapers. He assumed government officials wanted to keep the gangster activities quiet so citizens wouldn't be afraid and move away from Motor City. Or maybe they were hoping the mobsters would kill one another off. Or maybe they just liked the kickbacks the Purple Gang were giving them to stay out of their affairs.

Whatever the reason, Charlie believed Detroit to be the perfect place to make his fortune. The city was the entry port for whiskey, wine, and beer being smuggled in from Montreal. All he had to do was make the arrangements and get the booze in the hands of Shelton confidants. At least, until he could find smugglers who could avoid getting themselves killed as Ellis and Snyder had done so early in their careers.

"I hate this cold weather," Charlie's wife, Myrtle complained as she did most every day. She was a prostitute, so he couldn't figure out how low temperatures could do anything except benefit her occupation.

The two had met down in Phoenix, but their relationship had been interrupted one day when two plain-clothed detectives barged into her boudoir. Charlie reacted by pulling a blade and stabbing one of them. Since the officer lived, the judge gave him a one-year sentence in the Yuma lock-up. When he was released, Myrtle agreed to go with him to his hometown in Fairfield, Illinois, on the condition he marry her. Charlie agreed only because he didn't see a marriage certificate any more binding than a handshake. He needed a cook and housekeeper. Plus, Myrtle's occupation while he was away would mean he didn't need to waste any of his own money on her. Then, when

Carl offered Charlie Detroit, Myrtle came along, though reluctantly.

"Why do you keep taking me further and further north?" Myrtle slapped her hands on her ironing board. "I suppose our next stop will be Alaska! Besides, I thought you were supposed to be buildin' houses."

"I can make more money running one load of hooch than I can in a whole year of carpentry," Charlie said. "If you don't like it—leave."

When Charlie got home the next morning, his wife was gone. He started taking his meals at Johnny Reid's tavern.

He was sitting alone eating his lunch the day Bernie Shelton walked in with his new girlfriend, Carrie Stevenson. Burke, Reid, and Carey immediately left the bar and greeted Bernie with handshakes and slaps on the back. Charlie knew from previous conversations with the St. Louis boys that they would have preferred to shoot him.

"This place is nice, Johnny," Bernie quipped as he looked around the big room. "But can't you have an exterminator do something about all these Egan Rats?"

Charlie ignored the boyish bantering and hurried to finish his meal. He detested childish behavior, especially from grown men. Seeing a beauty like the Stevenson woman on the arm of a Shelton only added to his envy.

The front door slammed open and the Blonde Bombshell strutted in wearing a mink fur. The coat was worth more than Charlie had paid for the flivver he drove. Blondie had turned him down once when he asked for a free poke. She then set the price so high he had to take a walk. A double sawbuck seemed a goodly sum to be spending on a two-dollar whore.

"Throw some more coal in that furnace, Johnny," Blondie ordered, "unless you want me to leave this fur on. And, for your information, I'm wearing practically nothin' under it."

A young thug barely out of his teens was working the bar. He raced to the basement door, threw it open, and leapt in one bound to the bottom. When he returned from tossing extra coal into the furnace, his face and hands were black.

Blondie walked over to the handsome youngster and whispered in his ear, "Next time, use the shovel, dearie. Now, if you'll go get cleaned up, maybe later, I'll give you a poke for half price."

Charlie flushed with anger. The boy was barely out of school and most certainly could offer the blond beauty little more than a hard body and a quick finish.

"I have some business I need to discuss with Charlie." Bernie excused himself from the boys at the bar and took a chair at the table. Carrie and

Blondie joined the Rats doing shots and laughing at the youngster who was hurrying to wash his blackened face with a bar towel.

Charlie stopped eating. He sat up straight, not out of respect but because only when they were seated did he appear close to the same height as any of the Shelton brothers. They were all well over six feet, compared to his diminutive five feet, five inches. The sad thing was that Charlie had been five-five in fifth grade, the same year he and Bernie dropped out of school. Back then, Charlie had used his height to his advantage, although he was never anything like the bully the youngest Shelton became when he finally got his growth spurt during their teen years. Now, Charlie avoided getting so close to the brothers that he had to crane his neck back to look up the ten inches to their faces.

"I'm gonna need your help runnin' some alky down to Little Egypt," Bernie whispered to him. "Several of the boys is servin' time, and others are too busy."

"I'm listening," Charlie said. He poured a little sugar onto the table and began stirring it into different patterns with a spoon. Having grown up watching the youngest of the Sheltons develop his selfish, self-centered ways, he trusted Bernie the least of any of the brothers. Green paper was the only reason he would consider doing it.

"Carrie and Blondie is gonna run interference," Bernie explained. "They'll be in a souped-up Jeep that can cut across country if necessary. You'll follow behind in the farm truck. The hooch will be hidden in the gas tank. The only problem will be that you'll need to stop and refuel more often. I'll be behind you, drivin' the tanker. If any cops try to stop you, I'll jackknife and block the road. If we come upon a roadblock, Carrie will bribe the officers. If that don't work, Blondie will offer them her body. In the unlikely case that the cops are homos, I'll pass you and ram right on through. Your truck has iron doors, and the windows can be kicked out from the inside if they shatter from gun fire."

"What happens if they do catch me?" Over Bernie's shoulder he saw Blondie take the young boy's hand and lead him to a back room as the Rats hooted with delight.

"You claim you were just hired to drive the truck and didn't know what was in it." Bernie said. "You won't be packin' a gun, so there's a good chance you'll get less than a year."

"They don't have snakes in these jails up this way, do they?" Charlie asked. "Down in Yuma, the screws let snakes crawl around our cells at night."

"No snakes, Charlie. And we'll be sure to keep you in cigarettes and protection money if you go in the slammer. Plus, there will be a brand-new car and your share of the cash waitin' for you when you get out."

Black Charlie nodded acceptance of the assignment.

Carrie Stevenson walked up to their table. She removed her heavy coat and dropped it on a chair, then pulled her skirt up so she could straddle Bernie's lap. He threw his arms around her and kissed her.

Black Charlie rose, and without a word, left the bar. With nowhere else to go, he walked back to his empty apartment to take a nap.

***

"Are we taking the back roads?" Charlie asked Bernie the next morning after the hooch was loaded. The merchandise was almost entirely Canadian Whiskey with just a few cases of wine.

The truck he was to drive was parked in a wide alley. A long tanker was parked immediately behind it. It was the same type of rig the Sheltons had once drilled gun ports in the side to use against the Birger gang.

"Nope. Trucks the size of these would be a dead giveaway on a country road. We're gonna ride right down the hard road through Fort Wayne, Indianapolis, and straight on to Herrin."

The vehicle Charlie was to drive was much smaller and more mobile. Bernie told him that it had a powerful engine designed for a racecar. There was nothing conspicuous about the truck. It was loaded with stacks of wooden pallets.

Carrie and Blondie came out of the warehouse office. Carrie wore a simple, floral-print cotton wrap dress with a matching hat. Blondie, though, was dressed for her role as seductress in a sleeveless trumpet, her hair in side swept bangs with a bun pinned in back.

Neither lady even bothered to look at Charlie, a fact that bothered him immensely. Carrie gave Bernie a long, hard kiss and planted herself in the jeep behind the big steering wheel. Giggling like a school girl, Blondie hopped in the passenger's seat. She pointed her hand out the window as if she were directing a wagon train forward.

As Charlie started up the truck and followed the Jeep, he found his hands shaky and his mouth becoming dry. The memory of the snakes in the Yuma jail had haunted him all night. He kept waking up kicking his feet at imaginary wiggling under his blanket. Once, when he'd first got out of the lock up, he'd been awakened by Myrtle shaking his leg. He found himself standing up on the bed, tearing a hole in the wall two feet high and one foot wide all the way through to the water closet.

Now, as he guided the big truck, he tried to focus on the money he'd get if the delivery was successful. He kept telling himself that the Sheltons were old hats at this. They knew all the tricks. But then, *why was he the one driving the truck that would send him back to prison?* Snakes or no snakes.

The first six hours were uneventful. There were so many trucks coming and going from Detroit and Chicago, the law had their hands full. Because of the space the booze took in the gas tank, they stopped every hour to get fuel.

If not for the fear of getting caught the trip through Indiana might have been a pleasant drive. There was plenty of pretty, white snow on the barren branches of the trees and along the ground. Still, it had warmed enough that morning that the roadway was clear and only slightly damp.

It was when they dipped down past Indianapolis that Carrie began leading them off the main roads. Charlie wondered if they might be better off taking the longer route across to Danville before heading south. The two sirens in the Jeep in front of him had not stopped chatting since they left Detroit, their faces constantly looking toward one another. How Carrie could pay attention to the road was beyond him. He wondered if they might have forgotten they were leading a convoy.

Charlie saw the roadblock ahead just as they passed Evansville. He reviewed the procedures

Bernie had told him for dealing with such a situation. If needed, Carrie would bribe the officers first, Blondie would offer her body second, and, as a last resort, Bernie would run the roadblock.

When he saw Blondie get out of the Jeep and accompany a lawman to his squad car, he knew the third and more violent option would not be necessary. The remaining officer, who waved the next several cars on, seemed too preoccupied to worry about what illegal items any of them were carrying. Charlie was surprised, though, when Carrie continued on the journey, leaving Blondie to find her own way home the last ninety miles. The final two hours were without complications.

"There's a new sheriff in St. Clair County," Earl told them later as they drained the truck's gas line so they could unload the shipment. "Carl went to visit him."

The Shelton roadhouse they were parked behind was filled with automobiles. A dozen men began taking apart the truck and then unloaded the booze. Earl's dog, Hooch, ran around excitedly, barking and jumping up on anyone who displayed any kind of affection. Charlie smoked and stroked behind the dog's ear while he waited for Bernie to pay him.

"A new sheriff?" Bernie was surprised. "Who is he?"

"Jerome Munie."

"The hardware store clerk from O'Fallon?" Charlie asked. He was shocked. Munie seemed way too affable to be a lawman.

"That's the one." Earl laughed. "He was a long shot for the position. Folks are blaming Hoover and the Republicans for the depression, so, somehow, he slipped into the job. To show you the type of fella Munie is, they say he was sent dozens of flowers the day he took office. The jailhouse smelled like a funeral home."

"Sounds like a pushover," Bernie said.

6

Jeanene Munie liked to play in her daddy's jailhouse. When there were no bad men behind the bars, she got to use the jail cells as playhouses. Sometimes when there were bad men, if they weren't too bad, her daddy let her sit in a chair and sing to her doll, Maggie, as she combed Maggie's hair. The bad men liked to hear her sing and sometimes sang along with her, if they remembered the words from their troubled childhoods. Her daddy told her that he liked the bad men to see her and listen to her sing, because it would make them think of their own little boys and girls, and maybe they wouldn't be bad men anymore.

One day a bad man Jeanene had seen many times walked into the jailhouse while her daddy was working at his desk. Because he was the sheriff, her daddy did lots of homework.

"Hello, Jeanene," the tall bad man said to her as she changed Maggie's diaper. "Do you remember me?'

"Yes, I do. You're a bad man. Your name is Carl Shelton, and my daddy is going to put you in his jail. But don't worry. I can sing to you, and you won't want to be a bad man anymore."

"Well." Carl smiled. "Can I give you a nickel for your singing now, in case I don't have any money when your daddy arrests me?"

Jeanene looked at her daddy, who gave a slight nod of his head. With a petite curtsy, she accepted the coin.

"Thank you, Mr. Shelton. Do you have any special song I can sing for you so you won't want to be bad anymore?"

"Do you know *'Shall We Gather at the River'*?"

"No, but can you promise not to be bad for a while until I learn it?"

"I promise." Carl's boots clicked along the creaky wooden floor. He took a chair across the desk from Sheriff Jerome Munie. Carl had no children—as far as he knew. He envied Munie for his sweet, well-mannered, little girl. She made him think about Charlie Birger's advice to retire and enjoy life before a bullet caught up to him. He shook his head to clear such thoughts and tried to focus on why he was there.

The sheriff was a pleasant, middle-aged man. His wavy graying hair and glasses gave him the appearance of a college professor. A newspaper lay on his desk. The headline read: MORE DETROIT GANGLAND SLAYINGS!

"Detroit's getting worse than Little Egypt!" Carl said.

"I'd suspect having so many Egan Rats up there has something to do with it," Munie speculated. "I had hoped the gang wars ended in these parts when Birger swung."

"What can I do to get along with you?" Carl asked. The vision of Charlie at the end of the rope was still fresh in his mind. He hadn't come to talk about dying. Just living was hard enough.

"Nothing."

"How about a brand-new Cadillac and one hundred clams a month?"

"You're not Al Capone, Carl. I'm not afraid of you. The whole country is getting riled up against you mobsters."

"I heard they are bringing in some honest lawmen to take on Capone," Carl said. "Are you planning to be a southern Illinois version?'"

"Let's get this straight. There's nobody I know of who wants the Shelton boys in St. Clair County."

"How am I gonna make a livin'?"

"If I were you, I'd take your pistols and guns and go from town to town and say, 'Here is the notorious Shelton brothers in person.' You could make a million."

Jeanene walked over to Carl. Without any prompting, she crawled up on his lap and rested her head on his chest. She looked up at him with the greenest eyes he'd ever seen.

"Do you like my daddy?"

"Yes, I like him, Jeanene. Your daddy is a fine gentleman and a man of his word." Carl looked the Sheriff in the eyes. "I know what you're thinking, Sheriff. Don't worry. Your family will never be harmed by any of my men."

***

Sheriff Munie was as good as his word. The next day his deputies raided two of Carl's roadhouses. Unlike the Ku Klux Klan had done during their raids back in '25, these deputies smashed up all the alcohol bottles and barrels, never keeping even a drop for themselves.

Munie had personally selected every one of his men, most all veterans of the recent Great War and all devout Southern Baptists with a strong repugnance toward sins of most all kinds.

Even one of Carl's molls, the beautiful woman known only as the Blonde Bombshell, failed in her attempts to seduce the sheriff. Two of his deputies, however, did fall to her temptations, but being they were bachelors and from out of state, Carl found that blackmail didn't work with them. The two men simply resigned back to their hometowns with enough sensual memories of Blondie to make any future encounters with the opposite sex about as exciting as eating raw vegetables in a pastry shop.

7

Black Charlie had only been back in Detroit for a day when the Egan Rats drew him into another one of their crazy capers.

A band of Jewish hoodlums called the Purple Gang ran Detroit. Charlie didn't like them any better than he liked the Egan Rats. He'd run a while with Charlie Birger, another Jew he hadn't trusted, especially after Birger killed off half his own gang members. Fred Burke, though, was Black Charlie's main contact in Michigan, and he had affiliations with the Purples. So, Charlie bit his tongue and went along.

"The Sicilian mob is tryin' to extort protection money from me," Johnny Reid told Burke one day during a few after-hour drinks at the tavern. Black Charlie and several others were present, but Reid assumed Burke to be the leader. Charlie didn't mind, but he knew Gus Winkler resented being identified as only a lieutenant. Though Gus wasn't the cold-blooded killer his friend Burke was, he was smarter and knew how to plan better.

"Why don't you let the Purples take care of it for you?" Winkler asked.

Charlie thought this a good idea and one that a successful mobster like Carl Shelton would have come up with. Reid and Burke were more impulsive though, just like Bernie Shelton.

"We don't need those kikes," Reid said. "Mike Dipisa is the Sicilian boss. I just got a report that at this very moment he's at a blind pig down on Hunt Street. I say we do a drive-by and end this."

Black Charlie was the only one to not show enthusiasm for the plan. There was nothing in it for him. His job was to be middle man for the Canadian liquor. Besides, he was still edgy from transporting the truckload of booze hundreds of miles then turning around and driving back to Detroit. Still, it might be more dangerous to not go along with the Rats, so he joined Burke and Carey in the back of a sedan. Gus Winkler drove.

From the front seat, Reid directed. "Turn down this alley and stop before them trash barrels."

More than a little traffic filled the well-lighted streets. The many factories in the industrial area were changing over to the two-a.m. shift. Both workers who were late and those hurrying home made for somewhat hazardous driving. Having Winkler at the helm gave confidence to the men in the car. He'd been an ambulance driver during the Great War and was experienced at weaving in and out of traffic, as well as gunshots and even bombs, if necessary.

The Sicilians scared the hell out of Black Charlie. The ones in Chicago under Al Capone were terrorizing not only their own city but mobs in New York, Kansas City and a dozen other metropolitan areas in the United States. For Reid and Burke to want to hit a Sicilian boss in Detroit seemed a good way to bring the entire Italian mob down on top of them.

"Dipisa wears a straw hat," Reid told Gus. "You take the first watch for a couple of hours, then wake me."

The gangsters in the back relaxed and rested their eyes. Black Charlie doubted they would see action the first night of a stakeout. His only fear was that Burke or Carey would sleep-shoot the weapons they held in their laps. Both Carey and Charlie held pump-action shotguns. But Burke, who sat between them, caressed his gat, as he seemed to do every waking hour of the day. Charlie had a window seat on the passenger's side, so he rested his head against the window. It seemed his eyes had only been shut for a few moments, but it was three hours later when Reid yelled, "There he is!"

Gus started the engine. Carey and Charlie lowered the glass in their windows. Fred Burke sat up straight. He was a short man, so he needed to prepare himself to lean out whichever window offered the best opportunity. All five men in the vehicle placed plugs in their ears.

The sun peeked above the buildings in the east as Gus floored the accelerator and pulled the sedan into the early morning traffic. Dipisa and two bodyguards stood smoking on the sidewalk to their right. Burke leaned across Black Charlie as if he weren't there, his Tommy gun in position.

Charlie just had time to pump a load into his shotgun when Burke let loose a hail of bullets. Not wanting to be accused of shirking, Charlie fired blindly into the air, then pumped one more shot off before Gus sped them from the scene.

"Damn, Gus!" Burke smacked a palm on the back of the driver's head. "You drove too fast. We missed him completely."

"I might have got one of the guards," Reid said from the front seat. He was hastily reloading his revolver. "But I only got four shots off myself."

"Fine bunch of assassins you guys are," Carey yelled. "Get them on my side next time. I won't miss!"

"Hell, Bob," Gus bellowed over his shoulder, "if you'd had any guts, you'd have stood outside the car on the running board and fired."

"Stop by that hotel!" Burke ordered. "I need a shot of whiskey."

"It's morning, Fred," Reid tucked his revolver back in his shoulder holster. "You need to cut back on your boozin'."

After enjoying a leisurely breakfast washed down with Bloody Marys all around, the five gunmen returned to the car. No sooner were they back on the four-lane than a Cadillac sped up next to them. Bob Carey now had the opportunity he'd longed for—only the rapid fire of pistols from Dipisa's car drove Charlie and all his Egan Rat pals to duck low in their seats.

Winkler had often bragged about driving while under fire during the war, but never with quite as many bullets finding their mark on his vehicle. He too ducked below the dash, even as he pushed the brake to the floor so hard their vehicle slid sideways into a parked police car. The two policemen in the patrol car also ducked and stayed that way until Winkler had time to rise back up and give chase to Dipisa and his thugs.

Fred Burke was incensed. He rolled across Bob Carey, who was still on the floorboard, opened the back door, and leapt onto the running board. As Winkler sped within firing distance, Burke let loose a long volley of .45 caliber bullets until his cartridge ran dry.

"Give me the shotgun!" Burke yelled as he tossed the empty gat onto Carey's lap. Carey tried to reload the Tommy gun, but the barrel was so hot he burned his trousers.

Winkler used the traffic to his advantage. Seeing a bus blocking the Cadillac's lane, he swerved into oncoming traffic and then slowed just enough so Reid and Black Charlie could unleash a blizzard of lead into Dipisa's car.

Dipisa himself was driving with one hand and shooting with a revolver in the other. He pulled the steering wheel hard to the left and rammed the back side of the Egan Rat's sedan. Sparks flew from the metal against metal, but also from the lead being fired from the rival gangs.

Winkler again floored the accelerator. With little control of his damaged back end, he was forced to drive up on the sidewalk. Pedestrians screamed and leapt for safety into buildings and even into the street. One heavyset man was too slow. His body rolled over the hood and crashed through the windshield where he stuck, his butt inches from Winkler's steering wheel.

Despite the lack of visibility, Winkler managed to get the sedan back on the road. He quickly motored a few blocks before making a hard-right turn that sent the fat man rolling into a fruit vender's stand.

The vehicle looked like Swiss cheese. It coughed and sputtered, but eventually made it back to Reid's speakeasy. Burke said nothing as he entered the saloon ahead of the others. He went straight to the bar where he grabbed a full bottle of Irish Whiskey, downed half of it without taking a breath, then fell sideways onto the floor.

Reid rolled him onto his side. A bullet had found its way all the way through Burke's shoulder and out his back.

***

The next night, Fred Burke marched into Johnny's, Tommy gun in hand, wearing a bullet-proof vest over his bandaged wound. Black Charlie wanted to laugh, but didn't. No gangster he'd ever seen would stoop to wearing a flak jacket.

"Dipisa loves that dago food at Papa Leo Giorlando's Restaurant," Burke said. "It's in the basement of a sandstone. Even if he ain't there, I intend to ruin his appetite."

Reid was out of his chair with Carey steps behind. Black Charlie moved slower, but followed. He cursed himself for not leaving town after yesterdays fiasco. *But how could I know these idiots would be right back on the street twenty-four hours later?*

Since Winkler wasn't around, Reid drove. After parking the car down the street from Leo's, he turned to Burke. "Listen, Fred. Leave the gat. This is a small place. Hand guns should do the job this time."

Burke looked down at his Tommy gun like he was saying goodbye to a beloved pet. He tucked it down on the floorboard, got out of the car, and led the way into the building.

Inside, the four gunmen took just a moment to adjust their eyes to the candle light glowing from each table, the ambiance of the room a perfect setting for romance. A half dozen couples sat at individual tables. The ladies were dressed in low-cut gowns that left just enough to their dates' imagination to ensure an evening of attempted seductions.

At the cash register, Papa Leo conferred with his business partner and their master chef. The chef waved his arms as he argued something in Italian. A waitress with "Marion" on her name tag approached the four gangsters.

"You may sit anywhere you want. I'll be with you in a moment."

As she walked away, Burke pulled two pistols and unloaded them in the direction of the three men at the register.

Couples ducked and ran for the back door. Two of the men abandoned their high-heeled dates to fend for themselves. Reid, Carey, and Black Charlie followed Burke's lead, but aimed at mirrors, bottles of alcohol, and then at two men who had blown out the candle on their table so they could snuggle without notice.

Burke managed to cut down two of the men at the cash register, but somehow Papa Leo made it to the back door unscathed. He darted away into the darkness of an alley, even as a last fusillade of bullets flew all around him. The firing stopped.

Papa Leo's shouts faded as he ran down the street screaming in Italian, *"Dai! Qualcuno mi ha appena sparato."*

***

The next day, Black Charlie Harris visited one of his sisters who lived in Detroit. He could barely remember her from his childhood, since she was much older and out of the house before he even started school. Still, she and her husband were hospitable to him and he stayed with them for three days.

He spent the fourth night in a hotel before finally phoning Gus Winkler to report in.

Gus updated Black Charlie on what all had transpired. Mike Dipisa had asked for a meeting with Johnny Reid the day after the gunfight. A truce was obtained. Dipisa claimed two of his men had gone rogue. He blamed them for making the extortion demand on Reid without his consent. The next night, Reid, Burke, and Carey kidnapped and drove those two men to a private setting on Lake Huron and had them kneel with their backs to them. Then Johnny Reid pumped one bullet each into their skulls.

Charlie allowed the information to sink in. "You think Burke and Reid are mad at me for going AWOL?" he asked, struggling to keep his voice from cracking. "I did have to go help my sister, after all."

"They won't be as pissed at you as they are at me." Winkler laughed. "My wife and I drove over to Toledo and hid out for three days. Those guys are blood thirsty sons-of-bitches."

8

That summer saw Carl sitting on his tractor watching his nephews of ten- and twelve-years old running alongside a hay wagon pulled by a pickup truck. Grandpa Shelton drove the truck and never looked back or slowed down from his first-gear pace. Wearing leather gloves, the young boys grabbed fifty-pound-plus bales by the strings and dragged them to the wagon. Then they struggled to lift the bales to their legs, and using all their might, rolled them up one thigh. With a kick, lift, and flip, they tossed them onto the flatbed, which was near as high as they were tall.

Carl had no children. He admired Dalta's sons, especially since they were named after their uncles and called Little Carl and Little Earl. While brother Dalta didn't run much with the gang, he seemed unable to keep his sons from wanting to follow in his criminally-minded brothers' footsteps. Watching how hard they worked in the field, they would be able to succeed in anything they attempted.

Most farmers hated the baling season, but not Carl. He loved the sweat, the smell of the alfalfa, and especially the way his skin turned golden brown in the sun.

Earl loved it even more, and rode the hay wagon, where he expertly stacked the bales in crossing patterns so they would survive the bumpy ride through the field to the barn. Unlike Bernie, Earl was no lager when it came to physical farm work.

A sudden burst of high wind brushed the tall prairie grass sideways in happy waves across the endless prairie. It was moments like this that Carl considered taking Charlie Birger's advice and giving up the rackets to focusing full time on his farm. The cool breeze seemed to remind him it was lunch time.

While the boys joined their Grandpa Shelton at the farm truck, Earl walked over to the clearing to eat with his brother.

They had a lot to discuss. Despite Sheriff Munie's efforts, bootlegging was going well for the Sheltons. Their most recent problem being the East St. Louis boys known as the Cuckoo gang. The two sat on the ground beneath a shade tree.

"We're gonna need to do something about them Cuckoos," Carl told Earl as he handed him a sandwich.

"They didn't vamoose when you told them too, huh?" Earl asked. "We fixin' to get bloody, Big Carl?"

"Maybe not." Carl had been thinking a lot about the problem. Besides the money, problem solving was actually one of the few things he did enjoy about running the rackets. "I've been thinking we might get Tommy Hayworth to do our dirty work for us."

"Tommy's a cold-blooded killer." Earl nodded, a hint of respect in his words. "He could sure enough do it."

"Yeah, but he also wants to be top dog of the Cuckoos? I'll have a talk with him."

***

Tommy Hayworth had a crush on Lula. He was thinking about her shapely white skin while he sat in his Buick waiting for the rain to let up. It hadn't stopped for three solid days, but he was optimistic that it would slow down any minute.

The problem was he had worn his cowboy boots. They were hard to get off even when they were dry. He assumed they would be muddy by the time he tromped through the Shelton yard to the back door into the kitchen. Ma Shelton was a stickler for taking off muddy shoes. She didn't say much when Earl dragged in pig shit, but mud seemed to offend her.

Tommy was mostly concerned with getting the boots off. Once, when he and Lula had a romp in the barn, she had straddled his leg with her back to him, bent over and let him put his foot on her backside while she pulled them off one by one. The second boot had been the most fun, because he used his stocking foot against the soft pillows of her fine little ass. To this day he could conjure up the feel of his foot on that ass.

Today would be different. Lula had asked him to dine with her family. He hadn't eaten at the Shelton house since he and Lula started humping. Ma Shelton might not be very accommodating if he couldn't get his boots off. She might even send him home. He thought about trying to get his boots off in the car and going barefoot into the house. Pa Shelton and the boys might laugh at him and consider it a good joke.

Before he could decide what to do, it stopped raining. Tommy snatched his baseball cap off the dash, flung open his car door and splashed through the mud to the back porch. Lula threw open the door before he could knock.

"Land sakes!" she scolded. "It's about time you came inside. Supper's on the table."

"Don't bother with the boots," Ma Shelton said without looking back from the kitchen sink. "I ain't cleanin' the floor until it stops raining—that is, if we don't all drown first."

Carl and Bernie were already dishing food onto their plates. Pa Shelton sat with his eyes closed and his head tilted off to one side. Tommy took the empty chair next to Carl. Lula set a glass of sassafras tea in front of him and sat on the other side of him.

"Where's everyone else?" Tommy asked. He couldn't think of a time there had been so few Sheltons at their supper table.

"Probably treadin' water somewhere," Bernie said through a mouthful of food.

Ma Shelton gave Bernie's head a hard swat. "Don't be talkin' with your mouth full."

Bernie shoveled a big spoonful of fried potatoes into his mouth and kept quiet.

"Wake your pa up, Carl," Ma said as she sat down at the head of the table.

Carl gave his father a nudge on the shoulder.

"That was some good eatin'," Pa said as he opened his eyes and raised his head.

"You ain't ate yet, Pa," Ma said. "Now put your teeth in your glass and get to chompin'."

Tommy looked away while Pa pulled out his chompers and put them in a small glass bowl where they smiled up at everyone.

The room was uncharacteristically quiet while everyone ate. Tommy tried to play footsy with Lula, but she didn't respond back, so he quit trying to flirt and just ate his supper.

When everyone was finished and Pa had his teeth back in his mouth, Carl invited Tommy and Bernie into the den to have a smoke. That came as a surprise to Tommy, who'd assumed he and Lula would curl up on the loveseat and sneak a few smooches when no one was looking.

Instead, Lula helped her ma clean the table and barely gave even a comforting smile to her beau.

The walls of the den were filled with the stuffed heads of the brothers' prized kills. A gun rack held a half dozen rifles—one weapon for each of the five brothers and one for their pa.

Carl coaxed the fireplace into full flames while Tommy and Bernie lit up. He then poured each of them a glass of brandy and passed the drinks around.

"Here's to family and friends," Carl said, raising his glass.

Tommy felt the eyes of the brothers on him as he drank. He had an unsettling feeling. *Was Lula pregnant?*

"Tommy," Carl said matter-of-factly, "we want you to help Bernie kill a few Cuckoo gangsters."

Tommy staggered a moment, fighting the dizziness that almost took his breath away.

Carl reached out and steadied him by grasping his arm.

"Th-th-thank God, that's all it is." Tommy finally struggled to say. "For a moment there, I thought Lula was—was—oh, never mind."

***

Sending Bernie to do a job with Tommy Hayworth was like putting two mad dogs together in a chicken coop. In this case, the chickens were the five Cuckoo gang bootleggers sleeping soundly in the cabin near their big stillhouse on the Mississippi River.

The rattling of the Thompson machine guns drowned out the sickening sound of the death rattles coming from two of the men who awoke just long enough to pass into eternal sleep.

Of the other three, one made a spectacular dive through a glass window and escaped unharmed around the side of the building and into the woods. The two other survivors followed their comrade through the window, though with far less agility due to the half dozen bullet holes in each.

The entire ordeal took less than fifteen seconds. Bernie was pleased with the outcome. Having partly hidden his face with a kerchief just before the attack, he was pretty certain that those who escaped would, if they survived, identify only Tommy Hayworth as one of the shooters.

Tommy must've also been pleased. That night he treated Bernie to an evening of frolic at his favorite roadhouse, and even shared his main squeeze, a bodacious redhead with a set of legs befitting a dancehall girl. Bernie was glad he was able to spend one last evening with his partner in homicide.

The next week, Tommy Hayworth was machine gunned, along with three of his buddies, by the same fellow who'd made the infamous dive through the window at the Mississippi River cabin.

As always, Carl's manipulations worked. The only thing he regretted was that Lula seemed sadder about Tommy's death than he'd expected she would. She got over it quickly, however, when he presented her with a beautiful pinto gelding—though she did name him Tommy.

***

By mid-December, the Cuckoos had just about wiped out their own gang. Carl received a message from one of the survivors asking to meet him for a powwow at Wide-Open Smith's den of inequity in East St. Louis.

Erroring on the side of caution, Carl brought along Bernie, as well as their friends Tommy Gun and Smith and Wesson.

As they were leaving their motel for the meeting, an old driver with the Red Top Taxicab Company approached the brothers.

"Cab, Mr. Shelton?"

"Not tonight, Stan," Carl said, then listened for the message he expected from his longtime friend.

"You're right. You're being set up for an ambush!" the cab driver whispered, then continued on up the sidewalk to solicit the next people leaving the building.

"Damn them!" Carl said after he and Bernie were in their car and cruising down East Broadway.

Bernie said nothing. He reached in the backseat and extracted his gat from beneath a blanket. While he was checking it, Carl drove slowly, his mind racing through options.

Earl and most of the boys were on their way back from Florida with a shipment of rum. Those that remained were inexperienced gunmen.

What I wouldn't give to have Blackie Armes here tonight, Carl thought. Blackie had evolved into an efficient killer. The handsome youngster was proficient with bombs as well as the Thompson machine gun. He practiced at every opportunity, even firing the weapon from the backseat of an automobile while speeding down the road. Indeed, a sycamore tree near one of their hideouts was so full of holes it was teetering and expected to timber over when the next storm blew through southern Illinois.

By the time the brothers arrived at the near

empty parking lot in front of Wide-Open Smith's, Carl had devised a plan. One of the men scheduled to talk to them was Joseph Carroll, a friend and business partner of Bernie's. Carl knew Carroll well enough to believe he would want an opportunity to gloat to the brothers that he was about to kill them. That would be the only advantage that he and Bernie would need to get off the first shots.

Carl told Bernie the plan. They tucked their weapons beneath their long overcoats and entered the building. Carroll and two others were standing in front of the bar.

"Hey, Carl, Bernie," Carroll greeted them.

Bernie's Tommy gun was up and shooting flames, smoke, and a hail of bullets as he walked toward the men. The three Cuckoos immediately dropped to the floor. The young Shelton leapt on top of the barroom counter and continued firing down at the bodies until his weapon was empty.

"What the hell, Bernie!" Carl hadn't moved from in front of the doorway.

With a wide-eyed stare and breathing hard, Bernie placed a new magazine in his gat as he passed his big brother, went out the door, and back to the car.

9

Carl didn't like anyone around when he did the account books. If his brothers knew how much loot they were bringing in, they would just waste it on frivolous things they didn't need—Bernie on partying and being a big shot and Earl on farm equipment. The equipment wouldn't have mattered so much except that technology was improving so rapidly. What they bought today would often be outdated within six months. That didn't deter Earl. He bought a new tractor every time one came out with more power or better wheels.

With only one desk light on in his East St. Louis office, Carl studied the year's figures. Slot machines had brought in a cool two million; gambling, two and a half million; vices such as prostitution, car theft, and bank robberies, about two and a half million. Bootlegging, of course brought as much as all those combined.

Carl used a pencil to subtract figures. After payouts for gang members, bribes for government officials, and costs of materials such as vehicles, guns, and other equipment, the Shelton brothers' profit was right at five million dollars for the year. Not bad when the rest of the country was in an economic depression.

The decline in competition from other gangs accounted for much of the Shelton Gang success. The Cuckoos still had control on horse and dog racing but that didn't bother Carl. Those were enterprises that required more time and effort than he was willing to devote.

He took out a piece of paper and jotted ideas that would both make money and help him launder the illegal cash they had accumulated. His favorite investment was land. With oil becoming a much-needed commodity all across the world, the low lands of Little Egypt were teeming with rocking oil pump jacks. He read about Texas men who become rich when oil was found on their land. Illinois oil had less pressure deep underground than in Texas, so instead of a gusher, it had to be pumped up.

Carl's plan was to purchase land and then quickly resell it—but keep the mineral rights. Still, the problem was they had more cash than they could possibly launder. *Make sure you hang up your guns and enjoy life—before the bullet sends you to bootlegger heaven."* Charlie Birger's last words to him were haunting. There was no reason to risk an early death.

He raised the chain that was fastened to his trousers' and checked the time. He had to get ready to go to the racetrack. Slipping the timepiece back into his watch pocket, he stacked the papers neatly and tucked them away in the drawer, along with thoughts of giving up the rackets.

***

The one area of gambling the Sheltons all enjoyed and fought to keep uncorrupted was horseracing. Everyone from Ma and Pa to Lula loved horses. They liked to visit the Fairmount Race Track in Collinsville as a family at least once a month.

"Ma!" Hazel called down the stairwell as they prepared to leave, "Lula's wearin' trousers again."

"Well, if she wants to look like a boy, let her!" Ma hollered back. "At least she's past that flapper craze."

When going to the race tracks, Hazel and Ma Shelton liked to wear fancy hats with their cotton frocks. Ma was much more interested in her hat than which dress she wore with it. Hazel liked to show off her slim waistline, so she wore the tightest mid-calf skirts she could find. Since she couldn't stop her hips from filling out, she wore shoulder pads and high collars to give her a trimmer look.

"Pa!" Ma yelled, "Get that motor car around here before Hazel decides she wants to change clothes again."

Earl and Bernie had already left. They wanted to take a turn around the stables to get a feel for any horses looking lame or appearing particularly frisky.

"I want to drive." Lula ran from the house and opened the driver's side door. "Slide over, Pa!"

Pa stabbed his cigar at his youngest daughter. "I won't have no female telling me what to do."

"Move over, Daddy," Ma ordered. She got into the backseat beside Hazel. "How's a girl to learn if her own pa won't give her a chance?"

Pa gave in and moved over, but grumbled all the way to the racetrack. Lula had no sooner slid the vehicle into a parking spot than the three ladies took off for the fairgrounds, leaving half-crippled Pa to fend for himself.

They made straight for the grandstand. They had recently returned from the Kentucky Derby, where they watched a three-year-old named Gallant Fox win the race by two lengths on a muddy track. Mint juleps were the craze at Churchill Downs, so Hazel insisted on having them each time she went to the races. Since the drink looked so decorative and tasted sweet, they also fooled the law.

Hazel quickly found a spot where she could be seen by any eligible bachelors. With one hand holding her drink and her other arm bent luxuriously upwards to hold her hat in place, she assumed the pose of a Sears catalogue model.

"Move away from me, Lula," Hazel chastised her sister. "I don't want anyone thinking you're my little boy."

"Mommy! Oh, Mommy!" Lula whined to Hazel. "Can I have a dollar for some cotton candy? Please, Mommy?"

"Get away from me, you filthy brat!" Hazel looked to her mother, who had sat down to study the daily racing form.

"Give me a dollar, and I'll leave." Lula held out her hand.

"I'm not giving you a dollar!"

"Give her a dollar!" Ma said without looking up.

"Oooh!" Hazel reached in her purse and handed her sister a dollar.

"Thank you, Mommy!" Lula took the dollar and skipped along the grandstand toward the wagering windows.

As she waited in line, a tall, handsome man smoking a cigarette and wearing a cowboy hat smiled at Lula.

"Who was that pretty lady you were just talking to?" the cowboy asked, his voice deep, with a southern drawl.

"Oh, that's my Aunt Hazel. She's a sister of the Shelton brothers. You've heard of Carl, Earl, and Bernie, I suppose?"

"No, ma'am. I'm visiting here on business from Tucson. I'd like to meet her, though. I have a tip on the next race that might bring me into her good graces."

"Well, uh, you give me the tip and I'll guarantee a night with her that you will never forget." Lula leaned in and whispered, "She's a sportin' gal, you know."

A minute later, Lula ran down the grandstand steps to where Bernie was studying the racing forms.

"How much cash you got on you, Bernie?" Lula asked. "I've got a sure thing for an exacta in race four."

"How's that?"

"A cowboy from Arizona said that five horses in the next race have Monday morning sickness. The other two horses are fine but the one called Favorite should win easily and Early Bird is a cinch for second."

Bernie studied the racing form. Favorite was a two to one to win, but the other was a dark horse at sixty to one. He'd never been good at math like his brother Carl, but he could see that an exacta on a long shot would pay big money. He pulled his money clip from his pocket. "Five hundred dollars is all I got."

"Hurry, Bernie! The race is about to begin."

Lula snatched the money roll from his hand and ran to the wagering windows. She just got the money down as the post bell rang. With ticket in hand, she hurried back to Bernie. The horses were already finishing the clubhouse turn. Her picks were running one and two just as predicted.

The announcer's deep voice called the race.

"As they come down the backstretch, it's Favorite by a length, Early Bird in his shadow. Close behind is Last Testament on the rail. Baby Bowery coming hard on the outside."

"Come on, Early Bird!" Lula screamed.

"Into the turn, it's Favorite opening up a two-length lead, with Early Bird trying desperately to stay close."

With both hands, Lula sank her nails into her brother's forearm.

"And down the stretch they come!" the announcer barked, a hint of southern drawl in his voice.

"Hey, Bernie!" Lula pulled hard on his arm. "That guy's voice. He's the one who gave me the tip."

Bernie's face turned white. "That's the guy?" He slapped his forehead so hard his glasses fell off one ear. "That guy is a Cuckoo."

"You mean he's nuts?"

Bernie dropped his hand over his eyes.

"Early Bird fading fast. And now Baby Bowery on the outside is making his move, with Last Testament close behind. And across the finish line, it's Favorite by three lengths, Baby Bowery in second, and Last Testament will take third."

***

"Make me a bomb, Bernie," Carrie said that evening at Ma and Pa's home.

Lula sat on the chesterfield between Bernie and his girlfriend. Carrie held Lula's head on her shoulder as she cried. "I'll take it into that cowboy's place and blow him to kingdom come."

"That's crazy!" Bernie said. "There's still enough of the Cuckoo gang left to exact revenge."

"That guy insulted your sister." Carrie punched Bernie hard in the arm. "You gonna stand for that? What would Carl do if we told him?"

"Don't do that!" Bernie said. He didn't want his brothers to know how easily he'd been stung. "I know what Carl would do. He'd make it look like one group of Cuckoos were attacking the other. That way, we'd get our revenge and hurt their gang at the same time."

"Well, quit talkin' about it and just do it." Carrie smacked Bernie again.

He rose from the couch, went to the wall phone, and gave the operator Blackie Armes' number. A former coal miner, Blackie played with dynamite like it was firecrackers.

"I need an explosive on a timer," Bernie said into the speaker. "Yeah, four sticks should be fine."

***

The next day, dressed as flower shop delivery girls, Carrie and Lula carried two big vases full of plants into the East St. Louis building. So as to not attract attention, they had dressed down as much as two beautiful women could.

In the big office, businessmen rushed from one cubicle to another, trying to finish last minute assignments before the five o'clock hour. Since the goal was to further the Cuckoos fighting among themselves, the timer on the bomb was set for six o'clock. Even Bernie knew the loss of innocent lives would only cause public outrage and tougher law enforcement.

As they were carrying the pots across the room, Lula spotted the cowboy announcer behind his office partition. A coffee in one hand and cigarette in the other, he cupped a telephone beneath his chin as he spoke angrily. He glanced up at Lula. She froze. The cowboy hung up the phone and raced right past her to where a pretty secretary was typing.

"I told you to deliver those notes to the race track. Can't you bimbos do anything right?" The cowboy put down his coffee, leaned over her desk, and wrote on a piece of paper.

The secretary was so flustered she knocked over his coffee into a wastebasket. She quickly rose, and with shaking hands filled him a new cup from a cannister behind her desk.

After carefully placing the plants in the conference room, Carrie made sure the bomb was still covered with dirt while Lula walked casually behind the cowboy's room, took the coffee out of the secretary's hands, and spit in it. The eyes of the ladies met. They smiled.

"Make sure you leave no later than five o'clock," Lula whispered, then followed Carrie through the busy workroom.

Since it was a Friday, no one was on the workroom floor when the bomb went off. Word got out that it was an attack by rival Cuckoo gang members. A week later, the cowboy's bullet-riddled body was found in a parked car near the racetrack.

***

Only after two of the cowboy's fellow Cuckoo gang members were arrested for his murder did Bernie tell his brothers that he was the one who did the bombing. Earl gave Bernie a congratulatory slap on the back. Carl's slap came harder and across the face.

"You stupid bastard!" Carl gave one more backhand that sent Bernie rolling across the gravel floor. "I do my best to clean up your messes, but you just won't stop, will you?"

If the three brothers were not alone in the machine shed at the time, Bernie would've fought back. He was used to his elder brother's abuse, but wouldn't have tolerated it if it occurred in front of others.

"Why are you mad about this one?" Earl asked. "It sounds like it worked in our favor."

"I'm not mad about this one," Carl growled. "I'm fuming about this pipsqueak brother of ours doing things without checking with us first. Now, I know why I got called into the district attorney's office yesterday for questioning about the race-track bombing. They also told me that Bernie and me was under suspicion for the killings at Wide Open Smith's place. It seems that one of the East St. Louis police officers that I paid to dump the bodies squealed."

Carl lifted Bernie by the collar and threw him up against the side of the shed. "If we have to take the fall for this, so help me, brother, I'll see that you're the one who hangs for it."

Carl opened the machine shed door and stomped through a pile of cow shit on his way across the yard. Earl put a sympathetic hand on Bernie's shoulder but then followed his big brother back toward the house.

Bernie stood for several minutes, rubbing his jaw. His mind raced through his options. At first, he didn't believe that Carl would let him take the fall for the killings, but the more he thought about it, the less confident he became.

Something had changed in Carl. He hadn't been the same since Charlie Birger swung. Maybe he was losing his nerve. Bernie remembered how Birger had turned on his own men in the last days of his life. If Carl meant what he'd said, it wasn't just a Shelton gang problem. Bernie's own life was in jeopardy.

He paced around the machine shed studying the tractors and trailers as if one of them might hold the answer to his problems. There was no doubt the cop who betrayed them needed to be dealt with. If he paid the price, it would send a message that the Sheltons were not to be messed with.

Acting without Carl's permission would be chancy. Bernie may again find himself the odd man out. After all, all the members of the gang were loyal to Carl. He paid them enough. This, however, was a matter of Bernie's survival.

He found himself standing at a desk and chair near the back of the shed. A pad of paper and pencil used for writing telegrams lay beneath a heavy layer of dust. Tearing off the top sheet he wrote a hasty message to his old grade school friend, Black Charlie Harris.

10

Black Charlie didn't trust anyone, much less Mike Dipisa. The deal he'd made with the Egan Rats was only as good as their sweaty handshake. The Purple Gang were the ones most hurt by the car chase gun battle. Law enforcement was coming down hard on organized crime, and the Purples had the most to lose. The boys from Little Egypt were still somewhat an unknown in Detroit.

He and Burke were on their way to pick up Johnny Reid at his home. Both were on their toes for trouble. When they were within a few blocks of Johnny's place, they passed half a dozen police cars slowly cruising in different directions.

"Something's up, Fred." Charlie looked into the backseat to make certain their arsenal was hidden from view under a dark blanket. Neither Burke nor he could afford any more trouble with the law. They were both well known to local, state, and federal officials.

"Let's just drive by Johnny's house in case he's outside waiting for us," Burke said.

Since the Egan Rat was the one driving, Charlie didn't see any sense in disagreeing.

The lane leading up to Reid's home was dark, with a front lawn filled with trees and bushes. When they got close, Charlie saw a shadow move behind one of the evergreens.

"There he is." Charlie rolled down his window to signal Reid.

Just as Reid waved and stepped out from behind the tree, a shotgun blast struck at just the right spot on the back of his neck that his head was blown completely off his shoulders.

"Ambush!" Charlie ducked beneath the dash. "Floor it!"

At least one bullet ricocheted off their car as they drove away. They both knew they were in no position to make it a fight.

***

The following morning, Black Charlie and the Egan Rats were mourning Reid's murder by having a big breakfast at his place.

"The medical examiner gave Johnny's death a creative cause." Bob Carey looked up from the newspaper. "He called it 'traumatic cerebral hemorrhage'."

"They're trying to hide the gang war from the public," Gus Winkler suggested. Winkler prided himself on public relations. He'd already negotiated protection for his St. Louis friends by paying off several cops and government officials in Detroit.

"I found out that Frankie Wright was the one who blew Johnny's head off." Burke's assertion surprised no one. Wright was a newbie in the underworld of Detroit. His gambling debts were building up to where he could be easily bought. "The Purple Gang boss, Abe Bernstein, also has a hit out on Wright for knockin' off one of their kikes. Bernstein said he'd pay us—but good—to fix Wright."

"You gonna do it?" Charlie asked. He didn't like getting mixed up in gang wars. The East St. Louis hoods seemed like amateurs compared to the big-time city gangsters.

"*We*--are gonna do it," Burke corrected. He glared at Charlie as if seeing him for the first time. "You know, for a fella that's supposed to be such a tough guy, you seem mighty reluctant."

Charlie glared back but knew better than to argue. Since Bernie had just sent him a telegram calling him back to Little Egypt, Charlie had an excuse if he wanted out. Still, being labeled a coward was not something he could tolerate. The Sheltons could wait. "What's the plan?" he asked Burke.

"The Purple Gang will snatch Wright's friend. Wright pays the ransom, and Bernstein tells him to pick up his friend at the Milaflores Apartments.

We will have rented out the entire floor. When he goes to get him, we are waiting."Charlie found the plan workable.

The following week, he, Burke, and Carey waited on a fire escape until Wright showed up with two of his heavies. When Wright knocked on the door where he was told his friend was being held, Burke threw open the fire door and began blasting. Charlie and Carey stepped in next to him and unloaded their .38 caliber revolvers. After just a few moments, the gun smoke became so thick the assassins couldn't see their victims lying on the floor. One of the dying men moaned.

"Get him!" Carey yelled. With shaking hands, he struggled to reload his .38. "Get him again!"

Burke didn't need encouragement. He unloaded a torrent of lead into the bodies until his cartridge ran dry. The three hitmen turned and sprinted down the fire escape. Winkler had the motor running and, as the last car door slammed shut, he burnt rubber racing the vehicle out of the alley.

11

Hail hit the car hood like rounds from a Tommy gun. By the time Black Charlie arrived at the Shelton house, the sky was clearing with the ominous clouds moving off to the east. Charlie was glad to get away from Detroit. The Egan Rats were getting too bold. They had taken up kidnapping gangsters for ransom. It was a common enough racket. Gangs had the money to pay off, and as long as a fair price was asked, they paid up quickly. Still, it was just a matter of time before Fred Burke and his mob slipped up. Charlie didn't want to be there when they did.

Ma and Pa Shelton were sitting in the living room in rocking chairs, Ma crocheting and Pa smoking a pipe. Their girls were in the love seat, Lula reading a book while Hazel flipped her hair and day dreamed. Two identical gray tabby cats lay on their laps.

"I'm supposed to meet Bernie here to get some money," Charlie said to no one in particular.

"You might as well sit and rock awhile." Ma pointed at empty rockers on either side of the couple. "Mind the cat's tails. Bernie won't be back for a half hour or so."

The Shelton patriarch being the only family member he could tolerate, Charlie took a rocking chair next to Pa's. The girls didn't even look up, a fact that riled Charlie a little. They were both past their teen years and had the firm, hard bodies a man approaching middle age could appreciate. Hazel would be no fun at all, but Lula had spice. He kept glancing at her, and the more he glanced, the faster he rocked.

"There's nothin' makes me edgier than a person rockin' against me." Ma glared at him. "Now get in rhythm or move to a four-legged chair."

Charlie stopped rocking. Suddenly, Lula threw her book down on the coffee table. The cat in her lap shrieked and jumped toward the stairway. It bounded up the steps. Its twin in Hazel's lap raised its head with sleepy eyes, but dropped back down into the nook between her legs.

"I told you to quit reading that garbage!" Ma scolded.

"This isn't garbage, Ma. It's *The Great Gatsby*, and it's the rave everywhere. I just can't stand it that Daisy has to live life the way society tells her to. Be a good housewife, let your man take care of you. Why can't she live her life like a man? She should touch and taste the world. Then when she finds what she wants, take it and don't look back."

"We never should have given women the vote." Pa Shelton shook his head.

"If all we're gonna have is males in politics," Ma retorted, "we might want to give it back."

Lula rose from the chair, kicked the book off the coffee table and stormed toward the kitchen. Charlie waited about ten minutes, then said he was getting a glass of water in the kitchen.

"Don't announce it," Ma said. "Just do it."

Charlie got his water, then went searching for Lula. He found her in a backroom lying on her stomach on the chesterfield, a couch only available to the wealthy—and bootleggers. The twin mounds of her buttocks excited him.

"I-I was just getting a glass of water," Charlie stammered.

Lula looked up at Charlie as if seeing him for the first time. She leapt from the couch, went around behind it and stood with her back against the wall. Instead of recognizing her fear, Charlie mistook it for an invitation. He placed his glass on a table, came around and stood inches from her. He could smell her hair.

The softness of her face slowly turned hard. She seemed totally immune to Black Charlie's charms. It was a rejection he was unfamiliar with. He made a final move that had always worked in the past. Taking her in his arms, he put his mouth close to her neck.

She stiffened in his embrace. "I ain't gonna court an old man like you." Her voice was full of scorn. "Especially a shrimp that barely comes up to my eye level." Then she added a Daisy Buchanan-like line from F. Scott Fitzgerald's *Gatsby* that Black Charlie would never forget. "Rich girls don't marry poor boys."

Charlie wanted to strike her. He didn't. Violence toward a woman went against his personal code. As he was returning to the kitchen, Lula gave a snicker that was neither cute nor friendly. It was full of the absurdity that a short, aging man with no money thought he had a chance with a beauty like her.

***

That night, Bernie commissioned Charlie to find out how the law knew about his murderous spree at Wide Open Smith's place.

"I want the cop who snitched on me dead!" Bernie drew a finger across his throat as if his words weren't clear enough.

Charlie displayed no emotion one way or the other at hearing the youngest Shelton confess-ing to the murders. And killing the rancid cop was likely a mistake, an impulsive effort by Bernie to save face with his brothers. Nothing new about that. But, as long as Charlie could profit, he didn't care if Bernie dug himself a deeper grave.

"Start with the Sixth Street stationhouse," Bernie said over coffee in the kitchen. "I'm bettin' it's that young punk that just started in the jailhouse. Everyone there will know who the bum is who ratted. The night clerk at the desk is a pushover. He'll most likely tell you everything you need to know."

"I'm not really worried," Bernie added. "Carl is the worrier in the family. He worries enough for all of us. Carl had the bodies moved so nobody should have known where they got bumped off. If you can find out who snitched, we can take care of him. That is, unless you'd like to make the extra cash yourself."

"I'll take care of it," Charlie said. He took one last sip of coffee, rose and left the kitchen. When he passed through the living room, Ma, Pa, and the girls were back in the same seats as earlier, minus both cats. Lula was the only one to look up. She stuck her tongue out at him.

***

Charlie figured that the Sixth Street jailhouse would be empty at four o'clock in the morning except for the desk clerk and the jailer. He was right.

"Who ratted about the shooting at Wide Open's place?" With hand on the man's throat, Charlie had the police officer pinned up against the wall.

"I don't remember."

"Would a C-note help you remember?" He dangled a bill in front of his eyes.

"I wouldn't snitch on a friend to save my life."

Charlie's hand slowly returned the bill to his pocket, but came back out fast. A four-inch blade popped up directly under the policeman's nose. Charlie drew a thin line of blood then moved it under his neck.

"He's in the backroom."

Charlie closed the switchblade and turned toward the door.

"Hey," the man yelled. "Don't I still get the C-note?"

Charlie ignored him and made his way to the backroom. He found the officer cowering beneath his desk. Grabbing him by the shoulders he pulled him kicking and screaming to his feet. The officer clutched a small area rug he'd tried to hide beneath.

"They think the murders took place that Sunday around noon," the cop said as fast as he could make the words come out of his mouth.

"What I want to know is who reported the murders at all?" Charlie asked.

"All I did was report a lot of blood on the floor at Wide Open Smith's place. I just said it was more than normal after a Saturday night brawl."

"So, you took the money from Carl to hide the bodies, then thought you'd play the smart cop to get credit for discovering the murder site."

"I couldn't see how it could hurt." The jailor brought the dirty rug to his mouth, bit it and shut his eyes.

It was easy for Black Charlie to find the officer's jugular vein, since it was almost throbbing out of his neck. Putting the rug over the knife, he plunged it into the artery, then held it in his throat for nearly a minute until the pulsating geyser of blood had soaked the rug. By then, the officer was on his knees with Charlie easing him slowly into a more comfortable position for his eternal sleep.

At last, the killer wiped the bloody knife clean against the dead man's shirt, folded it, and returned it to his pocket. Just as Charlie was rising, the officer who had been out front walked into the room.

"Do I get the C-note now?" he asked.

"No." Black Charlie walked past him and wiped a trace of blood off his hand onto his shirt. "What you get is a chance to live to be a grandpa."

Outside, Charlie walked calmly to the car and got in on the passenger side.

"How much it cost us?" Bernie asked, opening his wallet.

"Two Cs for the bribe," Charlie lied. "Three more for cutting the bastard's throat."

Bernie smiled as he counted out five one-hundred-dollar bills. "You want to join Carrie and me at the Pine? Lula and Blondie will be there."

"Not tonight, Bernie." Lula was the last person he wanted to be around. "Carl's got me heading back to Detroit this evening to set up a purchase."

That afternoon, Charlie made a visit to a dentist. "I want you to replace my good eye tooth with a gold one to match the other."

"Why would you want me to replace a perfectly good tooth?"

"I want my smile to be the last thing people see before they die."

***

Carl dropped his head into his hands. "Of all people, why did you send Black Charlie?" He felt guilty for slapping Bernie over the racetrack bombing, but now he just might kill his little brother if he didn't get himself under control. "Why couldn't you have just let me take care of it?"

"Why are you worried?" Bernie threw some peanuts in his mouth. "The snitch is dead and Charlie ain't gonna confess to murder."

"Black Charlie Harris hates us, you idiot."

"No more than anyone else, I don't imagine."

"Get out, Bernie!" Carl bellowed. "Take Carrie and go up to Peoria until you have some good news."

Grumbling beneath his breath, Bernie left his brother alone in his office. Carl looked down at the money that was wrapped in white paper with Charlie's name on it. It was to be used in the whiskey purchase in Detroit. He turned sideways in his chair, leaned down to a three-foot high safe and spun the combination in different directions. Opening it, he extracted two thousand dollars in twenties. They appeared perfect except the print quality on Andrew Jackson's coat was slightly faded.

After several more moments of contemplation, Carl wrapped the counterfeit money in a new sheet of paper and wrote Charlie Harris's name on it.

***

Just after the new year, Black Charlie got word that Lula had got pregnant and moved to Indiana. He'd been dwelling on her rejection of late. It seemed his hate for the Sheltons ran straight through the entire brood. He blamed Ma Shelton's bad parenting for allowing her children to become the way they were. Her husband and the entire community tried to warn her but she would hear nothing negative about any of her seven brats.

Just when he thought his hatred for the Sheltons could get no worse, two policemen picked him up one day as he was leaving his apartment. They took him straight downtown for a show-up. Charlie was shocked when he was picked out of the line-up and charged with distributing counterfeit money. That afternoon, he found himself standing before a judge in a courthouse.

"I'm not much on reading," Charlie told the magistrate after the constable handed him a long list of charges, "but I'd expect I can do my own talking."

"Then tell us, Mr. Harris," the judge said, "what possible excuse could you have for passing counterfeit money?"

"Them dirty rat Shelton brothers set me up! I ain't no paperhanger! You let me go and I'll rid the law of their scum."

12

"They gave Black Charlie ten years in Leavenworth for counterfeiting," Bernie reported during dinner one evening. As Carl had instructed, he'd stayed in Peoria until he could bring back good news.

Carl and Earl showed more interest in their corn-on-the-cob than they did Bernie's report. The rest of their family had gone down to DuQuoin. Ma and Pa Shelton were big bluegrass fans. Some of the best from the Ozarks had come up to perform.

"That's not the only thing, Carl." Bernie brought out his second piece of exciting news. "Fred Burke used that Tommy gun you gave him to kill Frankie Wright and two other thugs in Detroit. Wright was shot fourteen times, but lived long enough to tell the cops, 'The machine gun worked. That's all I can remember.' Then he croaked. I hope that cop wasn't hankerin' for no long conversation."

Bernie chuckled, but Carl and Earl started gnawing on their turkey legs.

"Anyway, here's the funny part. Burke's gone into a new line of work. Kidnapping."

"Kidnapping?" Earl said as he filled his coffee cup. "What so funny about that? We've done our share of it, haven't we?"

"Sure. But we never kidnapped one of Scarface's thugs."

"You're kidding!" Carl stopped eating and was now paying full attention. "One of Al Capone's boys? And Burke is still alive?"

"Get this, Carl. I guess Capone was so impressed by Burke's balls, he invited him and his boys to dinner."

"Whose Burke got in his gang now?" Earl asked.

"You remember Gus Winkler?"

"Sure, I always liked his wife." Earl smiled. "Sweet gal."

"Well, you'll remember them from being in the Egan Rats gang from St. Louie. We've done jobs with all of them. Besides Winkler, there's Byron Bolton and Ray Nugent and Bob Carey."

"Carey?" Carl glanced toward the ceiling for a memory. "Is he the one who liked to watch his wife having sex with other men?"

Bernie's face turned red. "Well, I wouldn't know about that. But anyway, Capone took them all into his rackets. He calls them his *American Boys*. It's being said that the first job Capone sent them on was to kill Frankie Yale in New York."

"The Egan Rats were the one's to knock off Yale, too?" Carl set back in his chair and tried to digest the information. "That's big news, Bernie. Why didn't you lead with that?"

"They ain't Egan Rats no more, Carl." Bernie corrected. "They's the American Boys now, and your gat is makin' 'em famous."

***

"That ain't Bugsy Moran!" Fred Burke whispered to George Goetz. He pointed his gat at the back of one of the seven men facing the wall. He'd been looking forward all night to again using the Thompson machine gun that Carl Shelton had traded him in exchange for a five-minute romp with a scar-faced whore.

"No shit!" Goetz whispered back. He raised his twelve-gauge pump action shotgun that he lovingly referred to as his Twelve Iron. "The lookouts must have been fooled by his brown fedora and that he's the right size."

Dressed in police uniforms, Burke and Goetz both raised a hand and loosened their collars at the same time. This was not the way things were supposed to go down. Capone had made it very clear that Bugsy Moran was the one he wanted dead.

Standing on either side of them were Ray Nugent and Bob Carey, wearing chinchilla topcoats and gray fedoras. After lining the seven men up facing the wall, Burke had opened the side door and let the two in. From beneath his topcoat, Nugent produced a gat and Carey a shotgun similar to the one Goetz held.

Ten feet in front of the four gunmen, six of the seven men were very relaxed. Three of them hadn't even extinguished their smokes. All had plenty of experience with shakedowns, plus they knew there were no illegal products in the building.

The nervous seventh man was John May, a mechanic. Though it was very cool in the building, May was perspiring heavily. Vapor exited his mouth and skin. He wished he'd stayed home that morning with his seven children, but his family needed the money for food as well as clothing for the winter. Those necessities had brought him into the underworld of Bugsy Moran and his henchmen.

It was deathly silent. May recognized the click of a safety catch being flipped. He had a shotgun at home that made a similar sound. While the other men tensed and clenched their teeth, John May turned his head and looked back over his shoulder at the four men aiming the barrels of their guns at the Moran men. A shotgun blast tore the left side of his face off. He fell to the ground as the six men beside him began a jerking, spasmodic death dance. Bullets tore into them, sometimes exiting and carrying pieces of bone and brain matter that splattered on the wall.

May survived the hail of lead from the first barrage, though he was numb and bleeding from a dozen holes in his body. Laying partially beneath another body, he saw from his good eye that the four men were reloading. The Tommy gun men completed the task first, one reloading with a fifty round ammo drum and the other a twenty round box clip. The box clip man knelt to one knee and let loose with another volley. The last thought of John May was, *I should have stayed home today.*

13

That following Tuesday was a surprisingly warm day for February. Carl set in the tonsorial parlor with a hot towel on his face as a pretty manicurist cleaned a day's farm work from under his finger nails.

"Nobody shot me!" Stan, the barber, said from behind the *St. Louis Post-Dispatch*. The headline read, ST. VALENTINES DAY MASSACRE! Stan had a few minutes to catch up on the news while waiting for Carl's whiskers to soften, though there was hardly a hair on the eldest Shelton's face. All three brothers had just been shaved that morning.

"Frank Gusenberg's last words," Stan continued when no one commented. "Hard to believe, ain't it? He was the only one out of the seven victims to live long enough to tell who killed them, and even on his death bed he wouldn't rat on a rat! Code of the outlaws."

The barber took his spectacles off and pinched the end of his own nose. He'd just insulted the king of outlaws, who was sitting four feet away from him. Carl slowly took the towel off his face and glared at Stan.

"I'd 'spect you're ready for that shave now, Mr. Shelton." With shaking hands, Stan picked up the straight edge.

"I believe we'll wait a few minutes until your screaming trembles subside." Carl tipped the manicurist who picked up her supply tray and gracefully swung out of the room.

The massacre in Chicago was good news to the Sheltons, since fewer people were discussing Bernie's bloody Saturday night fiasco from two months before. Carl was feeling clever for the way he'd covered it up. Fortunately, several East St. Louis cops were on his payroll. It cost less than a thousand dollars to get them to discretely dispose of the bodies for him.

"It also says here they found three bodies in a ditch when the snow melted the other day," Stan said to change the subject until his hands steadied. "They think they were kilt at Wide-Open Smith's place. The cops got a tip that Monday morning and were checking out Smith's roadhouse—to find ol' Floyd cleaning up the blood. You know ol' Floyd ain't too smart, and when he seen a mess, he didn't think nothin' of it and just started mopping."

Carl hadn't been happy to hear that someone had tipped the law as to where the crime had occurred, but Black Charlie had taken care of the snitching police officer and Carl had taken care of Black Charlie. Matters improved, though, when the coroner set the time of death for the three gangsters as sometime late on the Sunday morning before Christmas. He figured the fact that he'd moved the bodies to the freezer might have caused that miscalculation. That would be a trick he'd need to remember for future homicides.

A newspaper reporter looked up from a magazine he was reading. "Where were you boys that Sunday, Carl?" He wasn't afraid to ask, since he got along fine with the notorious brothers. He was a regular in that same barber's chair most every day, waiting for a juicy piece of gossip. The Sheltons had become friendly acquaintances.

"Why, funny you should ask. Sheriff Munie is heading out to the farm to bring Bernie in for questioning this very afternoon. I'd expect all Bernie needs to tell him is that he was sitting in church at the time of the murders."

***

Sheriff Munie's mouth dropped when Bernie strolled casually out to his car to greet him. The bootlegger was wearing scapular medals that jingled around his neck as he walked. The religious medallions draped from a gold chain weren't what surprised the Sheriff. He expected such buttery behavior from the Sheltons, who knew that the Munie family were devout believers.

What surprised the lawman was that he thought he finally had Bernie dead to rights for the murder of the three thugs. The mobster's calm demeanor suggested otherwise. He decided to go along with the game. The youngest Shelton was just dumb enough to believe he could buy his way out of any murder rap, but he was smart enough to know that killing a lawman would be his undoing.

"I heard you was lookin' to bring me in, Jerome." Bernie was dressed in Farmer Johns and smelled bad. "You mind if I finish sloppin' the hogs before we go?"

"As long as you bathe afterwards. I don't need my car or my jail smelling like pig shit."

"Well, we could leave a lot quicker if you'd slop them hogs while I get cleaned up and dressed." Bernie leaned in as close as he could so the sheriff could get a good whiff of his pungent eau de shoat cologne.

"Okay, okay!" Munie pulled back and raised a hand to his face. "No funny business, Bernie! Just make it quick. And for God's sake, use plenty of soap!"

Bernie handed a bucket to the sheriff, then turned and hurried back to the house. Munie had plenty of experience feeding livestock, and was done by the time the suspect emerged from the house wearing a suit and carrying a small grip.

"Oh, crap, Jerome. Why the hell didn't I toss a few bales of hay down from the hayloft before I got all cleaned up. And them two dairy cows ain't gonna be able to milk themselves."

Since the Sheriff was already sweating through his shirt and coat, he told Bernie to hurry up and milk the cows while he tossed the hay.

"Then we're leaving no matter what else you need done."

"Yes, sir, Sheriff. I sure do appreciate your understanding."

Twenty minutes later, when Munie slid down the loft ladder, he held a bleeding hand against his once white shirt.

"What happened, Jerome?" Bernie asked.

"Ah, one of them twine bales busted when I lifted it, and I fell back into a pitch fork."

Just then a car sped toward them along the dirt road leading up to the house. As it swerved sideways and came to a stop, Bernie ducked behind a tractor. Munie, though, took the full force of the dust and dirt to his face, which was still dripping with sweat.

The driver's side door opened, and Carrie Stevenson spun her well-defined bared calves to the side. When she saw it was the County Sheriff covered with dirt and sweat who was staring at her ankles, she paused a moment, pulled her skirt up to the top of her thigh, and pretended she was adjusting a garter.

"Morning, Jerome. You come to help Bernie with the chores?"

"No, ma'am. I came to arrest him." The sheriff was now irritable enough to bring charges, even if he had no evidence yet.

"Arrest him?" Carrie gave Bernie a hard punch to the chest. "What'd you do now, you big, dumb ox?"

"Ouch! Would you quit hitting me? I don't know why he's arresting me, Carrie. Why you arrestin' me this time, Jerome?"

"For the triple murder at Wide Open Smith's the Sunday before Christmas."

"The Sunday before Christmas?" Carrie gave a laugh so shrill the livestock bellowed and backed away. "Sorry to disappoint you, but me and Bernie and his whole clan was in church from five o'clock that morning until late that evenin'. We was gettin' our preachin' from a travelin' evangelist. The Sheltons and me made breakfast and lunch for the entire congregation. You can check with the folks at the church if you want."

Munie gave Bernie a long, hard, filthy-faced glare. "You made me do all this farm work and cut my hand, and you knew all the time that you had an alibi?"

"Sorry about that, Jerome. If'n you'd told me why you was arrestin' me, I could have told you."

"Why the hell didn't you ask?" Munie grabbed his hat off his head, slapped it against his filthy trousers, then leapt into his squad car. He tried to spin his tires to repay Carrie for the dusting she'd given him, but gave the car too much gas, causing it to slide sideways against the metal support of a windmill. The side of the car grinded like fingernails on a chalkboard as it came free. It snaked back and forth along the sooty lane and then finally headed toward town.

14

Black Charlie didn't care for Leavenworth, but at least it didn't have snakes. Not the reptile kind, anyway.

The first thing the guards did when he was brought into the facility was dip his fingertips one at a time into ink and then rolled them onto a piece of paper.

"What are you doing, screw?" Charlie asked. He was being treated like a child at a doctor's office.

"We are called HACKS at Leavenworth, not screws. It stands for Hard Ass Carrying Keys."

"Okay, hack, so what's with the ink?"

"Everyone in the world has a different finger-print," the officer said. "You commit another offense and we'll know if you were at the crime scene by your fingerprints."

"I'll remember to wear gloves. Why don't other prisons do this?"

"They will. In fact, a smart federal fella named Hoover is already making copies of the ones we have on file. We've been doin' this at Leavenworth for two decades."

Next, he was shaved, showered, and issued dark blue cotton clothing. It was a far sight better than the striped suit he'd worn in Arizona, but it was still ill fitting and uncomfortable.

Each of the four main cell houses had a wide corridor for the hacks to supervise the five gallery levels that rose up on either side in the long buildings. Charlie's cell, like all the others, consisted of bunk beds on one side and a toilet on the other. At the end of the room was a built-in table and stool.

The first twenty-four hours in a prison cell were the hardest. Many convicts cried that first night. Charlie avoided that by thinking about how much he hated the Shelton brothers for his being there. He imagined and reimagined killing them over and over again until his eyelids grew heavy. He even hated their little sister, young Lula Shelton. She'd always called him Blackie and made-up silly rhymes about him. Plus, she'd rejected his advances, an insult he could not abide.

He was thinking about Lula when the guards shut most of the lights out across Cell House D. Only a series of individual lights in the corridors remained on. Instantly came voices making haunting sounds. Then a childlike voice called out, "Oh, Nicky, have you seen Babykins? Are you there, Baby Snooks?"

"That's the Fanny Brice Fan Club." Charlie's cell mate, Frank Nash, whispered to him. "Nicky is Julius Amstein. He's married to Fanny Brice."

"Fanny Brice? The vaudeville star?" Charlie whispered back. "I've seen her on stage. So—they're imitating Baby Snookums?"

"Amstein's getting paroled next week." Nash flicked a cigarette stub toward the head but missed. Tiny sparks spit onto the floor then instantly faded. "He ain't leaving soon enough for me. I don't want to listen to that racket any more than I have to. You just make sure you don't give them any reason to make fun of you or it'll be a long ten years."

Charlie had no intention of being there for ten years. Like his cell mate, he intended to be a model prisoner. Nash served as chef for the deputy warden at his home, which was outside the prison gates. A nearly bald, middle-aged man, there was nothing about Nash that would make the average citizen look twice at him.

"I could walk outta this joint anytime I want," Nash said, then changed back to a whisper. "Some of the boys down in Cell House B are planning on going out, if you want to get in on it."

Charlie didn't need to even think twice about it. He'd been doing a lot of studying and thought he'd be able to convince a judge to give him a new trial. After all, the whole counterfeit thing was the Sheltons' doing. Until then, he planned on being a model prisoner. Just like his cell mate.

For the most part, Leavenworth was a self-sufficient community. Over the next several weeks, Charlie was bounced around to different departments. First, they tried him in the electrical shop where he quickly burnt his hand by crossing the wrong wires. Before that was even healed, he went into a factory where inmates made shoes for the military. Next came the boiler room, then a furniture factory.

Finally, they settled him into the laundry room, placing him next to a mountain of a man who folded laundry while sitting on a stool. Back in their cell that night, Nash warned Charlie about the big man. "Don't even make eye contact with Carl Panzram. He will either want to rape you or kill you. He brags that he's killed twenty-one men and boys and raped over one thousand. He has to sit because his legs are bad. Remember that. He can't catch his butt buddies unless they get close to him."

Nash was in a talkative mood. He launched next into his own story about how he came to be in Leavenworth. "Me and my partner, Al Spencer, were caught back in twenty-three pulling one of the last train robberies in the United States. I had warned Spencer to leave the government bonds alone and take only cash. During the robbery, while my partner was filling a satchel, I stood guard outside the caboose. You know how I like to gab. So, I started havin' a political argument with the fireman. I found out too late that I should have focused more on the job at hand. Spencer had gotten overconfident and greedy and took all the government bonds. That mistake brought the feds into the case, and the two of us were apprehended a year later."

The lesson Charlie learned from Nash's larceny failures was to never trust a partner. A second thing he learned from his cell mate was how to charm. Charlie always tried to act a gentleman, but Nash assumed a level far beyond simple politeness. He'd a personality that could win over anyone. On several occasions, Nash talked himself out of trouble. A month after his incarceration, Black Charlie had an opportunity to practice what he'd learned—but he didn't.

15

His hand bandaged, Sheriff Jerome Munie followed his wife Mary and daughter Jeanene into the
Methodist Church in Fairfield. Infection had set in
from the rusty pitchfork puncture and required a
thorough and painful cleaning, two stitches, and a
swig of laudanum every few hours.

Finding himself and his entire congregation
the guests of a church that included the infamous
Shelton family was an excuse for a shot of the
laudanum.

"Morning, Jerome." Carl Shelton shook the
good hand of the lawman.

"Carl." Munie's head swam from the opium.

"Sorry to hear about the mix up at Bernie's place
the other day. He was sure enough grateful to you,
though, for helping him with his chores."

Munie's silent glare was still on his face a
moment later when the pastor greeted him.

"Sheriff," said the pastor. "I can see you're perturbed by the delay in getting our church repaired
after the recent flood. But you need not worry. We
shall be back in our hallowed halls next Sunday."

Munie nodded, attempted to clear the look of disgust from his face, and continued on into the sanctuary. Mary was talking fashions with several of her own congregation's church ladies. Jeanene had found several children to visit. Shelton gang children.

At that moment, Bernie Shelton leaned into the group of youngsters and said something that made them all laugh. When Jeanene dropped her head back to join in, Bernie placed his hand on the top of her head and gave her father a glare that sent chills down the lawman's spine.

As the service began, Carl Shelton's soft playing of the church organ, followed by the gentle voice of the preacher, put Munie to sleep. At least he thought it was the preaching that caused him to doze. It was a weakness that Mary tolerated since he didn't snore and his head seldom drooped. The laudanum brought dreams of Carrie Stevenson's shapely limbs. Normally, he dreamt of fishing or bird hunting, but since Carrie had been singing in the front row of the choir when he nodded off, she remained in his thoughts when his eyes grew heavy.

His pleasant reverie ended with the sound of mumbling and movement around him. Avoiding the temptation to raise his arms and stretch, the sheriff stood to join the exiting congregation. He struggled to think of something pleasant to say to the two preachers who would be standing on the church steps shaking hands. The stairwell in front of this Methodist church was much too narrow to sneak past without at least some sort of acknowledgment. Then he saw his wife moving sideways through the crowd toward him.

"Where is Jeanene?" Mary asked, panic in her voice. "She always returns before the service is over. I've searched everywhere for her."

Munie shrugged. Then he saw Bernie standing near the doorway watching him.

Your family will never be harmed by any of my men, Carl Shelton had told him. *But did Carl tell Bernie he'd promised that?*

When terror set in, the dreamlike effects of the laudanum were suddenly diminished. Munie pushed through those in the aisle to get to Bernie, who had turned around. The sheriff grabbed the bootlegger by the arm and spun him.

"What the hell did you do with my daughter?"

Munie had never been hit with a handbag before, but when Carrie Stevenson brought hers down on top of his head, it felt like she'd split his skull.

For just a moment, he saw the twinkling of stars between his ears. His recovery was swift though, perhaps thanks to the laudanum still in his system.

"You leave my man alone," Mary Munie screamed, "you ol' witch!"

Mary and Carrie had one another by the hair when Carl and the two ministers pulled them apart.

"Ladies, ladies!" the Methodist minister pleaded. "For goodness sake, it's God's day!"

Several parishioners who had made it to their cars or buggies were returning to see what the commotion was about.

"These Sheltons kidnapped my Jeanene." Munie shouted. His eyes were wide but his vision had gone black, not because of the heavy purse on his head but out of fear and anger.

"No one took your daughter, Jerome," Carl said. "I promised you that no one would bother your family."

"Yeh, but what if, what if some of your gang didn't know that you had promised that?"

"Bernie," Carl turned to his youngest brother. "Round up the boys and tell them to check the woods around the church for the girl." He turned to one of Munie's deputies who attended the Methodist Church. "You get hold of all the cops in the area. Tell them to stop every car within thirty miles of here and give them a description of Jeanene."

Ma Shelton leapt into action. "Margaret," she said to Carl's wife, "have all the church youngin's search the building. Earl, take some of the men and look in that old well that I've been trying to get you to fill in for the past month."

Mary Munie fainted right into the preacher's arms. His face turned red when the gasp of some of the church ladies made him realize that one of his hands was cupping her breast.

Both the inside and outside of the church was suddenly a flurry of activity. Mary was laid down in a pew and a wet towel placed on her forehead. Sheriff Munie regained his composure and accompanied Earl to the uncovered well. To their relief it was empty except for a family of toads that had found refuge in the muddy bottom. Some of the men immediately began boarding up the hazardous opening.

When the sheriff returned to the church to check on his wife, he found her sitting up in the pew with several Shelton women at her side.

"Did you find her?" Mary screamed at her husband.

"Not yet. But we will."

"Did they check in the outhouse?" Mary's hands shook as she covered her mouth.

"Yes, and down in the shitter too," Carl said.

"My God, Carl!" Ma Shelton reprimanded. "Show a little class!"

"Check inside the church one more time! *Please*!" Mary slapped her hands over her eyes.

"Well, you heard her!" Ma Shelton hollered at Carl and the sheriff. "Get moving!"

Carl nodded and Munie followed him.

"It's best to always oblige Ma," Carl whispered. "She's a holy terror when she's riled."

"You didn't take my daughter, did you, Carl?"

"No!"

"Did any of your gang?"

Carl ignored the question. "Let's check the balcony."

The church balcony seemed the last place anyone would expect to find a missing child, plus it had already been searched by the children. Carl just wanted the sheriff to shut up about the possibility that one of his men had kidnapped the girl. That was because Carl himself wasn't sure. He'd enough trouble just keeping the men from ransacking all of Little Egypt when they were drunk. Several of the gang had run-ins with the law outside of the normal Shelton rackets. Any one of them might have a grudge against many a lawman, much less a county sheriff.

There were only six rows of pews in the loft, so Carl and Munie walked through them to a water closet, which they opened and peered inside. They passed back through the rows of pews and were about to descend the stairs when Carl stopped dead in his tracks.

"What?" the sheriff asked.

Carl raised a hand, then slowly stepped back into the second row. Munie heard it then and recognized it. A familiar soft snore. The two men squatted and lowered their heads to the floor.

Curled up between two legs of a pew was little Jeanene Munie with her doll Maggie clutched tight against her chest. Sound asleep.

16

That next Saturday, Jerome Munie thanked the Sheltons for their help finding Jeanene by taking them bird hunting at a farm near Gillespie, Illinois. In fact, he was so appreciative, he was debating whether or not to continue his raids on their road-houses. But then Carl and Bernie showed up with Fred Burke, Gus Winkler, and Al Capone himself.

Munie was standing beside a pickup, having a smoke with the landowner, Maynard Eisley, when the big Lincoln stopped on the dirt road in front of them. Maynard had been talking non-stop since they arrived in the grassy glen. The old farmer hurried to finish his story while the five men exited the vehicle and retrieved their shotguns out of the trunk of the car.

"So, I woke up this morning with a piss hard-on," Maynard boasted proudly. "I told the old lady to jump on quick while she had the chance. Yes, sir. You shoulda seen the smile on her face for the next sixty seconds."

When Munie didn't even break a smile, Maynard grumbled and went to the back of the pickup truck to release the bird dogs. The sheriff was as mad as he'd ever been. It seemed that every time he tried to like the Shelton brothers, they found a way to ruin it.

Capone was a stout bull of a man of average height. He was dressed in his bird hunter's coat and wore a hunter's cap instead of the light-gray fedora he was famous for. He moved easily across the stubbly field toward Munie, loading his shotgun with two shells as he approached. Then leaving the action open, he flipped the gun into a side carry position.

"Al, meet Sheriff Munie," Carl said casually.

Munie was certain Carl introduced him with his title as a way to let the Chicago boss believe he'd the local law in his hip pocket. Capone's hand felt smooth but powerful when they shook. The famous scar on his face seemed more prominent than in his newspaper photos, the morning sun exposing the jaggedness from a long-ago knife slashing. But it was Capone's coal black eyes that most startled the sheriff. Perhaps it was only the well-publicized stories of the men he'd personally killed, but Munie felt he was peering into a soulless pit.

"Where's Earl?" Munie asked.

"Did he chicken out when he heard Killer Burke was coming?" Burke said as he stumbled a little in the tall grass.

"Earl is bringing in some rum from Jamaica," Carl said.

Though it was early morning, Fred Burke was half drunk. Munie couldn't decide if the famous machine gun killer was coming down from a night of frolicking or just getting started after too many Bloody Marys for breakfast. He decided it was most likely both. Burke was a stocky fellow with more than a hint of a beer belly. Hatless, his jet-black hair, combed straight back and held down with oil, defied even the strongest gusts of wind.

When the dogs were released, Gus Winkler stuck close to Capone, the two talking quietly as they shared stories.

"I came this way quite a bit when I first hit Chicago in nineteen," Capone reminisced. "Dees folks down here made some mighty fine bathtub gin for our joints."

"You didn't buy the white lightning?" Winkler asked. Winkler was the more athletic looking of the three guests from Chicago. Tall and slim with a hard enough face to make Munie glad the former Egan Rat had left St. Clair County. Rumor was he'd been the getaway driver after the St. Valentine's Day massacre.

"Nah, at that time Charlie Birger had that market pretty well wrapped up," Capone said.

"I met Charlie Birger," the old farmer said. "He walked right out of those woods one day while I was plowin' that field. Yes, sir, right outta them there woods over yonder. I remember it like it was yesterday. He strolled right up to me carryin' a satchel full of money he'd just stolen from the Gillespie Bank. 'Old timer,' he says to me. 'You bury this money and I'll split it with you if'n you tell the cops that I've been workin' with you all morning.'

"'How much you got, young fella?' I asked him.

"'I don't rightly know,' Charlie says, 'but I saw a couple of twenties before they started shootin' at me.'

"So, I agreed, and Charlie buried the suit he was wearin' along with the satchel. He took to that mule and that plow like he knowed what he was doin'. About an hour later, sure enough, here comes the sheriff and one of his men. They ask me if I'd seen a hide nor hair of a car passing by that mornin'. I told 'em no, and they never even asked about the fella plowing my field 'cause he was so covered with dirt and sweat.

"Well, sir, just to be on the safe side, Ol' Charlie worked all day, and when it came dark, he dug up that money. He let me count it while he cleaned up in that creek down yonder. He had near on a thousand dollars. 'Here's your half, Ol' timer,' he says.

"Yes, sir, that Charlie was an honest criminal. I made near on to five hundred dollars that day—and got my field plowed to boot. Yes, sir, by golly, no one had better say a bad word about Charlie Birger around me."

"Did you know that Charlie's ghost sometimes visits folks in Harrisburg and Benton?" Bernie chimed in when the old farmer stopped to take a breath. He wanted desperately to impress Fred Burke. Though Burke was only a suspect in Frankie Yale's murder, as well as the Detroit and Chicago massacres, his reputation with the Tommy gun Carl had given him was becoming international. "Mrs. Steinheimer took Charlie meals when he was waitin' to be hanged. His ghost visited her and thanked her for her kindness. She fainted."

"I heard it was Charlie hisself visited her," Burke said, slurring a little with his "s" words. "They say he's still alive, and it was a look alike who died on that scaffold."

"It was Charlie all right," Carl said. "I was there and saw him swing."

"Well, maybe they used a trick rope and switched bodies when he was being bagged and taken to the morgue," Burke added, clearly enjoying the stories. He pulled a flask from his vest and took a swig.

"If Charlie were alive, he'd be causing us trouble," Carl said, shaking his head. "He was one bootleggin' son-of-a-bitch who would never been able to lay low. He liked the limelight too much."

"Eh, Sheriff," Al Capone interrupted the conversation. "What say youse and me take a walk through that prairie grass down yonder and get away from all this yappin'?'"

Munie's eyes met Carl's. He'd heard of Capone's love for personally knocking off opposition, especially lawmen. The most famous story was that Scarface had taken a baseball bat to the heads of two members of his own gang.

Carl, though, didn't show any signs that the sheriff was in danger. Munie whistled his dogs in and followed the mobster into the grassy glen. Within moments the dogs pointed, then flushed two fat pheasants, which Capone and Munie dispatched with simultaneous shots.

"I knew we'd be better off gettin' away from them others," Capone said with a slap to his thigh. Munie's dogs retrieved the birds, each bringing the fowl to the man who'd shot them. "These dogs are smart. You trained 'em well. What's their names?"

"This one I call Lum and the one sniffing at your heels is Abner."

"Ah, you named 'em after the radio show! I love dem guys." Capone leaned down and scratched Abner behind the ears. "The Jot-em Down Store. No? Am I right, or am I right?"

"You're right!" Munie couldn't suppress a smile. Abner was usually shy around strangers, but not with America's most notorious gangster. The bird dog wagged his tail as furiously as if he were about to be fed a big ham bone.

"So, da Shelton boys payin' you good, are dey?" Capone asked matter-of-factly.

"Nope." Munie worried about how to answer. "We keep our private and professional lives pretty separate."

"I don't understand youse country folks." Capone shook his head. "But I admire your honesty."

The next day, Sheriff Munie's untouchables raided three Shelton roadhouses.

17

Chow in the Leavenworth mess hall seemed to get worse every day. Rumors that it was saltpeter that made the food so bad were denounced by Frank Nash.

"I've cooked for years, and I can tell you saltpeter is a myth," Nash told Charlie. "All it would do is make you sick, maybe even kill you if you got enough."

The day macaroni was served, Charlie made the mistake of asking a server for a second helping. It was the first good chow he'd had since being incarcerated.

Unfortunately, a guard nearby heard him and announced he would write him up for trying to cause trouble. The blood rushing to Charlie's head made him forget everything Frank Nash had taught him about talking his way out of trouble. Standing up without permission was bad enough, but the fact that he accidently dropped his dinner plate when he did it was enough to have him placed in segregation. Charlie's only consolation was that his mistake brought a rousing applause from his fellow inmates even as four burly hacks dragged him out of the dining hall.

Thirty minutes later, Black Charlie found himself in Segregation Building 63 with his wrists shackled to the top of cell door number ten. His back against the iron bars, Charlie's feet were tied several inches above the floor. The guard from the dining room took his best five shots at him with his night stick.

"Knock his gold teeth out!" screeched the inmate in the cell that was across the corridor cata-cornered to Charlie. His voice was shrill and girl like.

"Shutup, Stroud!" the prisoner in cell twelve next to Charlie's shouted in a deep baritone voice. "I want to hear him crying."

Charlie felt dreamy from one of the blows to his head. He saw canaries flying in the cell across from him. Then he lost consciousness.

Later, when he regained his senses, Black Charlie's shoulders were nearly dislocated. He struggled to raise his head.

"Good morning, sweetheart" the feminine voice again chimed.

Charlie was still seeing birds. They were sitting on and flying around the shoulders, head, and arms of the man in the cell across from him.

"Is our pretty boy awake?" came the deep voice from the cell next to Charlie. "Maybe they'll let us have him, Stroud. Do you want heads or tails? I prefer tails myself."

"You're the canary man, Robert Stroud." Charlie groaned when he heard the birdman's name. "I heard you were a homo."

"Oh, listen to gold tooth," Stroud hissed, giving a kiss to a canary on his shoulder. "It will be so sweet to hear his moans again when they beat him."

"They already beat me." Charlie forced a laugh. "Didn't hurt near as bad as my pa's whoopin's."

"Oh, it gets worse, gold teeth," Stroud said. "They hang you outside your cell from sunup to sundown every day and beat you every hour. The hacks draw straws to see who gets the next crack at you."

Stroud didn't lie. A few minutes later a group of officers arrived in the narrow hallway to watch Black Charlie Harris receive his second beating. They hooted and hollered with each blow. Afterwards, he didn't have the strength in his legs to push himself back up.

"Wrap your arms between the bars," the deep voice advised from cell twelve. "Keep your upper body stiff so the blows don't damage your insides."

Charlie couldn't see him, but now recognized the deep voice as belonging to Carl Panzram, who sometimes worked near him in the laundry room. He was the biggest, most powerful person Charlie had ever seen.

"Stay away from Panzram," he remembered Frank Nash telling him. "If he doesn't rape you, it means he's thinking of ways to kill you instead."

Still, Charlie decided that the murderous rapist's advice was sound. By the time the next hour came around, he was able to get his arms far enough between the bars he didn't crumple as bad when the beating came. Then the hacks were gone again.

Stroud provided his own unique advice. "Tonight, break the glass in your window and get a nice big piece. Then lay on your back and use it to cut the femoral artery that runs just below your nuts and down your legs. You will bleed out in ten minutes, and it won't hurt one bit."

"Shut up, Stroud," Panzram said. "I ain't even seen him yet. If he ain't so beat up by the end of the week, I may want to plow his field for him."

Stroud cackled and went back to tending his canaries.

"Convince your brain that you like the pain," Panzram whispered, his voice eviler and more sinister in the lower pitch. "Spend your hour making yourself look forward to the next beating."

"Why are you telling him that?" Stroud whined. "I want to hear him scream. It excites my darlings and their songs become screeches that sends blood to my genitals. Oh, how I love screams."

"I like the screams too, but I hate the hacks more," Panzram said. "Make them work for it."

When the sun finally went down, Black Charlie was unshackled, his broken body thrown on the cot in his cell. He had wet and shit in his pants all day long, but he couldn't move to clean himself. Lying in the face-down position they had flung him, his arms and legs were only partly on the cot. The only consolation he had before his brain turned itself off for the night was that the nineteen cells in the first floor segregation gallery were slightly cooler than his cell had been in the upper galleries of D house.

Hours seemed like seconds. Then he was lifted by his arms and shackled back to the door. He was unconscious through the first beating of the day.

"You'd better scream," Stroud's childlike voice said again. "They've placed bets on how long until you scream. Tomorrow is Sunday. The Sunday boys like to win the bet by using red hot pokers up your anus and pinchers on your balls. They'll be easier on you once you scream."

"Listen to me, you wart," Panzram yelled at Stroud. "I was in Africa and know how to make a pea shooter out of a roll of paper. I will start blowing shit at your damned pets if you don't shut up."

"Oh, Carl." Stroud rubbed his crotch against his cell bars. "Do tell Black Charlie Harris how you hired six natives to take you alligator hunting, then murdered them, raped them, and threw their bodies to the gators. I so love that story."

"That is a good one, ain't it?" Panzram laughed. "I prefer the one when I killed them ten sailors in their sleep. That was my record, you know. I spent the whole night lovin' them boys before sending them to their watery graves."

"Why?" Charlie groaned. He was struggling to wrap his arms up around the bars, but his legs wouldn't support his weight.

"I murdered twenty-one people and raped over one thousand boys and men," Panzram bragged. "For all these things I'm not the least bit sorry. I have no conscious, so that doesn't worry me. I don't believe in man, God, nor devil. I hate the whole damned human race, including myself."

Hour after hour, beating after beating, Black Charlie endured. Water was poured into his mouth often to prevent him from dying of dehydration. When he was thrown onto the cot that night, he knew that if he didn't eat something he might not last until morning. The tray of stale water, bread, and dry cheese that was on the floor was covered with cock roaches.

"Eat the cockroaches," Panzram said. "During one of my tortures, I once lived for a week on nothing but cockroaches."

His eyes swollen nearly shut from the beatings, Charlie crawled down next to the tray and devoured the food, not knowing what went down his throat. Then he slept, embracing the coolness of the hard floor.

He awoke with a piercing pain on his testicles, not realizing he'd been returned to the shackles. His screams were heard in many of the work-rooms and by the second shift of inmates lining up for morning chow.

Immediately, the Sunday crew of hacks left him to divide up their winnings. Robert Stroud's shrill laughter was heard above the screeches of his canaries. Carl Panzram returned to his cot, grasped what he lovingly called his sword, and reminisced that the screams were coming from the one thousand young boys he'd raped, tortured, and so often murdered.

18

Earl enjoyed running rum from Jamaica. Sitting in the sun on the deck of the banana boat with a pair of field glasses at his side was a life he could get used to.

"Why don't you Sheltons buy yourselves one of them speed boats?" the captain asked one starlit night as they edged closer to the St. Augustine shoreline. "I know a rumrunner that has three Liberty airplane engines on his. They can outrun any Coast Guard schooner on the water."

"We've never had any trouble sneakin' in at night." Earl didn't really like Captain Muir. He found his constant suggestions tiresome.

"Well, runnin' at night with no lights wears heavy on my nerves." The captain stood at the helm guiding the boat slowly toward the distant shore. "There's a German submarine that's been deliverin' for that Kennedy fella up Massachusetts way. Yes, sir, them German U-boats is sure enough torpedoing the Eighteenth Amendment with liquor and beer. His boat's got pipes runnin' through it so if they get chased, they can make a smoke screen when they pour oil on the red-hot coils. Why, with them big engines, they can travel up to forty miles per hour. All they have to do is circle around, and by the time the smoke clears, they's out of sight."

Earl ignored the old pirate. Raising his binoculars, he peered toward a single house on a lonely beach. "The lights are on in the left window of the watch house. Coast is clear."

"I don't like how this boat sits so low in the water," the captain said for the fifth time that night. "You over loaded it again, and this tide don't seem right tonight."

"You want your cut or not?" Earl growled. "If not, I'll just have the boys heft the alky barrels over the side and float them ashore."

Captain Muir grumbled, then eased the schooner toward the shoreline. Feeling his job done, Earl lay back on the deck chair and shut his eyes. The gentle rocking of the boat and the salty mist of sea breeze was so relaxing he thought about moving to Florida permanently. He especially loved the Jacksonville area where the temperatures were more moderate.

The sound of waves clapping against the hull became rhythmic as they reached shallow water. Out of nowhere came a faint scrapping noise like a razor on a heavy beard.

"We're running aground," Captain Muir warned his crew. "Prepare to heft barrels overboard!"

Earl leapt to his feet. The four ship mates were quickly forming a line from below deck to the starboard side of the boat.

"Not the barrels!" Earl pleaded.

"Would you rather be a sittin' duck for the Coast Guard?" the captain yelled. "Or worse yet, would you rather go down with the ship?"

Earl looked to the beach. They were still a half mile out. He was thrown to the deck as the boat rolled to its port side and stopped dead in the water. When he tried to stand, his feet slipped, and he slid on his bottom to the starboard rail.

The sailors, though, barely staggered. They relayed the big barrels to the deck by turning them on their sides and rolling them up from the cargo hold.

Earl flinched each time an expensive barrel of bootlegged rum splashed into the ocean. To make matters worse, instead of floating toward shore, they got caught up in a rip tide and moved swiftly out to deeper water.

"Damn my luck!" Earl muttered as he jumped to his feet. He watched a half dozen barrels floating toward the sun rise in the east.

"Coast Guard cutter!" the sailor hefting the barrels overboard warned. Suddenly the four sailors dove head first into the waves and swam toward shore.

"Too bad you insisted on leavin' the lifeboat so we'd have more room for rum!" Captain Muir said as he removed his jacket and kicked off his boots. "If you're a fast enough swimmer, you'll make the beach in about half an hour. That cutter won't dare follow you that close to shore."

"I can't swim!" Earl yelled as the captain dove into a wave.

Seeing the Coast Guard cutter was fast approaching, Earl lifted his deck chair and moved it to a position where he would be facing the authorities when they pulled alongside his vessel.

"Ahoy," a Coast Guard officer's voice bellowed from a bullhorn. "What's your cargo?"

"Party time favors," Earl raised a bottle. "Would you boys like to come aboard for a belt?"

***

Three months later, Carl and Bernie were meeting for a late supper at an all-night diner. It was right off a dirt crossroads near where Charlie Birger's Shady Rest fortress had once stood.

An elderly lady with warts on her face brought them their ham and eggs. The old man who had just finished cooking returned to a rocking chair next to a pot-bellied stove. He seemed so tired he didn't even remove his dirty apron and was fast asleep while sitting in the same position he'd been in when the brothers arrived.

"Ma and Hazel wired us from Georgia this morning. The judge gave Earl eighteen months," Bernie told Carl. He spoke openly since there were no other patrons in the place. "They said the Coast Guard laughed at him when he said he couldn't swim and that was why he didn't try to escape with the others."

"Why, they shouldn't have laughed at him just because he can't swim." Carl stabbed at his ham with his fork and tossed it in his mouth. He didn't like the idea of his own kin being made fun of, especially since he wasn't partial to swimming himself.

"Oh, that's not what they was laughing about." Bernie smiled. "They was a laughing because the water was only about three or four foot deep all the way to the beach."

"Well, that makes it even worse, Bernie." Carl spoke with his mouth full. "We don't need to be laughing stocks for lawmen. Folks have been talking mighty highly of Charlie Birger since he swung. They only remember things like the time he saved all those prisoners when the Saline County jail caught fire. I'd expect the Shelton name could use a few such stories; you just remember that."

Bernie was shocked. His big brother was talking about Charlie Birger like they had been good friends instead of sworn enemies. Anymore, Carl always seemed to get blue when Birger's name was mentioned.

Then Bernie remembered that Carl and Charlie Birger had survived the 1925 tri-state tornado together. They had hidden in a fruit cellar during the worse of it, then rode an old mule into Murphysboro, and for three days helped pull bodies out of the rubbish. Animosity between the two was set aside for several months after that as both gangs helped rebuild the two-mile-wide destruction that extended through southern Illinois.

It was only after the bloody war with the Ku Klux Klan had ended in 1926 that the Shelton and Birger gangs began fighting for bootlegging territory.

Carl finished his food. He took his coffee cup in hand, rose, and walked over to the big plate glass window that faced the direction that Shady Rest had once been. A fog blurred the outside world, making the forest where Birger had lived seem all the more haunting.

Bernie watched in wonder as his brother raised his cup in a private toast to the memories that lingered between his mind and those shadowy woods. The Shelton crime boss muttered five words that Bernie couldn't quite hear. Then turned and walked out the door without saying another word.

19

A few months later, Carl got thrown in the Vermillion County jail for transporting alcohol across state lines. He thought it would be a cake walk. Years before, Charlie Birger had been mollycoddled during the six months he served in Danville, Illinois. Deputies had given up their own comfortable workroom and supplied the famous gangster with booze, drugs, and women—they even allowed his wife and children to visit on a regular basis.

By the time Carl got to that same county jail, it was under the management of a new sheriff with somewhat honest deputies.

"These officers won't tolerate bad behavior," an inmate named Bubba told Carl on his first day in lockup. Being a career thief, Bubba was a three-time guest of the county jail. The enormous heft around his mid-section made quick getaways from crime scenes all the more difficult.

"You ever thought of a different way to make drinking money that would be more appropriate for a man of your stature?" Carl asked one day as they walked to the exercise yard. He'd been thinking about Charlie Birger's famous escapade in the Saline County lockup. When a fire got started in a jail cell, Birger convinced the sheriff's wife to let them out, with the assurance that none of the prisoners would escape. He had to threaten them with death, but when the sheriff returned that night, every prisoner was accounted for.

"You don't appear to have the stealth to be a cat burglar," Carl explained to Bubba. "Ever thought of bootlegging?"

"I wasn't so bad at thievin' twenty years ago before I got married. Now my wife drives me so batty, all I want to do is eat food and drink beer."

"Well, what if I make you a proposition that might give you a little more vacation time from your wife, but guarantees you a job where you can drink all the hooch you can carry in that big belly when you get out?"

***

Deputy Wojcik was afraid of Big Bubba. He'd seen the man take on three lumberjacks at one time in a barfight down in Marion. His assailants got in their fair share of body punches, but their fists seemed to bounce off his blubber like a pebble thrown at a rubber ball.

At six-foot, six-inches, the criminal also had an arm span that prevented the lumberjacks, who were all a foot shorter than Bubba, from reaching his head, which was safely tucked about a foot behind his beer-belly girth.

Wojcik walked well behind Bubba as he returned his four prisoners to the cells after their bi-weekly stroll around the exercise yard. There had been very little conversation between the cell mates during that twenty-minute recess, somewhat unusual, but not totally uncommon. The men got plenty of each other's company while confined to their ten-by-eight cells.

When Big Bubba tripped one of the other cons, the deputy pulled his night stick. That was all he remembered until he felt cool water on his face. When he opened his eyes twenty minutes later, he was shocked to see Carl Shelton on one side of him holding a wet rag and the sheriff on the other side, scowling at him.

"What happened?" Wojcik mumbled.

"I'll tell you what happened, deputy. These prisoners got in a fight, and Big Bubba knocked you out cold. Lucky for you, Mr. Shelton saved your life by subduing the cons and locking them back in their cells."

"Thank you, Mr. Shelton." The deputy's thoughts were still floating so he couldn't piece together how Shelton, who was standing slightly behind him when the trouble started, could have reached Bubba before he did, much less wrangle the giant back into his cell.

***

"Mr. Shelton, you are a man of intelligence and ability," Judge Lindley said at Carl's hearing a week later, "And from your appearances in court here and your conduct while in jail, I believe you are not without character. I am sure that the same amount of energy applied to some legitimate pursuit would be more satisfactory to you, and I know it would be much less dangerous.

"Now before I make a decision on the request to reduce your sentence, I want to know if you are prepared to lead a better life and learn respect for the law and property of others."

"Yes sir." Carl assumed his Sunday school teacher face. "Someone once said that, 'Good judgment is forced upon us by age and experience.' I'd expect I've accumulated a good deal of both."

There were a dozen newspapermen waiting when Carl walked out of the county lockup. The hallway was filled with the flashing of bulbs as cameramen danced around, jockeying for position to get the best side of the tall, handsome gangster.

"Mr. Shelton, Mr. Shelton."

"Mr. Shelton, why did you help the deputies lock up the prisoners?"

"Mr. Shelton, is it true you plan to go legit?"

"It's true, boys," Carl said. When he finally made it outside, he stopped walking and stood at the top of the courthouse steps. Reporters and curious onlookers gathered below him. "My bootlegging days are behind me. What about you fellas? I'd expect that bulge in your breast pockets would be a flask, rather than a rod. Am I right?"

Bernie waited in a Cadillac at the curb. Carl smiled at the crowd. Ignoring the rest of the questions, he made his way slowly through them toward the car. His brother reached over and opened the passenger's side door. Carl gave one last tip of his gray fedora to the crowd, keeping his fingers on the brim for a long moment to allow just a few more clicks from the camera.

20

The first thing Carl wanted to do was pay a visit to the Blonde Bombshell.

"She won't be back in town until tomorrow," Bernie informed his brother as they drove south toward Fairfield. He knew better than to suggest he go home to his wife. "What about another gal?"

"No, I've had my mind on Blondie for weeks. I'll wait until tomorrow."

"How about a picture show then?" Bernie suggested.

"A movie?"

"This ain't another Western, Carl. This is one you'll like." Bernie parked along the street in front of a theater that had a marque reading *Little Caesar* starring Edward G. Robinson. Bernie brought popcorn and drinks to Carl just as the picture started. An opening line for the story appeared on the screen.

"...for all then that take the sword shall perish with the sword." Matthew: 26.52

"That must be written for you," Bernie quipped.

"You first, brother." After watching Charlie Birger swing, Carl didn't like thinking about being killed for his sins. Church was mostly just a habit. Something Ma insisted upon, although he wondered if she thought many of her seven children would ever see the pearly gates. Pa certainly didn't give them much hope, except for maybe Dalta and Hazel.

Carl enjoyed church mainly so he'd have a captive audience while he performed on the piano and organ. But when it came down to giving up his somewhat extravagant lifestyle for eternity, he was counting on a death bed repentance in hopes of salvation. Or, maybe there would be a special heaven for bootleggers as Charlie Birger had suggested.

He could see why Bernie liked the picture show. In some ways, Rico, the character nicknamed "Little Caesar" and played by Edward G. Robinson, was a mirror of his youngest brother. Both Bernie and Rico liked being the tough guy. And Bernie longed to be in charge. Not to the point of knocking off his big brothers, but the youngest Shelton had often talked about staking out his own territory further north into Illinois. He and Carrie had been spending much of their time in Peoria and were looking at buying a farm up that way.

When the scene came where Rico was about to get plugged, Bernie got up and went to the restroom. He was still in the theater's lounge when the credits ran and Carl joined him.

"That Rico was a homo," Carl said as they got in the automobile.

"Why you say that?" Bernie shot back.

"Hell, he didn't have no dames, and he liked Joey way too much. He wouldn't even kill him when he needed to."

"There's another picture called *The Public Enemy,* but it ain't as good," Bernie grumbled. "That James Cagney guy plays the gangster like a crazy man." It irritated him that his big brother thought Rico was a faggot. He imagined the movie gangster had plenty of broads and was just too busy killing people to enjoy them. Bernie felt a sudden urge to drive up to Peoria and nail Carrie.

"Say, I haven't told you about the Fed that I saved, have I?"

"What Fed?" Carl was enjoying the feel of driving the big Cadillac and really didn't want to hear his brother fishing for compliments. He was keeping his mind off Blondie by focusing on the power of the L-Head engine.

"You remember old Matt Dunlap? Well, he's still as big a doper as they come. Anyway, Matt got arrested outside the Fairfield Post Office for vagrancy and disorderly conduct. He pulled a knife and slashed the lawman's gun hand, then raised his knife to stab him in the head. There was a park bench nearby so I clobbered Matt over the head with it. The newspapers called me a hero. Imagine that! A Shelton a hero!"

"Your heroics sure didn't stop Sheriff Munie from shutting down a half dozen roadhouses though, did it?"

"There you go again, Carl. I can't never do nothing right, can I? Well, you know, with Earl still in that Georgia prison and you gone, I couldn't be everywhere, could I?"

"But you still think you could handle running operations up around Peoria all by yourself?"

"I'd 'spect Carrie would be of some help." Bernie tried to relax and bring color back into his face.

"Listen, you moron, didn't you hear what Little Caesar told his pal Joey in that film? Joey wanted to run away from the rackets and be with that dame. Well, dames are a dime a dozen. All that matters is blood. You hear me?"

"No, Carl. Carrie and me is gettin' married."

"You know she's only marrying you for your money."

"That's okay. I'm only marryin' her for her looks. Sounds like a fair trade to me."

"And you think Carrie is gonna let you whore around?"

"Yes, I do." Bernie raised his chin a full inch. "She said I could, long as she can come with me."

***

Things were rocky between Bernie and Carrie despite their spending every evening together as well as attending church on Sundays.

"He's gonna pay plenty for the milk if he wants this cow," Carrie told her friends.

Though she admitted to no one, including Bernie, that they were an item, when Sheriff Munie arrested Bernie one day for vagrancy, Carrie stormed into the jailhouse.

"What the hell did you lock my man up for?" Carrie spotted little Jeanene playing with her doll. "Oh, hello, Jeanene. Why don't you go look in my brand new car? I have some candy on the front seat."

Once the child was out of the room, Carrie launched into a tirade of profanity that made Bernie, who could hear her from his cell down the hall, smile.

"Now you'd better calm down there, Carrie," Munie said when the beauty stopped to catch her breath. The lawman had never seen a woman who seemed to look more ravishing the angrier she got. Still, he didn't want to see just how attractive his harsh words could make her, so he tried some of the deescalating techniques he'd learned.

"How about a drink, Carrie?"

The softening of her facial muscles made the sheriff think he may have succeeded. Carrie tossed her hips as she moved around the desk to the chair where he sat. He tilted it back a little to look up. Then she seductively reached to the wall, took the photo of him that had been taken on his first day in office, and smashed it over his head.

***

Mary Munie was in the courthouse kitchen fixing supper for the inmates when three deputies dragged a kicking and screaming Carrie into the room. Since the two ladies had once sang next to one another in the church choir, Mary was familiar with the off-key notes she often heard from the blond beauty, but she didn't suspect that today's chorus of swear words would make it into any church hymn.

When Carrie kicked over Mary's favorite lamp and busted it, the sheriff's wife unloaded her own barrage of colorful language—as well as a few well-placed blows. That only served to infuriate the prisoner more. But when Mary produced a pair of scissors and threatened to cut the woman's golden locks, the room quickly became quiet.

Mary's search of the prisoner produced a small box cutter in her garter belt and golden brass knuckles that matched the locket that Bernie had given her. The weapons, along with the locket, were secured in a safe, but neither Mary nor the deputies anticipated that Carrie would make good use of the high heels of her shoes, which found their way into a deputy's arm and then into the panes of glass inches behind the window bars.

The next day both Bernie and Carrie were released on bond. They appeared the happy couple as they paid the Justice of the Peace two dollars to marry them. The deputy with the bandaged arm stood up for Bernie, and Mary for the bride. Little Jeanene proudly spread dandelion flowers on the floor as her father pronounced the two man and wife.

21

By the end of his first year, Black Charlie was beginning to understand two facts. First, his appeals for a retrial might not happen. Despite the overwhelming evidence he provided showing that he'd no connection to the counterfeit money, no one seemed to care.

The second realization was just as troubling. The Shelton brothers were hanging him out to dry. They had sent a few dollars and plenty of cigarettes, but little else. Leavenworth, without some form of contraband, was nearly unbearable. Pleasures as simple as chewing gum, candy bars, blocks of ice, or letters from home were worth their weight in gold. The prison dispensary offered candy bars, tobacco, soap, and other personal items for cash.

To make extra money, Charlie thought about forgery. He'd some experience with that during his year in the Yuma jail. But an inmate named George Kelly worked in records and had a monopoly on forgeries of hall passes. Most hacks either turned their backs to such illegal activities or found a way to profit themselves.

Charlie, though, was interested in valuable items like alcohol, marijuana, or other drugs. Since tobacco was the thing the Sheltons provided most, he decided to use it as his source of revenue.

Inmates liked to keep up on baseball scores. Each had a favorite hometown team they rooted for. Using the cigarettes the Sheltons sent, Charlie began betting on games. He knew little about any sport, but that didn't matter. Many inmates recklessly bet on their favorite teams regardless of odds. The payoffs for a bookie were enormous by prison standards. So enormous, in fact, that eventually Charlie needed an accomplice to help him hide and distribute payouts. Transferring and exchanging contraband throughout the prison was a logistical problem. The most unlikely accomplice presented himself to Charlie in the laundry room one morning during work detail.

Carl Panzram was so big and mean the hacks didn't even bother torturing him anymore when he was in segregation, mainly because the convict seemed to like being abused. It just made him madder and more determined to one day kill them. A giant of a man with muscles that couldn't be kept hidden beneath his prison blues, he'd been crippled when he fell off a thirty-foot prison wall in upstate New York. After the fall, he'd been locked away in an isolation cell for eight months without medical treatment to set his broken legs. He survived by crawling around the floor in his own defecation and on a diet of nothing but bread and water.

When Charlie saw Panzram's smoky gray eyes staring at him one day in the laundry room, he figured the killer was sizing him up to either be his bitch or to kill him. Either option seemed equally unpleasant.

"What you looking at?" Charlie said. He raised himself up to his full five-feet, five-inch height and looked the con straight into the eyes—although he left himself plenty of distance between them to run if need be.

"You the one running the lottery?" Panzram asked.

"What of it?"

"I want in on the action."

From that day on, Black Charlie had the most notorious killer in the country stashing chewing tobacco and other items and distributing them. Payoffs were easily delivered to winners hidden within the weekly delivery of linen and clothing. Not hacks nor inmates seemed willing to challenge Carl Panzram until months later when a civilian in charge of the laundry room found eight packs of Camel cigarettes and four bags of Bull Durham tobacco rolled up in the linen Panzram was folding.

"Where did you get these?" Robert Warnke asked after calling on four guards to back him up.

He was a short, balding man with a history of writing up inmates for any violation he could find.

Carl Panzram's upper lip curled into a snarl. "I don't care to tell."

"Take him back to his cell," Warnke ordered.

Had the civilian known more about Panzram, he almost surely would have chosen a better place to confront the inmate than in an area of the laundry room that housed heavy, four-foot-long iron pipes.

Any one of the five hard blows that immediately arrived on Warnke's head would have killed him. While Warnke's body quivered spasmodically in death, Panzram swung the bloody bar at the hacks, who being unarmed, quickly scattered in different directions.

Panzram's roar of anger froze every living person in the laundry room. With blood splattered across his face and clothes, the killer rose to his full height. He limped toward those too stunned to move and swung his pipe at their heads. Those not quick enough to duck or run were knocked unconscious. Panzram didn't bother finishing them off, but continued on his murderous rant through the room, looking for his next victim.

Standing nearby, Black Charlie scooped up the contraband he'd been folding for delivery and threw them down the laundry chute to the wash area on the floor below.

When he finished, he looked up to find himself staring into the cold gray eyes of the killer. If he expected any sympathy from his partner, he was mistaken. Panzram swung the bloody pipe with as much malice as he'd had toward the others. Charlie ducked and ran as fast as he could toward the door. The killer followed in his slow, monstrous limp, swinging the bar murderously at every piece of equipment that he could smash or that would make a noise loud enough to symbolize the hate and evil he possessed inside him.

When Charlie was far enough away, he turned back and saw that a heavy mist was escaping in a loud hiss from the pipes that Panzram had busted open. Then, through a cloud of steam, emerged the killer; his face so full of venom he looked nothing like a human.

Panzram raced as best he could on crippled limbs, smashing through the doors and bellowing as he entered the courtyard. Inmates scattered. They rushed into the closest cell houses and huddled together, trying to physically force the iron bars closed behind them.

The killer wanted to murder hacks and chased the ones he saw, first in one direction, then another. Then, as suddenly as the slaughter of humanity came, it seemed to pass. He lowered the iron weapon and his shoulders relaxed. In an instant, he appeared to age twenty years. He turned toward Segregation Building 63 and approached the iron gate.

"I just killed Warnke. Let me in."

"I will never let you in with that in your hand."

"Oh." Panzram looked down at the bar that was still dripping blood. "This is my lucky day."

He flung the bar into the courtyard. The guard opened the gate, and then found a place to hide. The man who had just killed his twenty-second man walked through the corridor and into cell number twelve. From the far side of the room, the guard pushed the lever that closed the cell door.

Panzram stood with his bloody hands on the bars. They dripped crimson that coated the rusty iron with Warnke's life fluids.

Robert Stroud was busy at his desk, giving a canary a dose of medicine. "Oh, hello, Carl. Did you kill many today?"

"I guess I got all I could get."

22

"I'm looking for an Elliot Ness to take down the Shelton gang and clean up southern Illinois," Governor Henry Horner announced to the two men sitting in leather chairs in front of his cluttered desk. Each of them smoked one of the governor's favorite cigars while they sipped coffee.

"Oh, hell! Ness had to use tax collectors to take down Capone." The cop named Joe Schrader tapped his shoulder harness, which held a pearl-handled pistol. He smiled. "All I need is this."

Horner wasn't sure he liked or trusted Schrader, who seemed more interested in his stogie than talking strategy, but St. Clair County Sheriff Jerome Munie, the third person sitting in the room, recommended the man, and that was enough. Horner only wished the two lawmen would *smoke* the expensive cigars and quit chewing on them.

"Shoot first," Officer Schrader added, "and ask questions later."

"Maybe." Horner didn't like the look of surprise on Munie's face. The governor lifted a set of bulky instruments from his desk. "But these will help—two-way radios."

"Ya think we can talk the Sheltons to death?" Schrader laughed.

"It will allow you and your deputies to stay in touch with one another on the backroads that the gang travels." Sheriff Munie's voice was more forceful than usual. "They would be useful if one of your men gets out-manned and needs some backup."

Schrader leaned forward in his chair and inspected the radios. The word was that Munie was a straight shooter. The sheriff had reportedly turned down a hundred-dollars-a-day bribe to leave the Shelton family's crime syndicate alone.

"Governor," an immaculately dressed aide interrupted from the doorway. "The Women's Auxiliary just rounded the corner and are coming down Capitol Avenue."

"Well, good, right on time." The governor checked his pocket watch. He didn't expect much of a problem from the coal mine wives who were protesting coal company abuse. "I like punctuality. How many are there? Two, three hundred?"

"Uh, w-well," the aide sputtered. He was a young man and, like the governor, new to his position. "I think you'd better see for yourself, sir."

Horner walked to the window, followed by his two untouchable lawmen. The capitol lawn and every street leading into the Illinois State Capitol building was filled with over ten thousand sign-carrying women. When they saw the governor standing in the window, the women began a chorus of chants.

"Down with Lewis's pay cuts!"

"Down with dictators!"

"Down with Peabody Coal Company!"

"Down with the state militia!"

Schrader spit a wad of chewed cigar into his coffee cup. "Wanna use one of them fancy radios to call for backup, there, Governor?"

A rabble rouser stood on a capitol step, a megaphone aimed at the window in which the governor stood.

"We have come to seek redress from the oppressive and intolerable conditions in the coal fields of Illinois!" The woman shouted. "Dare you fail us now, Governor Horner?"

"Oh, shit!" Sheriff Munie said under his breath. "We'll leave you to your constituents, Your Honor."

As the officers quickly departed, Horner put on his best baby-kissing smile and made a little wave to the mob below the window.

***

Three months later, the St. Clair County Courthouse steps were packed with spectators and reporters. Lawman Bill Miskell stepped into the courtroom just as the hearing for three bootleggers began.

Since all the seats were filled, he stood with several reporters along the back wall and scanned the faces, anxiously looking for Archie Norton. A short, red-headed, freckle-faced man like Norton would be easy to spot. The convicted murderer had escaped from the Atlanta Prison two weeks earlier, but had since been spotted in Joliet, Decatur, and, most recently, in Belleville, Illinois.

Governor Tanner's explicit orders were to find the escaped convict. If he didn't, Miskell was to join Joe Schrader's forces against the Shelton gang. Having formerly been with both Charlie Birger and Carl Shelton, Norton was expected to rejoin the infamous brothers at some point.

As those in the courtroom waited for the proceedings to begin, they smoked and talked. A gray cloud hovering above their heads grew so thick the ceiling fans were turned on and several windows opened. A cool rush of air filled the room.

Norton was nowhere to be seen. Miskell's hunch that the murderer might try to make contact with his fellow gang members at the trial appeared to be a dead end. Disappointed, the lawman turned his attention to the front of the room. Everyone in the gallery stood when the judge entered.

The first witness was Officer Joe Schrader. Miskell had read a lot about Schrader lately. The lawman was fast becoming a legend in the law enforcement field. He was credited with more arrests in the St. Louis area than any other policeman. When the St. Clair County Banker's Association paid him an exorbitant amount to moonlight for them as a private detective, Schrader displayed an aptitude for anticipating when and where robberies would take place. He claimed his personal acquaintance with the Shelton brothers gave him insight into their minds, but most suspected that he had an informant within the gang.

"These here boys are a plight on our society!" Schrader told the justice in a booming voice.

The three accused bootleggers all glared at the lawman, but the one who had been introduced as James Hickey gripped the end of the table in front of him with both hands. His fingers turned white and his face a bloody red.

"Running them out of the county is too good for this scum!" Schrader bellowed, his eyes now on Hickey alone. "They need to be locked up and the key thrown into the deep waters of the muddy Mississippi River."

"You son-of-a-bitch!" James Hickey screamed at Schrader. "If I get out of here, I'll kill you! I'm warning you, you son-of-a-bitch! I'll kill you! I swear I will!"

Blackie Armes, a second defendant, viciously grabbed Hickey around the neck and pulled him back down in his seat. "Hickey, you damned fool, shut up!" Blackie hissed. "You're signing your death warrant!" Blackie turned to Sheriff Munie, who casually sat in the front row, his arms and legs crossed.

"Sheriff, you're square, but keep that Schrader off us," the third defendant, Bad Eye Smith pleaded, white showing all around the pupil of his one good eye. "He'll kill us!"

Munie leaned farther back in his chair and gave a forced, twitchy smile. Miskell looked to the witness stand. Schrader lit a big stogie, never taking his eyes off James Hickey.

Despite a mountain of evidence, Hickey, Armes, and Smith were found innocent by the jury of twelve men. Convictions for bootleggers were few and far between in rural areas where liquor was considered an important part of life.

* * *

The first thing that Miskell noticed when he came into Officer Schrader's office were all the gun racks. Every type of automatic weapon he could imagine seemed to be either in a gun rack or piled on top of desks. He had to move a Thompson machine gun just to have a chair to sit in. He cradled it fondly as Schrader and Munie interviewed him.

"So, you infiltrated the Capone mob, did ya?" Schrader looked doubtfully at Miskell. "You understand Italian?"

"Only their screams as I kill them."

"You a good enough shot?" Munie asked.

"I can put a hole where your second button oughta be," Miskell stated matter-of-factly. He held up the Thompson. "But I prefer a gat. That way I can get all the buttons."

Schrader smiled at Munie. "I like this fella. Well, Mr. Miskell, I'm gonna give you a crash course on how to deal with crime. Five words. Shoot first and talk later. That's all you need to know. Shelton and company don't have the intestinal fortitude to stomach their own medicine."

Bill Miskell had a personal grudge against Carl Shelton. They'd had a fistfight several years ago over a moll. Miskell started it with a sucker punch. His haymaker hit Carl flush on the tip of his jaw, a spot that usually resulted in a knock out. This time though, Miskell's hand took the worst of it. After that, the knuckle on the lawman's pointer finger was about a half inch back from where it belonged. What vexed him most was that it would no longer serve as a proper fighting tool. Then one day a few months later, he saw a knobby ring in a hock joint.

The ring fit perfectly. Even better, it had a big letter M in its center. In his next Donnybrook, his prosthetic knuckle left a nice impression of Miskell's initial on the cheek of his opponent.

Miskell licked his lips. "You expecting to run into Carl Shelton too?"

"Oh, hell, no!" Schrader shook his head. "That's one Shelton we won't run into. Big Carl's a teetotaler. He only goes on one job in a hundred. Leaves it to his henchmen to do the dirty work, he does.

"Besides, now that James Hickey threw down the gauntlet, I'll go after him and his scummy friends first. Maybe we'll run into your Archie Norton in the process. As for the Sheltons, they can wait. I'd 'spect Carl won't want nothin' to do with Hickey's bunch after his tirade today."

* * *

The roadside tavern was set far enough back off the hard road only the locals frequented it. Carl Shelton sat at a table watching Ray Walker stuff his face with cookies as he sat counting a big pile of money. Two of Carl's men stood behind Carl, smoking cigarettes and drinking whiskey. Their pin-striped pants were held mid-belly by colorful suspenders against white, long-sleeved shirts. Both were glaring at the three men standing across the table from Carl.

Blackie Armes and Bad-Eye Smith kept their heads down as if they were children waiting for the school principal to decide on consequences. Holding their hats in front of them, they fidgeted with the brims while Blackie related the story of the court hearing. James Hickey, though, shifted his weight from one foot to the other like a fighter before a boxing match.

"Any man who can arrest you with a smile on his face can shoot you with a smile on his face," Carl said when Blackie finished talking. "You boys stay away from my joints. I don't want you getting blood on my floor when Schrader kills you."

"Come on, Blackie," Hickey said, his face frozen in a perpetual sneer. "We don't need this two-bit gangster. Let's go back to Signal Hill. We'll form our own gang."

"Shut up, Hickey!" Blackie said. "Just shut up!"

Blackie had been with the Sheltons since they pulled him away from his coal mining job when he was eighteen years old. He and Bernie had become fast friends in partying—and also in bombings and assassinations. Now Carl was put out with him. Blackie wasn't sure he'd be allowed back in the gang, but this was not the time to plead for a second chance.

When the three men left the room, Big Carl extracted a piece of paper and a short pencil from his shirt pocket, scribbled a quick note on it, and passed it over the table to Ray Walker, who had finished counting money. When Ray saw the note was addressed to Joe Schrader, he stood, took his white straw hat from the hat rack, and exited the building.

* * *

Riding in the back of the police car made Sheriff Jerome Munie feel like a child. The pecking order had changed immediately with the hiring of Bill Miskell. Schrader had a new drinking buddy who was as ruthless as was he. In their first raid, two bootleggers had come up unnecessarily dead. At least Munie thought it was unnecessary, since he'd arrived on the scene just a moment after the gunshots and saw that neither of the deceased had been armed.

Schrader usually smoked cigars non-stop throughout the day, but now as he drove along the darkened street, he clenched an unlit one between his teeth. Bill Miskell sat next to him in the front passenger seat, but never said a word. Instead, he concentrated on unloading and loading the two .44 caliber revolvers that he finally tucked into holsters on either side of his vest.

Munie had heard much squawking coming from the big radio attached to the dashboard, but from the backseat, could make out nothing the person on the other end was saying. Despite all the static, Schrader seemed to understand. He finally spoke into the microphone. "Signal Hill, check. Over and out."

Munie had no doubt his own pistol was primed for action, but his queasy stomach made him think maybe *he* wasn't. Killing didn't sit right with him. He'd been a simple store clerk until he won the 1930 St. Clair County Sheriff election. Even on the day he was sworn in, Munie felt ill-qualified to be a law enforcement officer. He decided that if he brought anything to the job it should be responsibility and honor.

Shoot first and talk later. Schrader's words had seemed so simple when Munie first heard them, but now he imagined complicated scenarios. What if an innocent person stood in his line of fire? Or what if civilians were behind his target and a miss could possibly hit one of them? The possibility of an errant bullet made a gunfight seem pretty chancy.

When Schrader stopped the car in an alleyway and turned the engine off, Munie was tempted to ask some questions about battle protocol. But when he started to speak, Schrader turned toward him and held a finger to his lips. The officers slowly and quietly opened their car doors and got out.

The neighborhood was alive with the sound of barking dogs, but none seemed to be directed toward them. An occasional cat shrieked, and the sound of crickets and bull frogs filled the air. Though it was now well after midnight, lights were still on in several of the homes they walked past. After about five minutes, they hunched low and crept up on a two-story house on the hill. The musty smell of leaves burnt earlier that day still hung in the damp air.

Schrader quietly gave a sweeping hand signal to Miskell, who pulled out both guns and pointed them toward the sky. As he disappeared around the side of the house, Schrader raised himself up on his toes and peered into a window next to the back door. He then stepped past the entrance and held up three fingers to Munie.

Munie found himself overthinking again. He didn't know if that meant three men were in the room or that the lawman planned on entering the building in three seconds. There was no time to ponder the question, because a moment later, Schrader pulled out his gun, kicked the door wide open, and rushed into the building. Before Munie could get a firm grip on his own pistol tucked inside the back of his belt, gunshots rang out. Munie was rammed by someone exiting through the open door. The collision knocked him several steps back, but he recovered immediately. He'd somehow been able to hang onto his weapon—which was now pointed directly into the pig-like, freckled faced of Archie Norton.

The little fugitive froze like a statue, his eyes crossed as he peered at the end of Munie's gun, which was only inches from his nose. Norton's hands sprung up in defeat.

A second series of gunshots came from inside the house, and Norton took a step backward. His eyes moved from the gun pointed toward his head to Munie's face. *Shoot first and talk later,* Munie thought. *But he has no weapon.*

Norton read the hesitancy on the sheriff's face. A second later, the thug ran around the side of a carriage house and out of sight.

* * *

Though a gun was found firmly grasped in his bloody hand, James Hickey never got a shot off. Two other men had tried to escape through the front door, but were arrested by Bill Miskell. They were charged with plotting a kidnapping. Schrader didn't criticize Munie much for his failure to apprehend Archie Norton. He seemed satisfied with the night's work and showed no signs of worry when it was pointed out that though Hickey died instantly with the first shot to his heart, he'd somehow been able to pick up his pistol with a bloody hand.

Munie wrote out an affidavit and was able to truthfully state he'd been outside the building the entire time and never saw any actual shooting. He had no doubt, though, that Schrader's philosophy of shoot first and talk later had been the sole reason for the raid's success.

***

Munie expected Schrader and Miskell to be tough on James Hickey's wife during the interrogation, but when Miskell punched the M mark from his ring onto her forehead, he thought they had gone too far.

When that didn't work, Schrader turned a bright light into Minnie Hickey's face, revealing pox marks and scars beneath her heavy makeup.

"You ain't so pretty up close, are you, doll?"

Minnie tried to shut her eyes, but Miskell placed two fingers on her eyebrows and forced them open.

"You better tell us what we want to know," Miskell said, "'cause I've got plenty of time but very little patience. Where are the Shelton gang distributing liquor from?"

Despite another punch in the face, Minnie Hickey screamed that she didn't know.

"Bring in the stiff, boys!" Schrader ordered.

Two state troopers shuffled into the room carrying a big rug. Hanging onto one end, they rolled it open. The bloody body of James Hickey toppled onto the floor in front of his wife. His dead, glassy eyes staring up at her.

Minnie screamed and fainted. Rather than catch her, Miskell stepped aside and allowed her to fall next to her husband.

"You boys were a little rough on her, weren't you?" Sheriff Munie asked, once again appalled by the brutality of the two men.

Schrader scoffed. "Why give those rats a break?"

Within an hour, the officers heard an exhausted and whimpering Minnie Hickey offer four words when asked about the Shelton gangs liquor distribution center. "Happy Hollow Dude Ranch."

23

Bernie and Carrie were especially proud of their Happy Hollow Dude Ranch near the village of Millstadt, Illinois. The ranch house sat on a hill with a barn, cabins for guests, and an in-ground swimming pool. A gently flowing creek gurgled into a small pond close by. Besides catering to gangsters, the ranch was also a working business with plenty of guests.

In addition to the usual gang members, there were plenty of well-off gentry riding horses, taking lessons on roping, or playing bocci ball and croquet on the lawn. The lawn games were dangerous. Bernie kept a coyote chained next to the concession stand by the pool. Being a yard game with no borders, it was not uncommon for an ornery player to toss the bocci pallino ball so it wound up inches from the coyote's bared teeth.

For nearly a week, Schrader, Munie, and Miskell hid in the woods where they could use field glasses to spy on the comings and goings.

The lawmen were amazed that no alcohol was spotted anywhere on the premises. There was, however, plenty of lemonade and homemade ice cream, as well as meats being smoked almost every day, causing the hiding lawmen to drool from the inviting odor.

"They must be keepin' the booze inside," Schrader snarled when Munie arrived one evening to relieve him of watch duty. "I'm just certain they are. Them folks are way too happy to be sober. I'll tell Miskell to have the boys in position before dawn. We go in at sunup!"

When the law man left, Munie settled down to take a nap. If any alky would be delivered to the ranch, the sound of the trucks would awaken him.

About two in the morning, screams came from the front porch of the ranch house. He rose just in time to see Carrie Stevenson fire a revolver at a half-naked woman who was making a bee-line toward an automobile. The bullet ricocheted off the car and appeared to clip the woman in the foot.

"You ain't woman enough to take my man, you damned hussy!" Carrie yelled. She fired another shot as the car beat it down the dusty drive.

A dozen curious onlookers emerged from the house and the cabins, including a slump-shouldered Bernie. Carrie took a swing at him with the hog leg of the gun, but Bernie ducked and then tackled her to the ground. When she came up kicking and swinging, Ma Shelton stepped forward. With broom in hand, she hit the two with all her might. The lovers separated, placed their hands on their knees and panted like out of breath hound dogs.

"You two!" Ma screamed. "Off to bed with both of you! And I'd better not hear a peep from you until morning."

Bernie and Carrie both dropped their heads and immediately followed the directions of the Shelton matriarch. But Ma didn't scold the couple when, five minutes later, Carrie screamed in delight as the bouncing bed springs played percussion for their lively jig.

With the excitement over and everyone returned to their cabins, Sheriff Munie settled back on the ground once more. It seemed only minutes later he was being shaken awake by Schrader.

"It's time!" Schrader said. "The sun will be up soon."

Munie tried to wink away the sleep in his eyes as he took up his gat and followed Schrader toward the main cabin. Throughout the clearing, the shadows of two dozen agents emerged from the wooded areas as each walked toward the cabins they had been assigned to. They held their preferred weapons at the ready, some with Thompson machine guns, others with Winchesters or shotguns.

Carl Shelton emerged from the main house just as Schrader put his foot on the first step.

"Morning, boys," Carl said while he stretched. "I was wondering when you fellas would come in from them woods. Hope the ticks didn't bother you much this past week. They've been nasty this season."

Schrader's face reddened, but he resisted the urge to remove his fedora and run his hand through his hair. Munie and Miskell were not so disciplined. When Miskell felt a tiny round bubble on his scalp, he pinched it between his thumb and forefinger and gave it a yank.

"Here now, deputy!" Carl warned. "You need to burn that critter off with a match, not yank him. You'll get an infection, sure as shoot."

Every door to every cabin opened. Dozens of men and women dressed in bathrobes filed out and gathered near a fire pit, where the ladies sat down in wicker chairs or on tree stumps while the men stoked up the embers until a roaring blaze lit the entire area.

"I hope you fellas won't wreck the place up too much!" Carl said to Schrader. "As I'm sure you know, we just redecorated the cockfight room this week and would hate to have to start over."

The lawmen searched every building and every room. It was noon by the time they were done. Other than a few empty bottles, they came up with nothing. By then, many of the guests were dressed and out riding or playing yard games.

"All through, boys?" Bernie grinned. "Then come on in. We got some fried chicken fixed inside."

"I could eat," Munie said. He'd had enough of his compatriot's nonsense.

With scowls on their faces, Schrader, Miskell, and their deputies turned to take the long walk through the tick-infested woods back to their cars. Munie remained behind.

"How appropriate that our Justice of the Peace is here," Carrie said from the doorway. She wrapped her arm around Munie's and led him into the ranch house. "This is Bernie and me's wedding anniversary. Oh, I wish Mary and Jeanene could be here. How is that little darling?"

24

The three canary eggs crackled, bubbled up and were burnt black within sixty seconds of landing on the hot pavement of the prison courtyard. Black Charlie lost the bet. He paid Red Rudensky the pack of cigarettes and followed him to chow.

Since he was with Big Red, Charlie didn't have to wait—a good thing on the hundred-and-ten-degree day. The line of inmates stepped aside to let their liaison to the warden gather his counsel at a dinner table for their daily conference. When the new warden took over, Big Red had become the spokesperson for the inmates. Part of the reason he was allowed that honor was because he'd had two of the most entertaining escape attempts.

One was with another inmate. They hid inside barrels being shipped by train. It would have worked had the other fellow not been stabbed in the foot by hacks with a ten-inch prod before loading. Though he made no noise and the guards didn't notice blood on their instrument, matters became unbearable for the escaping men when the loaders placed their barrels upside down in the train's storage compartment. Both men were unconscious four hours later when a train employee noticed blood leaking from the barrel of the escapee who had been stabbed.

Big Red's next escape attempt involved sneaking inside a canvas burial bag and spooning with a skinny corpse. That one would have also worked had the dead man not smelled so bad. Big Red eventually had to tear a hole in the draw strings to relieve himself of the stench. A guard happened to be sitting in the compartment having a smoke when Big Red's face appeared.

"What in the hell are you doing, Red; trying to steal the poor dead slob's gold teeth?"

Big Red had just enough time to laugh before vomiting.

He wasn't laughing on the intemperate day he led Black Charlie and the other members of his council through the noon chow line. It was the hottest day recorded since the prison opened nearly thirty years ago. After getting their trays, they took their customary seats in the big dining room. Soon nineteen hundred grumbling cons were picking at Spanish rice and boiled potatoes. Few ventured to try more than one bite of the food that was so overly seasoned it made the feverish temperature in the mouth every bit as intolerable as that within the room.

Black Charlie had assumed his place on the council after Frank Nash left Leavenworth. Nash escaped exactly the way he'd so often said he would. Having used his pleasant personality to gain trust and favor with the hacks, he simply reported to the gate one morning for his daily trip to the deputy warden's house to cook, and then just kept walking. By the time the evening roll call came and he was reported missing, Nash was well on his way to St. Louis.

Since Charlie had survived time in solitary confinement for his macaroni revolt, he was assigned to Nash's former position as the chow councilman. Now, he noticed angry eyes glaring at him as he forked the spicy Spanish rice into his mouth. There was already tension in the prison from the new warden's crackdown on privileges concerning mail and visitation. Carl Panzram's murderous rant and the anticipation of his upcoming hanging added to the anxiety. The unbearable heat and bad food made Charlie realize he'd better take action before he wound up a dead chow councilman.

"This shit ain't fit for a pig!" Charlie screamed. He threw his plate against the wall. "You bastards can keep your slop!"

The nearly two thousand hardened criminals in the room grew eerily quiet. The hacks patrolling between the tables looked around to see what had happened. Then, cons began yelling and throwing cups, plates, and utensils. They rose from their seats as one, some of them attacking guards who were too slow to escape through the doorways. Blood from the hacks quickly pooled on the floor.

Some inmates leapt onto the tables to dance or jump up and down. A large number rushed into the kitchen and returned carrying meat cleavers, knives and even pots and pans heavy enough to wield as weapons. From the gun gallery above, guards armed with heavy artillery aimed their weapons down at the chaos below them.

Other cons rushed to the windows, their shouts telegraphing to the inmates who were lounging in the exercise yard that a riot had begun. Despite the stifling heat, that area also became a living hell for the security guards, many of whom were beaten and left without aide. Other prisoners took advantage of the chaos to settle old grudges with fellow inmates. They fought their bloody personal battles to the delight of their friends, who gathered around chanting encouragement.

Black Charlie did not expect that reaction. He and Big Red remained seated as they watched. Charlie's hands trembled a little when the leader finally stood and stepped up on top of the table. Big Red looked around as if he were doing an inspection. If he was upset with Charlie, he didn't show it. Instead, he stood staring through the window toward Warden Thomas White's office. A faint smile came to his face when White, his deputy warden, and the prison chaplain walked calmly from the building and across the rioting exercise yard. Guards in towers threw canvases off big belt-loaded machine guns and pointed them down at the inmates. Prisoners screamed and cussed at the three men but gave them room to walk to the mess hall and enter.

"Kill the dirty bastards and string them up right here!" one prisoner screamed above the shouting.

White's party walked into the dining area and right up to where Charlie had joined Big Red standing on the table. The room grew quieter. Prisoners watched to see what would happen.

"It's not my doing, Father," Big Red said. "And I'm damned tired of being blamed for everything. Since I'm always catching hell, I might as well enjoy the fun!"

"What is it these men want?" White asked. "Tell me, and maybe I can straighten it out?"

"Let the warden have it," an inmate yelled. "Him and his goddamned goons."

The inmates' cheer ended abruptly when Big Red raised a hand.

"Tell him what we all want, Red," another con demanded. "If they don't give it to us, then let's chop them up and cook them for a snack. But give them a chance."

"Listen guys, listen a second," Black Charlie shouted. "Let Big Red give the pitch to the man. If he doesn't accept our deal, then let somebody else get up here."

"Warden," Big Red said in a voice that echoed across the room, "we want our mail and visiting privileges back immediately."

Cheers.

"And, we've got to have some decent cooks," Big Red continued. "This shit isn't worth feeding pigs, and you know it. Either get us some decent grub or we'll tear this place apart. We don't deserve this slop, and you can't expect men to live on it."

"You just made a bargain," Warden White said. "Tell the men to ease off, and I'll look into the food situation right now. You can have all your privileges back too, but first get your men back in their cells."

Some of the men grumbled and began getting loud again.

"Knock it off," Big Red ordered. The room grew quiet again. "The man says we'll get new food and our privileges back. White's never crossed us. Let's give him a chance."

Big Red stepped down off the table and began walking. The men in the room moved aside for him, then formed a line back to their cells.

"Not you," White said to Black Charlie. "You come with me."

Charlie raised his chin as he joined White leaving the room. Several inmates patted him on the back. He knew the consequence for starting the riot would be time in Segregation Building 63.

In the courtyard, guards had brought out fire hoses with enough water force to push back inmates trying to storm the gates. From the east tower, a shot brought down a convict who was trying to throw knives at the guards manning the hoses.

That brought some quiet to the yard, although personal fistfights were allowed to continue until the loser lay unconscious in their own blood. Word spread slowly among the four thousand inmates that an agreement had been made between the Warden and Big Red. Medical staff were allowed to enter the courtyard to treat or evacuate injured officers and convicts.

Walking with his head held high, Black Charlie strode like a king past his fellow inmates. His escort moved more swiftly as they were joined by four guards carrying shotguns loaded with buckshot.

A con stuck out his foot and tripped White. Even as the warden went down, one of the guards let loose a blast that took the end of the inmate's foot off.

As the wounded man screamed in agony, a dozen heavily-armed guards raced across the yard and formed a circle around the warden. Charlie placed his hands behind his head, as did dozens of other cons who were hurrying back to their cell houses.

Another shot came from a building, causing even more cons to hurry to the safety of their cells. Twenty-four hours of screams, shouting, and gunshots followed. Black Charlie heard it all as he was again shackled and suspended from his cell door in Building 63.

25

When Earl got out of the big house in Atlanta, he needed to lay low for a while. He returned to Fairfield in Wayne County and poured all his energy into farming.

Getting back on a tractor was a much bigger treat than he'd imagined. He expected that part of his enjoyment was being away from the hazing he had been subjected to while in prison. As if getting caught because he couldn't swim wasn't bad enough, the fact that he could have walked to shore in the three feet of water made his capture all the more embarrassing.

"I hope you'll feel safe being in an Atlanta Prison, Mr. Shelton," the warden had greeted him during cell count his first day. "We thought about having you placed down at Savannah, but the judge feared you'd have a heart attack being so close to the ocean."

Earl down-shifted and turned for the next row. He was glad to get back to Illinois, where there was less talk about the circumstances of his capture.

His Farmall F-20 tractor had put Henry Ford's Fordson machine out of business, and Earl had just bought the first one in the county. He finished plowing one twenty-acre field and was puttering along the drainage ditch to the south forty when a shiny black Packard came up from behind him and stopped along the road. Earl shaded the sunlight out of his eyes and watched as his brother Roy emerged and walked toward him.

"Why ain't you traveling on the hard road, Brother Earl?" Roy asked.

Earl found his brother's question perplexing. Roy had been in prison for eight years, and though Earl had visited him occasionally, he had thought at least a handshake would've been appropriate.

"I'd rather do eight seconds on a Brahma bull," Earl responded with nary a head nod. "Them jagged steel wheels makes for a mighty comfort on soft ground, but firm roads, well, I don't know, you'd have to see fer yourself, Brother Roy."

"Then slide off that ass-shaped seat and let me have a go."

Roy plowed fields until sunset.

***

It was during the five brother's drunk-fest celebration of Roy's return that Earl met Earline. The first memory he would have of her, though, was when he woke up beside the beautiful redhead the next morning.

"Your brothers is sure all different," Earline said later as she made grits and gravy for breakfast.

"How's that?" Earl was trying to remember how he'd wound up sleeping with the comely woman. Though she was pretty enough and made a decent cup of coffee, he didn't think he could ever get attached to a girl whose name might be appropriate for his daughter, but never his wife.

"Well, Carl is about as exciting as a waveless fish pond," Earline said without turning away from the stove. "Useful but boring. I doubt he was drinkin' anything but juice all night. At least, it never affected his walk or his piano playing. Doesn't he ever play anything but church songs?"

"Carl's a tea toddler, that's a fact."

"And that brother, Bernie! Boy! I wouldn't want to cross that guy! He slapped Carrie twice last night. I would've come to her defense, but she didn't seem to mind. In fact, I saw her lead him into the bedroom soon after, both times."

Earl chuckled.

"And your brother, Dalta!" Earline set an overflowing plate on the table in front of him. "Are you sure he's your brother? He acted more like a school teacher than a Shelton."

"Dalta don't run with the gang. What did you think of Roy?" Earl asked. Since he couldn't remember much about the festivities, and his reunion with Roy in the field was fleeting, he wondered how eight years of prison life had affected him.

"Well, Roy's personality was all over the place. One minute he'd be hoopin' and hollerin' with Bernie and your sister Lula, and the next he'd be broodin' in a corner with your other sister Hazel holdin' his hand. I don't really know what to think about Roy."

Earl forked a big scoop of grits and gravy into his mouth. Tasting that food was the moment he decided a woman with a name so close to his might not be so bad after all. The real test came though thirty minutes later when they found their way back into the bedroom.

The rutting suited him. Two weeks later, Earl and Earline were married.

***

Carl knew Carrie was mad by the way she whipped her horse, Buttermilk, up the lane to the farm house. He was currying a mule and had to grasp the halter with both hands to prevent the animal from running off.

"Did you tell them Chicago boys they could hunt on your land?"

"Yes."

"Come with me." Carrie had given her command. She gave Buttermilk a hard neck rein and cantered back in the direction she'd come.

Carl threw a hackamore bridle onto the mule, swung onto its bare back, and kicked it into a fast lope. As he neared the top of the hill overlooking the glen, he heard shotgun blasts coming from the bottoms, the field being an eighty-acre patch of prairie grass surrounded by timber on three sides.

"Ha, now that's a sight you don't see every day." Carl laughed.

With five men spread out on each side of the field, twenty hunters walked slowly toward the center, shooting anything that moved in the tall prairie grass. Fred Burke was the only one Carl could recognize from that distance. Killer Burke had a flask on a string draped over one shoulder while he fired randomly, staggered a few steps, took a drink, reloaded, then repeated. Most of the other hunters were moving with similar staggering steps.

"They're shooting anything that moves," Carrie said. "And they're not even using bird dogs."

"Lucky for the bird dogs, I'd say."

"Carl Shelton! You are way too affable. I say we let them kill each other off in their little circle jerk, then we finish any that are still standin'." Carrie spurred Buttermilk and rode hard back toward the farm house.

Late that afternoon, five very expensive automobiles wound down the grassy lane between two pastures. Their kills were bagged so high on the front, top, and back ends, Carl didn't know how they could see to drive. He took a seat beside Bernie on the porch and laughed.

Carrie was livid. "What the hell are they gonna do with all that?" she demanded. "I'll wager that none of them—or any of their city fe-mule wives—even knows how to skin them varmints."

Carl laughed.

She and Bernie walked down to the cars and inspected the kills. Killer Burke was the only one to get out of his vehicle. He walked proudly up to the porch. The rest of the men in the cars were passed out, except for the drivers who were so drunk they lay their heads on the steering wheels for a quick cat nap.

"They got one dog, three cats, and I don't know how many chickens," Carrie yelled back to her brother-in-law.

Carl laughed.

"Carl," Bernie called when he reached the last car, "you'd better come see what these bums assassinated."

Curious, Carl got up from the swing and walked slowly past each car, laughing at all the rabbits, squirrels, racoons, turkeys and even one very large snapping turtle without a head. Fred Burke followed, pointing out some of his personal kills.

When they came to the last vehicle, Carl's laughs stopped.

"Ain't that the biggest buck you ever saw?" Burke said proudly, pointing at Carl's prize donkey. The jack was stretched out on the hood on its stomach, its legs out to either side and its head resting on the hood ornament, a long tongue hanging out of its mouth. "I just wish it had some horns."

Killer Burke awoke ten minutes later with his chin resting on the hood ornament, his arms and legs tied down to the car hood as his vehicle led their Chicago safari off the Shelton property.

26

Finding his wife Margaret lying dead in their bed startled Carl more than anything he'd ever known.

He'd just returned home from church when he found her lying on her back, her eyes looking straight up at the ceiling. She'd skipped the Sunday school class she and Carl taught together.

"I've got a terrible headache," Margaret had told Carl as they walked down the church hallway to their class.

"Go home then."

Carl realized as he sat on the edge of the bed holding his wife's cold hand that his last words to her must have seemed harsh. He regretted that.

Though his only phone call was to Earl, all his four brothers and two sisters arrived within the hour.

"How's Big Carl wanna get rid of the body?" Bernie asked Earl when Roy and Dalta finally convinced Carl to leave the bedroom.

"Bernie, she's not a stiff we need to hide." Earl was used to his youngest brother's insensitive remarks, but this was a new low even for Bernie.

"Oh, I didn't mean it that way." Bernie flipped his hand in the air like he was swatting away the dumb question. "I've just not had a lot of experience in this type of thing. Folks I know just don't usually die the normal way. You know what I mean?"

"Well, in the future just try to say the same words you would use if Ma or Pa died. Be sensitive, Bernie."

"Okay, but I'm not sure Carrie will like me if I get all sentimental."

Downstairs, Carl took a seat at the kitchen table, Hazel and Dalta on either side. Lula, home for a visit from Indiana, made coffee, and Roy went outside to get more firewood for the cooking stove.

"I thought that with Earl and Roy home from prison, life was going to get back to normal." Carl cradled his forehead in the palms of his big hands. "Sometimes life just doesn't seem to want us to ever get ahead."

Sounds seemed so loud to Carl; the rustling of his shirt sleeve, the perking of the coffee. Every tick of the clock on the wall echoed through his brain like a gunshot. His wife's death made him realize he had more years behind him than in front. Charlie Birger's advice to retire and enjoy life seemed more poignant than ever. He glanced at the clock again. Running out of time.

***

"Goodbye, Margaret," Ma Shelton said. She tossed a handful of gravelly dirt down into the grave. The pebble's bounced off the wooden coffin as if the spirit of Carl's dead wife were trying to reject her mother-in-law's tribute.

Ma showed little affection for any of her sons' choices in mates. Not even Carrie, the one who most closely resembled the matriarch's sassy personality, was safe when Ma wasn't happy.

***

"Wed in haste, repent at leisure." That was all Ma Shelton had to say when she heard her youngest child, Lula, crying about her divorce.

Ma and Earline were hustling about the kitchen preparing breakfast. Carrie didn't want to look up at the pathetic scene, so she sat at the table breaking green beans into a bowl. Lamenting over men was a pastime she could do without.

Sister Hazel was the only one showing sympathy for Lula. She stopped shucking corn and rubbed her baby sister's shoulder.

"But, ain't it nice that Guy Pennington stopped by to comfort you, Lula?" Hazel whispered, since the men were nearby in the living room. "He's a might clumsy, of course. Born with two left hands, I reckon. But he really cares about you, don't he?"

"He's sure enough been showin' his church door face around here lately," Carrie said. Hazel gave her a glare that went unnoticed.

While Lula lamented to the women in the kitchen, Guy paced in the living room. Carl was half asleep on the davenport, while Earl and Bernie cleaned shotguns at the dining room table.

"I sure do love Lula, Bernie." Guy said while he paced. "Can you give me some advice?"

"I sure can," Bernie said. "Never squat with your spurs on."

Earl snickered.

"Where is Lula's little boy, Jimmy?" Carl asked from behind closed eyelids. An anger was burning inside Carl. Even after three months, he was still mourning Margaret's passing. He actually looked forward to a distraction.

"Jimmy's in Satan's sanctum sanctorum." Being a failed Shakespearean actor, Guy put as much drama into the sentence as he could muster. Then, seeing Earl and Bernie's puzzled expressions, he added, "In Evansville, Indiana. At his pa's house."

"I'm plumb tuckered out," Carl muttered, rolling onto his side. He saw no way he'd get any easy stress release. Besides, he'd always liked Lula's soon-to-be former husband.

"Someone's been greenin' you, Guy." Earl said. "The court gave custody of Jimmy to Lula's husband. She was deemed unfit because she likes the night life."

"Well," Bernie said, "that would be a fact undenied." He and his youngest sister were two peas in a pod when it came to partying.

"That didn't give him the right to hit Lula," Guy said.

Carl raised up and opened his eyes for the first time in an hour. Earl and Bernie simultaneously closed the action on their shotguns with a louder than normal click.

Five minutes later, Carl's Ford sedan was skidding in the loose gravel as he floored the accelerator and cat-tailed the car down the long dirt drive from the farmhouse.

Bernie figured Guy must really love Lula. No one but a man in love would get in the backseat of a sedan carrying three well-armed and pissed-off Shelton brothers, go into another state, and kidnap a young boy. But what Lula wanted, Lula got, and she wanted her son Jimmy back from her husband who was living in Indiana.

Ma Shelton didn't even wave when the car carrying four of her children skidded out of the driveway in front of her farm house. Pa, though, stood and watched the car until it was clean out of sight.

"Them boys is no good," Pa said to himself. His sour expression was indigestion as much as grumpiness. "No good a-t'all."

Carl was driving like a mad man and would continue to do so for the first hour of the adventure. Earl sat quietly in the front seat, wondering if it would do any good in an accident to somehow wrap the back of his suspenders over the back of his seat. One day several years before, he'd been sitting on his porch when two cars met head on in front of his house. The drivers of both cars flew out in opposite directions through their windshields and into the trees. It took an extension ladder and nearly two hours for the dead men to be retrieved. Since then, Earl had thought about trying to invent a way to keep folks from trying to be birds during a crash. The best idea he could come up with was to build a car in the shape of a ball so it could just bounce around during a wreck.

Bernie was in the backseat with Lula sitting between him and her boyfriend, Guy. He was thinking about having Ray Walker or one of the other boys knock off Guy—on the sly, of course, so Lula wouldn't know. Bernie was pretty sure Guy only wanted to get his fingers in the Shelton money. Carrie had provided him that bit of information, although Bernie was confident he could have figured it out for himself if he'd had a little more time.

All the youngest Shelton brother's fears and suspicions had faded by the time Carl's temper lessened and he let up on the accelerator. In fact, the three in the backseat were fast asleep when Carl eased the vehicle in front of the long driveway to the Indiana farmhouse and cut the engine.

It was decided that Lula would sneak up to the home from the woods, and try to find out if her son was in his bedroom. If she could get him alone, she was certain the three-year-old would come running into his mother's arms and she could whisk him away to the car.

Guy Pennington watched from the backseat of the Ford. Without a word, the woman he loved left him alone with her brothers. Matters became even more frightening as soon as Lula was out of sight. The three Shelton men exited the car. With meticulous precision they opened the trunk, extracted weapons, and donned gun belts around their waists and shoulders. Bernie chose his favorite Tommy gun and Earl a pump-action shotgun. Carl chose to keep his hands free, although he had two revolvers in his waist belt and one in a shoulder harness. The three disappeared into the woods, leaving Guy sitting alone and wondering what he'd gotten himself into.

Meanwhile, Lula had located Jimmy. He was in the backyard hitting a tether ball suspended from a clothesline. Several pairs of men's long underwear and trousers hung from the line.

Assuming her husband might glance out the kitchen window, Lula hunkered down low and used the clothes as cover. She got as close to Jimmy as she could without being in direct view from anyone looking out of the house.

"Jimmy!" Lula said as loudly as she dared. The result was not what she'd hoped for. The boy screamed and raced for the house.

"What's going on out there?" Jimmy's father hollered from the back doorway.

Lula froze. Her son rushed toward his father, who was now standing with open arms. From out of nowhere, Carl raced up to his nephew, scooped him up with one arm and ran toward the wooded area in the direction of the car, Jimmy's father in hot pursuit.

Crouching beneath the clothesline, Lula reached up just as Carl passed carrying her son. That was the moment she pulled the line down. When the rope hit his neck, her husband's legs flew in the air and back over his head. At the same moment that he landed on his back came the sound of Earl and Bernie blasting the unconscious man's car with their shotgun and Tommy gun.

Little Jimmy screamed all the way to the Ford, his mother following close behind. When Carl tossed the boy in the front seat, Lula jumped in and took her son in her arms. Earl and Bernie were laughing as they piled into the back on either side of an awe-shocked Guy.

"Did you laughing hyenas cut the telephone wire like I told you?" Carl yelled as he sped the Ford away from the scene of the crime.

The laughing stopped.

"Wow!" Little Jimmy shouted a few moments later. His crying had ended abruptly when he saw how fast his Uncle Carl was motoring them past the houses and hills.

"Why you goin' so fast, Carl?" Lula asked.

"As far as I know, kidnapping is still illegal in Indiana. They won't pursue us into Illinois though."

The bridge crossing the Wabash River between Indiana and Illinois was almost in the shape of an inverted U. Little Jimmy would always remember that moment between the two states as being the closest he would ever get to flying in an airplane.

27

Carl found Earl in the barn nursing a sick calf. During the night, several cows had rubbed their backsides through the wooden fence and got into the barn. Someone had not sealed the grain box securely, and they ate so much the calf and a full-grown cow had foundered. They sent the cow off to be slaughtered. Earl was busy hand-feeding hay to the calf to counteract the grain.

"The Collinsville whiskey still is gonna get raided tonight," Carl said.

"How'd you learn that?" Earl asked.

"Jeanene told me."

"A child told you her pa was going to raid our still?"

"More or less." Carl's brain was racing through various scenarios even as his mouth explained. "She told me her pa said he was goin' to Collinsville tonight with her Uncle Joe to..."

Carl stopped talking. He closed his eyes, a hand on his forehead. "Who's working those stills tonight?"

"Blackie Armes and Buster Wortman. Ray Walker's in charge." Earl smiled as the calf began munching happily. He was more worried about the animal than their still. "You gonna warn 'em?"

"Buster and Blackie have been getting mighty chummy here lately. They've been spending a lot of time together down in East St. Louis." Carl gave his ear lobe a little tug. "Get Jerome Munie on the telephone for me. Then go tell Ray Walker I want to talk to him."

***

Joe Schrader knew the bootleggers were inside the cabin the moment he smelled the vinegarish fragrance of sour mash. He sighed in relief, knowing there wouldn't be a long stakeout before they could apprehend the outlaws.

"Go back to the car and radio Munie to cover the south road," Schrader told one of his deputies.

Schrader proceeded to draw a dip of snuff from his jacket pocket. It would be forty minutes before the men would be in position.

The second deputy produced a pipe and deftly drew a match along his trousers.

Schrader swung the barrel of his shotgun, knocking the lighted match out of his hand. "They might smell a smoke," the lawman said as he stomped the lighted match out, then handed the rookie a plug of tobacco.

Miskell appeared from behind a hill, crouching as he approached. When he arrived next to Schrader and the deputy, he pulled a flask from his coat and took a long swig.

"I don't know why Munie insisted on covering the wooded side of the cabin." Miskell offered the nervous deputy his flask. "Do you think he's losing his nerve?"

"Not likely." Schrader accepted the flask from the deputy for his turn at a draw. "I'm not sure he has his heart into bustin' another Shelton place though. He seems a little too friendly with them lately."

"Want me to tell him we need him here?"

"Nah, let's just see how he does."

***

"Don't be calling me Bust Wad no more," Buster Wortman warned Ray Walker for the third time that week. It was bad enough being confined in the cabin with Walker and Blackie Armes, but to constantly be reminded of his one mistake from years ago was getting under his skin.

Blackie was sitting quietly in a rocking chair in front of a roaring fireplace; his two bootlegging partners lay on the cots nearby. Blackie and Ray had been through plenty of gunfights together, not to mention a tank attack and even an aerial bombing on Charlie Birger's Shady Rest fortress. Still, Blackie didn't really care much for Ray's bullying. It seemed that Walker thought that since he often played the role of Carl's personal bodyguard, he was better than everyone else.

"You should have been there, Blackie." Ray laughed even louder than he had when he'd told the story three days before. "Carl told Bust Wad to duck down under the seat of the car and not rise up to fire unless shooting started." Ray rolled to his side on the cot and held his side. "And when the tractor backfired—" He laughed harder. "Bust Wad rose up and kilt the tractor dead."

Wortman had had enough. He rose from his cot, stormed across the room, opened the door, and slammed it hard behind him. The cool bite of the morning air helped him overcome the light-headedness he always experienced when Walker got to teasing. A fog developing from the nearby creek lay low to the ground, providing a shivering reminder of the film he'd recently seen called *The Wolf Man.*

He decided to go sit in the outhouse and read *Detective* magazine for a third time. Re-reading it by lantern light didn't take long, since most of the pages were missing. The magazine also doubled as toilet paper. It was the last magazine left in the outhouse, so Wortman made a mental note to pick up some more magazines on his next trip to town.

As he rose from the toilet to leave, there was a flicker from the first rays of sunlight that were streaming through the crescent shaped hole in the door. Since his bootlegging partners had once before roped the outhouse shut with him inside, he quickly looked through the hole to see if they were again acting like juveniles. A uniformed state policeman carrying a Winchester disappeared around the side of the machine shed that housed the still.

Wortman's instinct was to run for the woods. He opened the outhouse door and stepped out into the dewy grass. Two hundred yards away, the trees seemed to be coming alive with lawmen cautiously making their way toward the cabin.

The gloomy prospect of surrender was short lived. A line of fog appeared in the middle of the approaching ranks. There was a thirty-foot-wide ravine running beneath that thick fog. To the lawmen, it might have appeared to be runoff from the creek bed. They seemed to be staying clear for fear it had water in it, or maybe they had also just been to the picture show to see Lon Chaney's werewolf gnawing on necks. Staying low in the fog, Wortman raced across the yard and into the cabin.

"Cops," was all he said, but it was enough to put his comrades into immediate action. All three men snatched up weapons and rushed to the door. "Stay low in the fog, and I think we can beat it through the culvert to the trees and get right past them."

"How many are there?" Blackie whispered.

"Enough," Wortman said. "Stay as quiet as you can."

Blackie fell in line just behind him with Walker guarding the rear. Making it to the ravine was easier than Wortman had imagined. He figured that if he couldn't see the lawmen, then they weren't seeing him either. His only concern was that the three of them might be leaving a wake-like disturbance through the fog above. He estimated they were about halfway to the wooded area when he ran head-on into a deputy. They were both knocked onto their backsides and set rubbing their foreheads. Before the lawman could shout, Blackie knocked him unconscious with a hard blow to the head from the butt of his shotgun. The solid thud echoed through the ravine.

"That you, Dave?" a voice called.

"Damn rock!" Blackie grumbled to disguise his voice.

When no one responded, Wortman got to his feet, grabbed Blackie's arm and pointed back in the direction they had just come. Blackie pointed the opposite way, then realized the problem. Ray Walker hadn't followed them.

"All right, boys," Sheriff Munie's voice came from above, "you're surrounded. Come along peaceable-like. Throw your guns down and walk up the hill with your hands up."

28

Because of his mess hall escapade, Black Charlie was again in segregation, this time in cell three next to Robert Stroud and across from Carl Panzram. As a return guest of the establishment, the bets among the hacks was that he would scream the first time he was beaten. They weren't disappointed.

Since there were also four first-time inmates serving in the adjoining cells, Charlie's beatings were far less brutal than his first experience. The guards relished, though, in making the new guests feel unwelcome. But even they received less harsh treatment than had Charlie on his first visit.

Carl Panzram's execution by hanging was scheduled for that next morning. He never acknowledged his old sports betting partner's presence. In light of his eminent demise, Charlie wondered if the killer's mind could even remember the role their partnership had played in his troubles.

The small courtyard separating Building 63 and the laundry facility was where the thirteen-stepped gallows was being built. The unsettling hammering went on all day and into the night. The balding, middle-aged hangman, Phil Hanna, oversaw the construction.

Charlie was suspended from his cell door when Hanna came into the segregation area to measure and weigh Panzram. Robert Stroud was so excited he even swatted his birds away so he could watch.

"They call you the humane hangman, is that not correct?" Stroud sniggered. "I heard you don't take pay but want the weapon the killer used."

"Ha!" Panzram laughed. "You plannin' on cuttin' my willie off? 'Cause that's what I used to kill twenty-two men. Choked 'em to death, I did."

Stroud gleefully fluttered his hands together in short butterfly-like claps.

"Do you have any special requests for the proceedings?" Hanna asked. He'd prepared over seventy hangings, including the famous Charlie Birger 1928 execution in Benton, Illinois.

"I don't want any of the goddamned chaplains around during the hanging. It's none of their damned business, and I have no use for them." Panzram glared at Hanna, and then spoke softly in his ear. "You know somethin', hangman? I heard you've hung more men than I've killed. I don't think you and me is so different. I'll bet you like seein' men dangle. Do you get all excited before your murders, like I do? Does your heart beat fast for days afterwards? Do you see the dead bodies at night when you sleep? And does your roundeye pucker? I should've thought about bein' a hangman myself. I like to keep a souvenir from my killin's, just like you do. Yes, sir. Maybe you and me ain't so different after all."

When Phil Hanna walked slowly past Black Charlie to leave, his legs almost gave out from under him. He caught himself by placing a hand on the wall. The hangman took a deep, gasping breath before continuing out of the building. Panzram was not like any condemned person he'd ever met.

That night, Charlie lay on his cot listening to Robert Stroud encouraging the doomed man on ways to commit suicide to save himself from having his neck snapped at the end of a rope. The canary man considered himself a medical authority, since he was writing articles on bird care. His cell was full of books from the prison library, many of which had pages torn out and shredded to be used as nests for his darlings.

"Make a paper quill," Stroud hissed. "Open a large vein anywhere and insert the quill. Blow a bubble or two into the vein. Or, add simple tap water. That would work, too. You'll go right to sleep, Carl. Just imagine it, Carl. You can go to sleep forever and ever and ever."

"Shut up, Stroud," Panzram growled. "I tried your idea of eating a big plate of beans that I had hidden and allowed to rot. And I cut a six-inch gash into my leg to boot. But I'm still here. I'm too evil to die easy."

"Yes, but you groaned and vomited so loud the hacks came running with a doctor. You need to die quietly, dear Carl. Quietly, I say."

"Don't bother me with that stuff!" Panzram yelled. "My part of the performance isn't ready yet, but I'll prance up those thirteen steps like a blooded stallion."

A guard came down the corridor and shut the thick wooden doors to the canary man's cell. His cackling laughter could still be heard along with muffled canary singing.

Panzram continued to busy himself writing appendix letters to his own life story, which he'd penned for a journalist several years before. The sadistic killer liked to read it aloud as he wrote. His deep baritone whispers carrying to Charlie's ears. Ears that understood the condemned man's suffering as well as anyone.

"My only regret in life is that the human race have but one neck and I can't get my hands around it. I have no desire whatever to reform myself. My only desire is to reform people who try to reform me. And I believe the only way to reform people is to kill 'em. My motto is, rob 'em all, rape 'em all, and kill 'em all.

"I have lived thirty-eight years in this world and soon expect to leave it. I hate all the fucking human race. I get a kick out of murdering people. All that I leave behind me is smoke, death, desolation, and damnation. Today I am dirty, but tomorrow, I'll just be dirt."

Listening to Panzram unnerved Charlie. His own childhood had been fairly normal. Like the Shelton brothers, his mother had doted on him. Unlike the Shelton brothers, Charlie parents died when he was young. He cursed the brothers for their luck on that too.

The next morning, Charlie and the others in segregation were not shackled to their doors. Six burly prison guards arrived early to give Panzram his last meal and then were to harness him for the walk to the gallows.

"I ain't goin'," Panzram said. "Tell the warden I want to see him."

Ten minutes later, Warden White walked into the corridor followed by twenty people, which included guards, newspaper reporters, and two chaplains.

One of the newspaper reporters broke protocol and screamed out a question. "Do you have any regrets, Carl?"

"Yeah," Panzram yelled back as he tossed a magazine at the reporter. "I regret I won't be able to read the end of this story. It's continued next issue."

"This is your party, and you've got to be there," White said. "You have two choices. You can either walk in there like a man, or you can be taken my way."

"I told you I didn't want any of those god-damned chaplains out there. I'll come as soon as you get them out of here. I don't mind being hanged, but I don't want any Bible-backed hypocrites around me! Run 'em out, Warden, or you're gonna have one hell of a time gettin' me outta this cell. Every man I get a hand on is goin' to a hospital."

Warden White motioned. As the clerics were leaving, Panzram stood at his window and shouted so those gathered around the gallows and inmates in their cells might hear. "All right, you son-of-a-bitches! You've come to see a show and now you're going to see it. They tell me when I drop and hit the end of the rope, I'll crap my pants. I just wish I could take them off so I could crap all over you dirty bastards."

The hacks quickly harnessed Panzram's elbows and then his hands in front of him. A long chain trailed behind it that two guards grasped tightly.

"Anything you want to say?" Hanna asked the condemned.

"Yeah, hurry it up, you Hoosier bastard. I could kill ten men while you're screwing around."

Though Panzram was harnessed he led the way down the corridor, out the door and straight to the gallows, shuffling in determined strides. Despite the prisoner being half crippled the guards holding his chains had to almost run to keep up. The reporters and witnesses who were gathered in the little courtyard quickly stepped aside so they wouldn't get run over. Panzram roared at the spectators and shuffled a few fast steps toward them, making them fall over one another to get out of his way. Most all the cellhouse windows in view of the gallows were whitewashed from the outside so inmates couldn't see. One, though, had somehow been missed. Every inch of that window was filled with faces of convicts watching the proceedings.

Panzram hopped up the thirteen steps on his healthier leg, then stepped upon the trap door. The condemned man snarled as Hanna placed the black hood over his head, then the rope with the thirteen notches. The hangman nodded to the deputy sheriff assigned to throw the lever. Carl Panzram dropped seven feet and eight inches, then danced for just a moment at the end of the rope.

Phil Hanna cursed himself for not making the drop six inches longer to get a good clean snap of the neck. Of the seventy-two hangings he had performed, only a handful had suffocated while dancing at the end of the rope. He attributed Panzram's muscular physique for the miscalculation.

As the hangman's heart pounded in his chest, he forced himself to think about what souvenir would best bring back the excitement of this moment. The iron bar had been wiped clean of Warnke's blood. He supposed it would have to do.

29

"I've a powerful lack of affection for G-men." George Kelly told the Shelton brothers.

"What are G-men?" Bernie asked.

"Government men." Kelly stroked the barrel of his gat with a dry cloth. "They think they can police the whole country, chasin' us from one state to another since the local lawmen don't have jurisdiction outside their own states. I don't know what they're thinking. Hell, them G-men ain't even allowed to carry guns unless the local municipality tells them they can."

Carl had trouble taking George Kelly seriously. He bragged way too much to have committed all the mayhem he claimed in his tales of bank robberies and kidnappings. Still, he was right about the problem lawmen had when a criminal escaped to a different state. Those limited jurisdictions were the main reason for thugs like Kelly's success.

The gangster's girlfriend, Vivian, called him Machine Gun Kelly, a total joke since he could barely change the box clip in his gat. She had him practicing daily, though, and his friend Vernon Miller was a good instructor. To show how good he was, Miller used one of Bernie's sheds at Happy Hollow as a backdrop to write his name with his Tommy gun's fifty-round ammo drum.

Bernie's excuse for not being able to do the same with his own name was that a B was harder to shoot since it required a lot more bullets than a V.

While the marksmanship competition went on, Carl took Frank Nash inside for a business meeting. They sat at the kitchen table cleaning their arsenal.

"So, you just walked right out of Leavenworth?" Carl asked. He thought that if Nash was lying, he may not tell the same story a second time.

"That's right. I was the deputy warden's cook. When I went to his house outside the prison grounds one morning, I just kept walking. Kelly, Miller, and me have pulled a few bank robberies since then. We've also got Charlie Floyd, Alvin Karpis, and the Barker brothers workin' with us. If we get some of these other boys out of Leavenworth, we could run everything from Missouri to Texas."

"You planning on anything in Illinois?" Carl asked, recalling Al Capone posing him a similar question.

"Nope." Nash made sure Carl was looking at his eyes. "We will have our hands full down south."

"So, what can I do for you?" Carl saw a business opportunity coming.

"How would you hide weapons inside a barrel of shoe paste?" Nash asked.

Asking why never occurred to Carl. He'd hidden liquor of all types inside gas tanks. Weapons would need a stronger layer of protection. After contemplating a few minutes, Carl answered. "A tire inner tube."

Nash studied on the idea as he eye-balled the cleanliness of a revolver barrel. Finally, he looked at Carl. "We need a dame to visit Charlie Harris inside Leavenworth."

"Black Charlie?" Carl shook his head. "How the hell did he get into this conversation?"

"He was my cell mate in the big top. He and I came up with this escape plan."

"Is he one of those going out?" Carl didn't like the idea of seeing the man he had betrayed back on the street.

"No, he's just a mailman. Two fellas I got sent up with for the train robbery are going out. They'll handpick five others to join them. The broad's job will be to visit Charlie three or four times to relay info in and out. We also have a hack who is in on it. Between those two, we shouldn't have any trouble with communications."

"What about the shoe paste barrel?" Carl asked. "How do you know you can get it inside the prison?"

"We already did a dry run and got two hundred dollars in." Nash said. "So, who should the gal be? It'll need to be someone who Charlie already knows. That way, if they ask personal stuff, they'll both have the same answers."

"Maybe Lula or Carrie." Carl's wheels were again turning in his head. "No, it has to be Blondie."

"What's her real name?"

"That's what makes her perfect. Even I don't know her real name. We just call her the Blonde Bombshell."

***

Charlie was glad it wasn't Lula waiting for him in the Leavenworth visitor's room. The two guards who summoned him treated him like royalty as they escorted him through the prison yard. The windows overlooking the meeting area was packed with guards and inmates trying to get a look at the woman seated behind the wire mesh.

When he sat down across from her, Blondie blew a breathy kiss at her admirers and then motioned for them to give her some privacy. Charlie had been rehearsing the code that he and Nash had created for this meeting.

"Do you want stuff sent to you by the usual method?" Blondie asked.

"Yes. I've found that to be the easiest route."

"Oh, darling, I can't wait until you get released." Blondie's acting was not as good as her singing. "We have the whole family coming to get you in a Lincoln and a Cadillac. But don't worry, they'll be sure not to bother you unless you ask."

"I just hope you know the roads to get us home."

"I should. I've been driving them enough." Blondie hesitated a moment to recall the next part of the message. "Mother and Frances are well. We will leave next week."

"What about Aunt Edna?"

"She's been very ill but she'll leave St. Louis tomorrow."

The guards barely noticed Charlie twenty minutes later when the visit ended. Blondie had hundreds of eyes on her all the way to her car.

"The shoe paste barrel is leaving St. Louis today," Charlie told Will Green the next day at work in the laundry room. "There will be a Cadillac and Lincoln full of red hots if the guards start shooting from the towers. They've got the escape route mapped and have been practicing."

"Good," Green said without looking up from his folding. "We'll need to stay on the hard roads. All this rain has the dirt roads soaked."

"I want to be one of those going out," Charlie said. The more he thought about Blondie being the messenger, the more certain he was that the Sheltons were working with Nash on the outside. If he wasn't being asked to join the escapees, it would be Carl's doing.

Green shook his head. "No way. The plan was for seven to go out. There's no room for more."

"Then leave one of the others." Charlie was louder than he intended.

"Shut up, Blackie!" Green hissed. "You'll be rewarded when you get out. You cause any trouble, though, and you'll be buried in the yard next to Panzram."

The next day, it took Charlie and Green thirty minutes to open the barrel and extract the inner tube. Inside it were six revolvers, seven sticks of dynamite, a box containing one hundred blasting caps, and approximately one hundred feet of fuse.

That night in his cell, Charlie smelled Green sweating nitroglycerin out of some of the dynamite. Every inmate in cell block D were smoking cigars to hide the odor. A hack came upstairs an hour before lights out, but was quickly distracted when a fight was staged between two cellmates. By the time the two men were finally dragged out to Building 63, the lights were out and the nitro bottles capped.

The day of the escape, Charlie volunteered for mop duty at the main entrance, a job few inmates wanted.

"What's taking you so long?" a hack yelled at him.

"Someone spilled some glue here," Charlie snapped back. "You want it clean, or should I just leave it for the supervisor to see?"

The guard nodded. Scuffling from the hallway drew his attention. Charlie set down his mop and backed up against the wall. No sooner had the hack stepped around the corner than he returned, walking backwards, Will Green with a .32-20 caliber revolver to his nose. Next came Warden White and a half dozen hostages, followed by six more well-armed inmates.

"Open the damn door!" Green shouted. He pointed his revolver at an elderly officer locked in the small outer foyer.

"I'll be damned if I will." The officer didn't even rise from the chair at his desk. "Only one man in this institution can make me unlock this door, and that's Warden White."

"If this gate isn't open by the time I light this fuse, I'll blow all of us to hell!" Green scratched a match along the wall and held the flame to a fuse attached to four sticks of dynamite. "You'll be dead and in hell in one second if you don't open this door!"

"I guess we'll all see each other in hell, then." The old guard cackled. Feigning disinterest, he began sorting through paperwork.

The escapees pushed Warden White toward the feisty old gatekeeper.

"All right, Officer Dempsey," White said calmly, "open the door."

Dempsey shook his head but slowly rose. The keys on his chain jingled as he limped toward them and fiddled to find the right one.

"Hurry it up, you damned hack!" Green screamed.

Dempsey gave the inmates a scowl but unlocked the door. Leaving the other hostages, they pushed the Warden in front of them. Green grabbed the keys and looked straight in Charlie's eyes as he locked it behind them. Charlie rushed to an outside window to watch their escape.

The inmates checked their weapons. Pushing Dempsey and the Warden in front of them, the seven escapees stepped through the outer door. A long, wide series of concrete steps lay before them with a guard tower just beyond.

"Don't shoot!" Dempsey screamed to the guards on the main tower. "They've got the warden."

The guards immediately removed a tarp from a Browning belt-fed machine gun and swung it toward the steps.

"If he fires, we'll kill you both," Green stuck his gun in the warden's ear. "Order him to hold it!"

"We've made it this far," White yelled to the guards. "There's no reason for bloodshed now."

The powerhouse whistle sounded the alarm. Gunshots echoed throughout the yard. The seven Leavenworth escapees stopped an Oakland Eight Sedan that was coming towards them, forced five black soldiers out of it, jumped in—along with the warden—and sped away.

30

Carl spent more time picking his wives than he did his whores. A wife had to be a good cook, clean, and stay out of his way when he wanted privacy. She also had to keep her mouth shut about his goings-on, especially his frolicking with other ladies. A woman who didn't like copulation would work, but Carl preferred one that enjoyed female companionship as much as he did.

When he tasted Pearl Vaughn's cooking, he thought he might have a winner with at least one of the traits he desired. Her parents owning the most popular restaurant in Fairfield, Pearl was a woman of exceptionally good stock. Carl longed for social acceptance almost as much as he did money.

"They caught the last of the seven convicts that escaped from Leavenworth," Bernie said as they waited for Pearl to bring their dinner. "He came walking up to two fellas in a garage and told them they could have his rifle in exchange for a cup of coffee."

"At least he didn't stay at the farmhouse with Will Green," Earl added. "I heard Green and two of the others committed suicide rather than get captured."

"Yeah." Bernie looked at Carl. "They had quite a gunfight first, though, didn't they?"

Their big brother wasn't paying attention to anything except the pretty waitress bringing a big tray of food and setting it on an empty table next to them.

Carl and Pearl had known one another for years. Their conversations had mostly involved the menu but occasionally they strayed into a flirtatious battle of wits that they both enjoyed.

"What's your opinion on matrimony?" Carl asked.

"True love gets you through the bad times," Pearl said as she set their food on the table, "and makes the good times even better."

"What happened to your first husband?" Bernie didn't like not being part of any conversation. "You run him off?"

"One night he went wivin' in town." Pearl poured Carl more coffee. "When he got home, he found his lawful wife gone. It weren't my cookin' that gave him the wanderin' eye."

"Then it musta been your bedroom habits." Bernie grinned at his own wit.

"Well, I declare!" Pearl forked a piece of meatloaf off Bernie's plate and put it on Carl's. "I sure do wish I was a man so I'd know everything."

"I know women." Bernie snatched a chicken leg from Earl's plate and began gnawing on it.

"Well, I'll admit you're learning about women, okay," Pearl said, putting her fists on her hips, "but you're sure enough takin' your time about it."

"Don't blame the night for being dark." Carl laughed. "So, are you gonna marry me, Pearl?"

"You're a thief, ain't you?"

"I have never laid my tongue to any meat that wasn't mine." Carl passed two crossed fingers over his chest. "And that's a truth."

"I'd 'magine in your case the truth is but a lie, undiscovered." Pearl noticed some corn meal on her arms and wiped it off with a wash rag. "What would the terms of matrimony be?"

"Well, let's see." Carl was shocked that she'd even joke about his offer. He thought fast. "You'll have my supper ready for me nights. Each morning I like to leave a list of meals I want for supper on the ice box."

"You get two choices for supper in my house." Pearl tossed her hair. "Take it or leave it."

Carl knew by Pearl's sassiness he was in trouble. Just like Bernie, he enjoyed sassy women. Margaret had been homespun, a trait Carl appreciated but wasn't really attracted to. He often wondered if he and Bernie were drawn to feisty women because of their mother's own brazen behavior.

Earl, on the other hand, was steadier in his use of women. He kept his liaisons on the down low, a factor that kept his marriages more stable than those of his siblings. Remembering how bold Earl had been in his courtship of Earline, Carl reverted to flirtatious sparring.

"So," Carl spoke hesitantly, "do you have to drive all the way home to get cleaned up for our wedding?"

"I 'magine I can put on my bridal agony over at the Tonsorial Parlor and Bath." Pearl said, removing her apron. "What about you?"

"I'll be ready as soon as I wet my dry." Carl grabbed the flask from Bernie and took a rare swig. "I'm ready, I guess."

Carl and Pearl were married that night. The next morning when she went in the kitchen, she found a note on the ice box with Carl's dinner order. She tore it up, threw it in the garbage, then taking a fresh sheet, wrote: *You're taking me out for supper tonight.*

***

"Can't you shut-up those damned birds?" Buster Wortman screamed from his Leavenworth Prison cell. He was standing with one hand on the window bars, the other cuffing a cigarette. It was just his luck to get stuck in the only cell house overlooking the little courtyard for Building 63. Black Charlie Harris, his cellmate, told him it was a historic room since it was the only window that cons had been able to see out during Carl Panzram's execution.

"I've learned to like their singing," Charlie said from his top bunk. During his many hours hanging by the cell doors in segregation he'd used the birds to help his mind escape the torture. "Reminds me of sitting on a porch swing on a Sunday morning."

"On a Sunday morning you oughta be in church," Wortman chortled then shouted through the cell window. "Not listenin' to a flock of fowl squawkin'."

"Shutup, you damned Wormman," a loud voice came from the courtyard, "or I'll cut you up and feed your innards to my darlings."

It was Robert Stroud's exercise time, and he didn't appreciate anyone disturbing his chance to give his birds some fresh air.

"You'd better do as he says, Buster," Charlie warned. "Robert Stroud's a born knife man. He's in solitare for life, so he doesn't care if he shivs one more."

"How the hell did we wind up in a joint that allows a damned birdman convict to have canaries?" Blackie Armes shouted from the cell directly across the corridor. He was standing facing them, his hands on the iron bars.

"We wound up here 'cause them damned Sheltons set us up," Wortman grumbled. "And so did Ray Walker, I'm guessin', since he got away." He tossed his magazine into the toilet. Since the plumbing had been turned off for the past two days, the facility was overflowing with Charlie's latest shit. Rumor was that an inmate had tried to escape through the sewage pipes and was stuck somewhere along the system, most likely dead by now, considering the foul smell emanating from the drains.

"Carl Shelton told me they would take care of me if I didn't rat on them," Wortman complained. "Besides putting a few dollars on my prison account this past year and a half, I ain't heard squat from them."

"Well, they hung me up to dry with funny money," Charlie said as he did at least once a day.

"You'd better keep it down," Wortman warned. "We've only got a few more months and we're out of here. The only good thing about being in the big top is I've got to know some of the Chicago boys that work for Jake Guzik. They tell me he's looking for some help organizing St. Louis for a national syndicate. Who better than us to take on a job like that?"

"If you need help with that, I can have my friend Red Rudensky talk to Capone," Charlie said. "They're cellmates in Atlanta. Rudensky was a former Capone man and is his personal body-guard in the joint."

"I've already started the ball rolling to get the Sheltons for the same tax evasion they got Capone for," Wortman bragged. "If that works, we may get a chance to shiv them up right here under the big top."

***

"You're kidding!" Bernie laughed. "They think they can get us for tax evasion?"

The Farmer's Club in Fairfield had done a booming business the night before, as had all the other roadhouses in Little Egypt. Carl hadn't looked up from counting cash and laying it in stacks for the monthly payroll. Earl squirmed and paced the room. Bernie snatched his gat from behind his chair and began caressing its barrel.

"They got Capone for it, didn't they?" the accountant's voice was shaky. His livelihood depended on the Shelton brothers staying out of jail. Three convictions for falsifying tax records had cost the accountant his credibility everywhere except in the criminal world.

"They have Earl owing eight-thousand, seven-hundred, and fourteen dollars," the accountant read directly from the subpoenas. "Carl's being charged with owing nine-thousand, two-hundred and seventy-two dollars."

"What we gonna do, Big Carl?" Earl asked.

Carl finished stacking the money, then stared at the big piles in search of the answer. Each had a small piece of paper denoting who it belonged to. He pushed off to one side cuts that were for family and gang members. "Since the government wants its money, let's give it to them from their own." He began counting out protection money set aside for policemen, councilmen, mayors, and the governors of Missouri and Illinois.

When he was done, he counted it twice, then, following a moment's hesitation, lifted half the money from brothers Dalta and Roy's pile. He handed the stack over to the accountant. "Tell the IRS to keep the change." Carl looked at Bernie and pushed the protection money that was leftover toward him. "You take this to our government friends and tell them that this will be the last payment if we have any more problems from the IRS."

31

Roy Shelton dropped the side of beef into the hog scalder. With head down, he silently walked toward the house. Stella sat comfortably on the porch when he arrived. She rose slowly, taking a moment to loosen her arthritic knees and hips before walking toward the pole barn to get her carving knife.

The two passed one another beneath the empty clothesline without so much as a nod. Roy liked that about his wife. She kept her brooding to herself, as he did with his own. The fact was, he'd come to know some of his cellmates better than he knew Stella, most likely because he'd spent so much more of his life with them than he had with anyone except his brothers.

Still, Stella had waited for him for the eight years he'd been in prison—six years longer than he'd known her before he was sent to the big house. Thanks to his brothers, she'd lived well enough while he was away. Perhaps better than she had since his return. Money was getting scarce now that Carl assumed Roy could hold his own.

Though he knew his brothers would give him money if he asked, he didn't think he should bother them while they were dealing with tax problems. After all, he and Stella were living comfortably— though lavishly would have been much better.

"Go fill the machine up with petrol," Roy told Stella when she came back into the house after butchering the beef and storing it in the ice house. He was cleaning his Colt forty-five at the kitchen table. "You're gonna drive for me tomorrow mornin'. Be ready at dawn."

Stella primed the faucet and hand pumped some water into the big kitchen basin, then washed her bloody arms with lye soap and dried them with a towel. She knew better than to ask what her husband had in mind, but thought she had an idea anyway. Roy didn't like being broke all the time, much less living off his brothers.

She decided that when he went out that night for his regular rendezvous with his friends, she would take her own revolver down to the creek and get in some target practice on the many rats that inhabited the hillside. Being in good form might come in handy if Roy was planning what she guessed.

The next morning, she woke her husband before daylight for some rousing and heartfelt love-making. He responded much better than he had in his first days after coming home. He'd blamed it on the saltpeter. She assumed from his present reaction that it had finally worn off. Stella was hoping that if he was going to go back to prison, he would at least leave her with a baby this time.

With that in mind, when Roy tried to pull her on top of him, his favorite position, she tossed him back into the missionary posture that would ensure deep penetration for the seeds to easily meet.

The two-hour drive to a remote small-town bank was quiet. Stella tried to imagine they were on a fall drive to look at the beautiful autumn colors. She imagined doing some similar sight-seeing one year from now. Only Roy would be driving with her beside him, breast feeding a three-month old baby.

Later, when Roy was preparing to leave the vehicle, he embraced her and gave her a lingering, open-mouthed kiss. He felt the salty tears on his wife's soft lips and tried to memorize them in case of a future without their warmth.

Without even a reminder for her to leave the Packard running, he opened the passenger side door, got out, pulled his kerchief up over his mouth and nose, and walked into the bank.

***

Four months later, Carl and Earl sat together on the porch swing of their parents' home. As usual,

Bernie messed with his Tommy gun while sitting on the top step.

"They gave Roy an undetermined sentence for robbery and kidnapping," Earl told his brothers. "He could be in the joint for the rest of his life."

"Why would they give him life just for offering a hostage a ride for a few blocks?" Bernie scoffed. "Don't they know the banker wouldn't be hurt as long as nobody shoots? And if they did, that would be the cop's fault, not ours."

"The law is trying to discourage bank robbin'," Earl explained. "Now that prohibition's over, they think they can drive us back into coal minin', I'd 'spect."

"Well, that ain't gonna happen!" Bernie quipped. "Is it, Carl?"

Carl had been studying their racketeering options ever since Franklin Roosevelt was elected and promised to end prohibition. Bootlegging had been a good living, especially when combined with the gambling and prostitution industry. An occasional carjacking or a bank job kept the money coming in. He figured the gambling and whores would always be an easy and lucrative business, but the other endeavors were getting dangerous now that J. Edgar Hoover was sending federal agents all over the country.

"Put Stella back on the payroll at her usual split," Carl said. "Now that she's pregnant, we may want to increase that. I'll figure it out later.

"In the meantime, I want you fellas to start getting to know some of the union boys as well as the company men."

"Why do we need to court both sides?"

"Bernie," Carl stared blankly ahead and spoke slowly as if trying to make something clear to a child, "'cause we'll work for whichever side pays us the most, of course."

32

"Carl Shelton offered me thirty thousand dollars to let him take over the Boilermaker's Union," Oliver Moore told the man sitting next to him in the backseat of the automobile. Three men armed with Tommy guns patrolled outside the car. They carefully watched both ends of the country road leading up to Moore's parked Cadillac. "When I told him no, he said I was a walking dead man."

St. Louis Post-Dispatch reporter Carl Goodwin wasn't sure what to think of the president of the East St. Louis Central Trades and Labor Union. Moore's hands didn't shake as he accepted the half-pint flask from Goodwin, but his head constantly darted back and forth from the back window to the front.

"The Sheltons sent for six carloads of red-hots from Peoria to bump me off," Moore lamented. "Well, let them try. They can't intimidate St. Louis labor."

The headlights of an automobile approached slowly from the east. The three bodyguards moved around to the ditch side of the Cadillac and readied their weapons. Moore ducked low in the seat.

"They've been drivin' past me all day long." Moore's sweating through his white shirt was turning it gray. "I think they're pointing me out to somebody."

Goodwin found himself holding his breath until the car passed. He saw it was a blue Lincoln with shades on the back and side windows.

"Let's continue the interview at my place," Moore suggested.

"How 'bout in the mornin'?" Goodwin replied. "I have a hot date for a Garbo flick."

Moore tapped his knuckles on the car window. The three big bodyguards squeezed into the front seat.

When they reached the Boilermaker Union's office building on St. Louis Avenue, Moore shook Goodwin's hand.

"My driver will drop you."

Goodwin followed Moore out onto the sidewalk.

"I'm meeting my date at the Majestic Theater right down the block," Goodwin said. "I'd enjoy the walk."

"Suit yourself. See you in the morning."

Twenty minutes later, Goodwin stood on the sidewalk with his date waiting for tickets. He was feeling uncharacteristically tongue-tied. Her large bosom and V-shaped waistline was the problem. For whatever reason, he always had more trouble performing with a beauty than a plain gal.

"You have the bluest eyes!" she said.

Glad the silence was finally broken, he smiled.

"Why they're the same color as that blue Lincoln," she added.

Goodwin turned his head toward the street just in time to see the blue Lincoln with the shades drawn passing by.

"That's the same car—" His words were interrupted by the rattle of machine guns made louder by the echo between buildings. It caused many of those on the street to scream and fall to the ground. Others ran into nearby stores.

Goodwin pulled his date into the protection of a doorway. Cars on the street pulled off to the side and those inside ducked down onto the floorboards. A moment later, the blue Lincoln roared past again, going in the opposite direction. Goodwin had been a reporter long enough to take note of as many details as he could. In the days to come he would question over and over in his mind if the face he saw in the car window before the curtain was drawn were that of Bernie Shelton.

***

"They're reporting that Moore was hit by twenty-seven machine-gun bullets!" Earl gloated that night. The brothers set in Carl's St. Louis office. "I don't think Blackie Armes could've done better! Way to go, Brother Bernie!"

Bernie grinned. He loved it when his big brothers were proud of him.

"One bullet, Bernie!" Carl shouted. "One bullet and they might think Moore was killed by an irate girlfriend or an errant gunshot. But no, Bernie had to shoot up half the block and wound two bodyguards to boot."

Bernie grunted. Things changed too quickly. "Well, it coulda been a girlfriend!" he grumbled back. His face was dark red. "He coulda been screwin' that little Bonnie Parker gal. Clyde Barrow says she's good with a gat. Besides, what does it matter?"

"Carl's right, Bernie. You really oughtn't not 've kilt Moore that a way!" Earl changed his tune as he always did when his big brother contradicted. "It matters because now public sympathy is against us."

"That's right!" Carl said, looking at the newspaper. "Listen to what this reporter writes: 'Carl Shelton has the softest tongue and the bloodiest hands of any gangster who ever operated on the East Side.'"

"Your tongue ain't so soft!" Bernie whispered.

33

Once, when Bernie worked in the coal mine, he quit swearing, but then the mules couldn't understand anything he said. When the animals started balking, he returned to swearing a blue streak as often as possible.

"Damn, shit, hell, bastard!" Bernie screamed at the thought of his oldest brother. Fortunately for him, he sat alone in his Lincoln, puttering along the hard road near Fairfield. Big Carl wouldn't have taken kindly to any of his siblings, much less his youngest brother, cussing at him.

The thing was, Bernie had learned to enjoy watching bodies bounce and dance a final jig, followed by their writhing as they struggled for life. Whenever possible, he also enjoyed sticking around for the inevitable death rattle, as he'd done when he Tommy-gunned the three men at Wide Open's den of inequity.

Carl was never satisfied with anything. Bernie never forgot the time in grade school when he'd awoken early from nap time. Seeing the children sprawled out across the room was just too tempting. Bernie leap frogged across the backs of the four older and bigger Barry brothers. Reaching the end of the room, he threw open the door and raced home to the protection of his big brothers. When he got there and told them what he'd done, Carl boxed his ears.

That hurt a lot more than anything the Barry boys did to him during the fistfight that evening when the two sets of brothers met at the Pond Creek bottom for the rumble. Bernie was pretty sure Carl allowed the youngest Barry named Jack to drag Bernie into the creek and baptize him a few times before coming to his rescue.

Now Bernie was thinking about that when he pulled into the narrow lane that led up to the Barry house. Jack was chopping wood, and his plump missus was taking in the wash from the clothesline.

"Don't even get out of that flivver if you ain't got the C-note you owe me!" Jack's warning was punctuated by the axe that he raised over his head with both hands.

"Got it right here, Jack." Bernie wasn't afraid. The two were now good friends, and he was pretty sure none of the Barry brothers remembered his grade school pranks, although they often reminisced about some of the good Donnybrooks the two clans had in their youth.

"I'd like some fresh eggs that ain't water glassed," Bernie demanded in exchange for the hundred-dollar bill he handed over.

"Well, come on in, Bernie," Ethel Barry said as she folded the last of the clothes into a wicker basket. "I was just gettin' ready to fix some biscuits and gravy topped off with fresh eggs and sorghum molasses. How's Carrie doing? I haven't seen her in a month of Sundays. Oh, look at me. I'm just jawin' away to a fare-thee-well. Come on in and wash up, Bernie. We just don't hardly never get guests in these backwoods."

"There she goes again." Jack rolled his eyes. "She gets the jabbers ever time we have visitors."

"Glad to oblige anytime you need a guest for eats." Bernie opened the car door and followed her toward the shanty house. "And might I add, you're looking lovelier than ever, Ethel."

"Has all that masturbation finally affected your eyesight?" Jack grumbled. "I didn't marry her for her looks. I married her cause she keeps me warm on cold nights, and I don't have to worry about scallywags like you runnin' off with her."

"Life is best when it's simple," Ethel continued rambling. "We had a traveling preacher stop by here a few weeks ago. He was south to the mouth, probably from Texas, I'd guess. Jack ran him off the next day when he caught him in the barn sucking eggs."

"Oh, twattlin' shite. I ran him off 'cause he drank a whole jug of my good corn liquor." Jack then looked at Bernie. "It's against my better judgment to let you in my house, you know?"

"Since when do you ever use good judgment?" Bernie retorted.

"Well, I might if'n you'd stay on your side of Pond Crick. You've been gettin' me in trouble ever since we was in grade school."

"Now I seem to remember it was you gettin' us both in trouble." Bernie took one end of the clothes-basket so Ethel wouldn't have to turn sideways to get through the door. "We had a two-seater outhouse at school, and Jack always challenged me to see who could grunt the loudest. That ol' Miss Foster sure didn't like us, did she, Jack?"

After breakfast, the men went down to the creek to shoot some of the frogs that had recently invaded southern Illinois—not a difficult task considering they both used Thompson machine guns. Jack lost back the C-note when Bernie bet he could make a frog jump with one blast and then hit him midair with another.

Bernie was glad that the trick was accomplished before the two finished off their first jug of sour mash. Then, Jack suggested a trip to a brothel in the Valley of East St. Louis. Bernie eagerly accepted. Carrie was in Peoria visiting friends, and he was feeling feisty.

At the brothel, Jack chose a fat Black whore who was almost as unattractive as Ethel.

"Ugly women try harder than pretty gals," Jack said later that evening as Bernie drove them down Michigan Avenue. "My experience with attractive women is they like to just lay there and say, 'look at how pretty I am.'"

A bullet shattered the windshield. Bernie swerved the Lincoln into oncoming traffic. It was a fortunate maneuver, since that caused the Buick coming toward them to also swerve to avoid a collision. The two gunmen hanging out the Buick's window to aim their gats almost fell out of their vehicle as it ran up on a sidewalk.

The audacity of the ambush brought Bernie's blood to a boiling point. When he reached the end of the street, he performed a hard, squealing, U-turn and took chase after the Buick. Despite the early morning hour, the sidewalk had several pedestrians and the street had more than just a few cars. He had to swerve in and out of lanes to get around them.

Jack rolled into the backseat where the two Tommy guns were and quickly passed one up to Bernie.

The four men in the Buick were caught off guard when the Lincoln pulled into the left lane beside them. To free both hands, Bernie jammed his knees beneath the steering wheel and fired the gat through the passenger window. Jack's weapon jammed, so he dropped to the floor board to work the mechanism free.

The Buick squealed to a stop. Bernie drove fast to the next street and again performed a careening U-turn that sent pedestrians running for cover. He floored the accelerator and raced through the gears. As they approached the stopped Buick, Bernie stuck half his body and the gat out the driver's side window and poured a barrage of bullets into the Buick. Jack was even more daring. He stepped out onto the running board on the passenger's side and used the roof as his armrest to allow for a steady aim at the men inside the enemy's vehicle.

Despite being under fire, one of the men in the Buick got off a shot that hit Bernie in the back of his shoulder. He managed to regain control of the careening Lincoln and sped out of the city toward Collinsville. Twenty minutes later, he pulled up in front of a Shelton roadhouse. Then, he fell into the steering wheel and lost consciousness.

34

"It was a good thing you fell onto the car horn or you and Jack would both have bled to death," Carrie told Bernie when he woke up the next morning.

"Where am I?"

"Peoria hospital. Carl was afraid to put you in a hospital down south. He remembered when Charlie Birger's boys tried to kill Earl at a hospital. Plus, your little Tommy gun duel has got the whole of St. Louis raring to lynch any Sheltons they come across."

"Is Carl mad?"

"What do you think?" Carrie laughed. "He said you'd better stay in Peoria, 'cause if he doesn't kill you himself, someone else will."

"Who were those guys that ambushed us?"

"Jack said the only one he recognized was Buster Wortman."

"What happened to Jack?"

"Oh, he was in surgery for about six hours down in St. Louis, but they say he'll come through."

"Did we get any of 'em?"

"Sounds like two of them may not make it. Carl said that if your intent is to kill, you might not want your next gunfight to be so close to a hospital."

***

Carl's one-on-one appointment with Buster Wortman reminded him of the meetings he used to have with Charlie Birger. They met alone in an abandoned Pinewoods Roadhouse near Bellville, Illinois. Wortman wasn't as predictable as Charlie. For that reason, Carl kept the revolver in his breast holster unhitched.

"You Sheltons have worn out your welcome in East St. Louis," Wortman said, after sharing a few preliminary niceties. "Bernie has made the Tommy gun as famous in the Valley as Fred Burke did in New York, Detroit, and Chicago."

"I hear they're callin' him Killer Burke now." Carl laughed. "I remember when both you and him were just snot-nosed kids."

Wortman's neck turned crimson, the memories of being teased in his youth by the Sheltons still fresh. When his hand went to his neck to loosen his tie, Carl readied his own for a shootout.

"Let's not get petty." Wortman returned his hand to the table. "I know that your interests are moving north. So, you need to let me and my boys take over your operations in East St. Louis."

"Who are your boys, by the way?"

"Jake Guzik is providing some muscle."

"Greasy Thumb? I heard he's moving in on Frank Nitti's territory."

"Not hardly. Guzik is an organizer. Besides Chicago, he's payin' off political contacts in Kansas City, St. Louis, and New York."

"And you want to be his man in St. Louis?"

"Carl, I already am."

***

"What you want to do that for?" Bernie asked Carl one day when his big brother suggested hooking up one of his donkeys with Carrie's prize Palomino mare, named Buttermilk. "Them molly's you breed are infertile. What good are they?"

Mules fascinated Carl. He found that when a male donkey was bred to a female horse, the result was a colt that seemed to have all the best characteristics from both its parents. They were intelligent, strong, sure-footed, and fast. Not as fast as a horse in a short dash, but possessing an endurance that could run most horses into the ground over a long distance.

"You don't know that for sure, Bernie," Carl argued. "Why just last year a female mule produced a fine filly down Texas way."

"I don't know." Bernie ran his hand through his thick black hair. "Carrie would kill me if her favorite mare produced a foal that didn't know the difference between a whinny and a hee-haw."

"I'll help you buy that farm you wanted up there in Peoria County." Carl knew how to manipulate his little brother. He'd decided to fold his hand on East St. Louis graft. The end of prohibition, Earl's long stint in the big house, tax issues, and Bernie's shooting sprees, had put major dints in his operations. It was time to consolidate interests and reduce overhead. He was thinking a lot about Charlie Birger's last words of advice to him lately. Retiring to a life of leisure seemed more appealing than ever.

Over the next year, he spent more and more time on his Pond Creek farm. By the time Carrie's mare was ready to deliver, she and Bernie were living quite comfortably in their newly remodeled two-story home in Peoria County. They dubbed their three hundred acres the Golden Rule Farm.

Carrie slept in the barn with Buttermilk the night of the birth. Bernie had told his wife that Buttermilk had gotten out of her pasture and bred with his stallion, Lancelot—a union that didn't displease Carrie. As soon as the mare's water broke, she ran inside the farmhouse and screamed for Bernie. In anticipation of the delivery, Carl and Earl were visiting, and they also quickly dressed and came running. By the time they were all in the barn, Carrie's mare was lying on its side. Bernie's pet goat, Hill Billy, followed them into the stable and went straight to Buttermilk's head to give her a kiss.

"Get that damned goat outta here!" Carrie yelled at her husband. He quickly herded Hill Billy outside, gave his favorite pet a tickle under its whiskers, and shut the barn door.

Within moments, a single hoof emerged from the birth canal, followed several minutes later by the second front hoof a few inches behind. Then came the muzzle on top of the legs. It was all tightly encased by the amniotic sac.

"That's sure a big, ugly head," Carrie told Bernie and Earl as they worked to help the mare with the delivery.

"I imagine it's just a little out of shape from your mare's tight opening," Carl suggested from behind the stable wall. He was keeping a safe distance away, just in case the headstrong Carrie went off when she recognized the ruse. The brothers had already hidden the most lethal weapons that were scattered all around the farm.

Earl helped with the birth by pulling on the foal's legs. The sucking sound as the midsection slipped through the vaginal canal made Carrie gasp with excitement. The brothers, though, moved backwards a little to give Bernie's wife space for her anticipated explosion.

"Damn if it ain't short legged!" Carrie exclaimed. "Just my luck. Well, Bernie, looks like you got another polo pony—or maybe we could make her a cuttin' horse."

Earl was a little surprised Carrie was slow to recognize that the colt was a hybrid, especially after its long ears popped up. He guessed that she was too busy doctoring. While he tended the mare, his little brother cleared the amniotic sac from the foal.

"Let Buttermilk do that, Bernie," Carrie scolded. "That's how she'll get to know her youngin'."

Earl used straw to curry the foal so it could breathe more easily. At first the newborn shook its head, blinked, and looked around at its new world.

The mother and daughter rubbed noses to become acquainted, then Buttermilk licked at some of the birth fluids.

From the foal's mouth came a whimper, followed by a little whinny. The hew-haw that followed was expected by the brothers, but startled Carrie. Carl picked up a rope and quickly tied one end into a honda knot.

Carrie sat up on her knees staring at the newborn. Finally, she glared from Bernie to Carl. The moment she leapt to her feet, Carl tossed the lariat. It settled and tightened around her midsection, pinning her left arm. But that didn't stop the wild woman's right fist from connecting with Bernie's eye. When her husband grabbed around her waist and struggled to hold down her right arm, Carrie raised up both feet, catching Earl with a hard kick to the stomach and chest. While he slammed backwards into the wall of the stall, Carl rushed in with a piggin' string, and with two wraps and a hooey, had Carrie's feet tied down.

It took all three brothers to finish binding her arms. They then carried her wiggling and screaming into the house, where they left her tied up all night in the front room.

Bernie woke up the next morning in a pool of blood, as did Carl. Earl was spared the embarrassment, but rushed into the hallway when he heard the other two screaming obscenities. The three met there, and for several feverish moments checked one another's bodies for stab wounds.

Finding none, they dressed and descended the stairwell two steps at a time as they once did on Christmas mornings as children. The ropes that had held Carrie were lying in a pile in front of the fireplace.

"God, I hope she didn't kill the mule!" Carl shouted, rushing out of the house and to the barn.

There, they found Bernie's favorite goat, Hill Billy, hanging dead from a rope around a rafter, his head nearly severed by a deep cut around his neck. Carrie lay asleep in the hay, the little mule sleeping beside her.

Carl never got the mule away from Carrie. She named it Carl Ruth. For the next several years, Carl Ruth followed Carrie Stevenson around the yard like Hill Billy had once done with Bernie.

35

The first time melancholy really hit Carl was the day the Blonde Bombshell left town. Legs spread apart, his head hanging almost as low as his knees, he sat beside her at the bus depot.

"You sit there much longer," Blondie told Carl. "I might take a notion to puddle water on you."

Carl raised his head and stared at Blondie like he'd never seen her before. For the first time he noticed her big brimming eyes. The skin on her arms was smooth as custard. Embarrassed that she might see mist in his eyes, he looked back down. She had on high tab shoes with a large buckle. Her shapely ankles were too inviting, so he raised his eyes again. She wore a pink, ruffled, dotted-swiss dress, with leg of mutton sleeves and plenty of room for her bodacious cleavage to breathe. A parasol rested across her lap.

It made no sense to Carl that he had never really noticed how petitely beautiful her face was. Her nose and jaw line might have been created by a master sculpturer. Her hair was a large mass with a bun at the top of her head. The style gave her luxurious neck added dimension.

"Do you feel funny?" Blondie asked Carl.

"Yes, but I'm not laughing."

"You for sure got a snoot full last night."

"I'm just feeling a little green around the gills." Carl couldn't help rubbing his swollen face. He'd tied one on the night before as a result of Blondie's news that she was leaving Illinois for greener pastures out West. Since Carl rarely drank, the experience had left him sicker than it would a professional boozer.

"Make sure you don't delay puttin' some ice on that nose." Blondie raised his chin so she could better inspect his face. "Your behavior definitely put Pearl in a jaw-bustin' mood."

"I was sorta off-handed with her I suppose, but she shouldn't have talked to me like that."

"When a man takes to drinkin', there's just not a darn thing a woman can do about it, nothing at all."

"I'd expect I got my licks in."

"Carl, you need to quit makin' violence your first answer to everything." She sank her fingernails into his forearm to let him know she wasn't happy.

"I suppose that wrath was beaten into me as a child. Now it'll most likely be beaten outta me as a man."

"Why are you here, Carl?" Blondie lowered her head. "Why are you chasin' after a sportin' gal just as she's fixin' to go make a better life for herself?"

"You ain't no regular whore, Blondie."

"Ha! Where do you suppose that old coal miner expression came from?"

"What expression is that?"

"Why, fire in the hole, of course. My britches have been burnin' since I was first introduced to a man's pleasure."

"This ain't the time for any of your Tom foolery, Blondie. I love you. Why, I'd cut off my own right arm with a dehorning saw if it would get you to stay."

"I declare, your eyes are lit up like the full moon." Blondie gave him her sweetest smile. "The things that men will do in the name of love. You sure is a Johnny-come-lately, Carl. You should have said them words to me years ago."

"I suppose there's nothing more for us to talk about then. Is there?" Carl started to rise, but Blondie gently pulled him back down on the bench.

"Carl, before you go, can you make this moment last forever? This fancy dress didn't quite do all the things it was supposed to."

Carl didn't usually abide of smooching in public. He surprised even himself when he took Blondie in his arms and gave her a kiss to remember.

"I'll see you directly, I'd 'spect," Carl said. "You'll be back."

He walked out of the bus depot without turning around to look at her again.

"Not this time, lover," Blondie whispered.

***

Carl drove to St. Clair County. For a reason he couldn't fathom, he had a desire to visit Jerome Munie.

"You got a shoe on the wrong foot, you big, dumb lout," Carl said when he saw Munie putting on a new pair of boots.

Munie didn't even look up. He switched the boot over to the other foot. Carl noticed half-filled boxes on the desk. The photograph of the sheriff on his first day in office was missing from the wall. Instead of his uniform, Munie was wearing a blue cotton walking suit.

"You going somewhere, Sheriff?"

"Yep, I'm not running for reelection."

"You're being a little premature in your retirement, aren't you? The election won't be for another few weeks."

"Oh, I'll serve out my time until the next sheriff takes office. But, until then, you don't need to worry about me raiding anymore of your roadhouses. I'll be taking Jeanene fishing a lot more now."

Carl was as shocked by the news as he'd been by Blondie's leaving town. He walked over to the empty jail cells. They were unkempt. The cots were stained and smelled of sweaty body odor.

"Is Jeanene around?" Carl asked. "I'd like to say goodbye to the little jackanape."

"She doesn't need to hear any goodbyes from a criminal like you."

"What's got into your crawl?"

"You know you're a real shit-stirrer, Carl. Here you are pining away about a little girl and then you'll go out and rob a bank or shoot somebody. I'm fed up with trying to reform this county. Let someone else do it."

"Why, you did a fine job cleaning up St. Clair County. You sure put a damper on the Shelton gang enterprises."

"And what did it get me, Carl? Nights away from my wife and daughter, just so I can shut down one of your sawdust joints. Hell, half the time you knew I was coming and had already moved most everything to a new location. What good did I do?"

"Well, that's why they're called sawdust joints, Jerome. You know that. It's so we can move on a minute's notice. It was nothing personal. We liked you."

"I'll bet you did. Like when you introduced me to Scarface Capone as your pet sheriff."

"I said no such thing."

"You'd just as well have." Munie sat down at his desk, his hands over his face. "Now the governor has pulled Schrader and Miskell to do their dirty work up in Chicago. I'm glad the bastards are gone."

"Well, I'm sure sorry to see you go, Jerome." Carl held out his hand. "I was proud to have you as a nemesis these past four years. I hope there's no hard feelings."

Munie looked up at Carl's hand, but refused to offer his. The dejected Shelton boss turned and walked out of the jailhouse, never to see Jerome Munie or his daughter Jeanene again.

BOOTLEGGER HEAVEN

The Shelton Gang Story

BOOK TWO

1941-1950

1

"You wanna know what white supremacy is?" Carl asked the driver of the '28 Ford. "We are white in the winter, turn red in late spring, and a golden brown come summer. Now that's pretty supreme, I'd say."

"If you say so, Mr. Carl," Harry Sterns said. "But I'd still like to know what it's like to be White, if only for a day."

"It might disappoint you," Carl said. "Besides, you're smart. No one expects a nigger to be smart, so you've got an advantage there."

"Yes, Mr. Carl." Harry grimaced. "But what would you do if your little girl was as sick as mine?"

"I suppose that as a last resort, I could pray."

"Prayer shouldn't be the last resort," Harry chided. "It should be the first resource."

The flivver had been lurching for nearly two hours, so when it gave one final belch and came to a stop, it was no big surprise to either man. The surprise came when a squad car pulled up behind them a moment later.

"Well, if it ain't Carl Shelton," the deputy said when he arrived at the car window and looked inside. He immediately reached for his side arm, which he drew and held at his hip as he inspected Harry's identification. "Not a real fancy car for a big-time bootlegger, Mr. Shelton."

"I'm not dealing in white mule anymore," Carl told the officer. "I'm dealing with real mules now, and they bring a pretty good price on the hoof."

"You appear to have quite a bulge under your coat, Mr. Shelton. You got a permit for that cannon?"

"I only use it to dispatch animals to the afterlife. Kinda a veterinarian's tool."

The next day, the newspaper headlines ran with the story of southern Illinois' once notorious gangster falling so low as to be arrested in a beat-up old automobile while in association with a Negro.

Carl was furious as well as embarrassed by the insinuations that he was a failed racketeer. Never mind that Harry had only been giving him a ride because Carl's Cadillac had hit a deer and damaged the motor.

"Hell, we're still running all the gambling and prostitution in Little Egypt," Carl told his brothers when they bailed him out later that day. "I'm tempted to buy those newspapers and turn them into publishers of them silly comic books."

"We'd make a fortune." Bernie's eyes opened wide. "That new Superman comic is great!"

"A story about a guy who can jump high ain't the type of comic Carl's talkin' about, Bernie." Earl laughed.

"Did you hear Charlie Harris is back in town?" Carl asked to change the subject.

"Black Charlie?" Earl grimaced. "I wonder what new methods of murder he learned in the pen?"

"Well, you boys just keep clear of him until we see if he's changed any," Carl advised. "Black Charlie was never a real stable fella to begin with."

2

The desk drawer had been rifled with a letter opener. Mabel Bell knew this because the letter opener was lying on the floor bent into an L shape. Her first thought was that her brother Charlie had done it to find some money to take gambling.

Charlie Harris was fresh out of prison for the second time in his life. She hadn't seen much of him since they were children, so she wasn't sure he wouldn't go searching for cash or maybe even do something worse. Then Mabel saw her daughter, Beatrice, curled up in a corner alongside the bed.

"Who did this, Bea?"

"I ain't seen nary a soul," Bea said. The twelve-year-old reached quickly to her face and covered an eye.

"Who hit you?" Mabel wasn't usually the type of mother to express excessive concern over a simple black eye, but she'd never had an ex-con staying in her house before. "Did you get hit hard?"

"It was harder than I'd slam a door," Bea said. She rose from the corner, approached her mother in tiny steps, then lowered her hand from her face. "Are you mad, Mommy?"

"It just don't sit right with me, that's all," Mabel said. She made a rare gesture by taking her daughter's hand and pulled her to sit on the edge of the bed. Then dropping beside her, she put both hands on her face. "Don't forget what I learned you. If a man ever hits you, just roll with the punch, curl up on the floor with your hands over your head, and start crying. Even if it's your Uncle Charlie hittin' ya."

"I'll do it sure, Mama," Bea said. "But it weren't Uncle Charlie that struck me, Mama. It was Mr. Anderson did it."

"The oil rig man?" Mabel's mind raced through the surprising information. She often fed the workers that were installing the oil pumps on her land. Since the nearest restaurant was several miles away in Fairfield, they paid her well for a hot meal. "He must have spotted me payin' bills at the desk and thought I kept my cash there. But why did he strike you, girl?"

"Because he was drunk and I got in his way, I guess."

"Well, he didn't get nothin', and I'm glad it wasn't Charlie done it."

"Uncle Charlie's a bit of a queer old duck," Bea said. "He ain't talked three words to me since he got here."

"Oh, he picked up pretty quick when he seen you, child." Mabel rose and adjusted the long black braids folded up over her head. "Why, he said you're sweeter than a barrel full of corn squeezin's."

"What in hell blazes is goin' on here?" Black Charlie said from the doorway. His eyes darted from the letter opener that Mabel had placed back on the desk to the damaged desk drawer, then to Bea's swollen eye, which she quickly covered again.

"Did that Anderson fella do this?" Charlie demanded. "I saw him leaving here."

"He used to come around, now and again, but he won't be no more." Mabel returned to her daughter's side when she saw a darkness come over her brother's face. "He foremanned the mine when I was a girl. Now he's workin' the oil rigs and stops here for meals. He'll know better than to come around here again, Charlie, so don't be makin' no trouble. Ya hear?"

"And I can just about guarantee he won't be hittin' no more little girls, neither," Charlie said. "I aim to disabuse him of that notion once and for all."

***

"It never seems to fail," Charlie said when he saw the three Shelton brothers sitting together in a luxurious hotel dining room. "Them that's got always seems to get more."

"I've got no quarrel with you, Charlie." Carl gave his childhood friend little more than a glance, then proceeded to cut into a three-inch steak. "Sit a spell, if you've a mind."

"Obliged." Charlie took a chair that was facing the wall, turned it backwards, straddled it, and put his forearms on its back. A waitress brought him a cup of coffee.

"You fellas know a scumbag works the oil rigs named Anderson?"

"I used to know him," Earl said through a mouthful of food. "He's a triflin' little fella, but he used to be a coal miner. He givin' you trouble, Blackie?"

"He ain't givin' me no trouble at all." Charlie winced a little at the nickname. "He prefers to give trouble to little girls."

"How little?" Carl asked.

"'Bout twelve years old, I'd say." Charlie avoided mentioning she was his niece, since he was afraid the Sheltons might think it strange that he didn't know her age. "She ain't filled out in the womanly places yet, anyway."

"You fixin' to kill him, Blackie?" Bernie asked.

Charlie tolerated Carl and Earl calling him Blackie, but Bernie was still the runt of the brood. He gave Bernie a hard stare. "Might just beat his ass a little. I'll save my killin' for those who disrespect me."

"I'd expect you'll find him in Fairfield this Saturday night." Carl took a napkin from his lap and wiped his mouth. "There's gonna be a hootenanny at the tar paper shack. My sister Lula and me are setting up our portable roller rink at the warehouse next to it that morning. If you'd like to help us, it'd give you an excuse for being there. Plus, you could make a few bucks. I wouldn't think it would be too difficult to get Anderson outside for a whoopin'. He's usually drunk anyway. Just make sure you rumble in the parking lot, Blackie. We don't want to ruin the festivities."

***

For nearly five years, Carl had been dreaming about climbing on top of Blondie for just one more jaunt. She'd been missing for so long, some supposed she was kidnapped by a band of gypsies that came through town. He was one of the few who knew the truth but declined to offer the information to anyone.

Then, that Saturday night at the honky-tonk, an extremely large woman grabbed him and pulled him into a bear hug.

"Don't you remember me, Carl? It's Blondie. You boys used to call me the Blonde Bombshell."

When Carl saw the folks in the crowd grinning, his face turned as red as Blondie's lipstick. He was perplexed. The woman before him was well over two hundred pounds with graying hair—except for a little bit of a dark mustache between her nose and upper lip. Dark age spots filled her face. Her skin had patches of light and dark as if she'd peeled away large sections. She had a bosom even larger than he remembered, leaving a wrinkly cleavage over her lowcut dress along with several small, scabby scars that looked like burns. The mystery of the scars was revealed when ashes from the cigarette that was hanging straight down from her eye teeth suddenly fell into the deep valley between her breasts. Blondie didn't flinch. The cigarette bounced rhythmically with her constant chatter, most of which Carl didn't hear.

"His mother tried to name him Tarantula," she rambled, "but didn't know how to spell it, so it came out Turntula on his birth certificate."

"Why would a mother want to name her son Tarantula?" Carl asked.

"Well, her name was Spiderella, so who knows." Blondie hugged Carl again and whispered in his ear. "So, what ya say, Big Carl? Wanna go a few rounds for old time sake?" She said it a little wistfully. Her eyeballs jiggled nervously with excitement.

Carl blushed even redder. She was a brazen hussy. He once had liked that about her.

"What's wrong, Carl?" Blondie's voice was full of scorn. Her face turned as red as Carl's but much darker. "You don't like me now that I've filled out a little?"

"Why, n-no, that's not it." He tried to look startled by the accusation. She shrugged off his arm when he tried to put it around her. "It's just that I've got a reliable wife now, Blondie." Then, thinking she might feel sympathy for him, he added, "You heard that Margaret died, didn't you?"

Seeing the red draining from her face gave him hope. She poured some white powder from an envelope onto her finger, held one nostril, and snorted it up the other.

For a reason even he didn't know, Carl took a plug of tobacco from his trousers watch pocket and bit himself a chaw. The chaw wasn't his. In fact, he'd never chewed before. He'd brought it for Bernie, but Blondie made him nervous and he was looking for a distraction. What he'd told her was half true. He did feel lucky to have a reliable wife, as well as a lively girlfriend. But Blondie didn't need to know about the girlfriend.

The tobacco in his mouth burned and tasted horrible. Without realizing it, he swallowed. A mistake. The next thing he knew he was running outside where he spit a dozen times then stuck his mouth under the water spout next to the horse trough, and as he pumped, drank fast and long.

"Get a bad taste in your mouth?" Black Charlie asked. He stacked an empty keg onto the pallets of a fork lift. Perspiration had soaked through his dress shirt. He doused some of the water Carl was pumping onto his own head and combed his fingers through his graying hair.

"Anderson's got his no-account friends with him," Carl gasped when his throat quit burning. "You'd better be careful. They say he's become pretty crafty with a blade."

"Maybe you could tell him that there's a gal in the front parking lot that wants to talk to him," Charlie suggested.

Carl agreed. He wanted to see how Charlie handled himself. Considering their tenuous relationship, he had a feeling the information might be of use somewhere down the line. The Sheltons had always imagined Charlie would be a back shooter. It surprised Carl a little that the professed killer seemed to want to take this fight head on. Maybe he'd learned some things during his ten years in Leavenworth.

"I'll get him to come out," Carl agreed. "If his friends come with him, my brothers and I will be there to back you up."

"You owe me at least that, I reckon," Charlie grumbled. "Better than that wreck of a car you gave me when I got out of the big top."

That comment was interpreted as a stark warning to the Shelton boss. Carl had never mentioned to even his brothers that the notes he'd provided Charlie for the business deals in Detroit were funny money. Now he recognized that a showdown with Black Charlie Harris was inevitable. Still, he figured Charlie was right. He did owe him at least one instance of professional courtesy—before he killed him.

Convincing Anderson to step outside was easy. The oil rigger was staggering as he led three of his friends across the dance floor, shoved a couple of dancers out of his way, and headed for the rear exit.

Carl knew they were planning to circle the building. Probably just in case it was a setup. He guessed that the tough riggers had plenty of reasons of their own to suspect an ambush.

As they danced, Bernie and Earl were watching. They saw their brother nod, so they quickly left their wives and followed. When the brothers got outside, they saw the four men standing in front of Charlie, who was clenching and unclenching his fists.

"Charlie, you want them all at once or one at a time?" Carl's question caused a frown on the faces of Anderson's three comrades.

"I want Anderson first," Charlie said, a vein on his forehead throbbing. "Then I'll take the others all at the same time, if that's how they prefer it."

"What you want me for?" Anderson took a step to the side, his left hand slowly reaching behind his back.

"You hit the wrong little girl. Bea is my niece."

"Ah, I didn't swat her any harder than her ma has done. What you want me for?"

"I don't chew my cabbage twice," Charlie said, then lunched forward.

Anderson's hand came from behind his back, knife first. The blade sank deep into Charlie's hip, breaking off at the tip when Anderson forcefully drew it back out. Black Charlie's eyes turned black even while his face winced in pain. He quickly withdrew several feet until his back was against the side of a car.

"Charlie!" Carl hollered. "Catch!"

A revolver floated over Anderson's shoulder. Charlie caught it by the handle and fired twice, even as his assailant rammed the knife into his shoulder.

A bullet in his heart, Anderson went down like a fallen deer. His three friends raced to a parked car, opened the doors and leapt inside. The car kicked gravel as they made their getaway.

The pain in his hip caused Charlie to drop to one knee in front of the dead man's body. A few yards away, Carl Shelton also crumpled to one knee. Earl and Bernie were immediately beside him, each with a hand under a shoulder. Carl's fingers were grasped against the left side of his chest. His eyes locked with Charlie's as he extracted a silver spectacle case. When he opened it, out fell his broken reading glasses along with a .45 caliber slug.

***

Bea was sound asleep when she heard her mother give a soft shriek, followed by commotion coming from the front room. She got out of bed and walked to the bedroom door in her bare feet. Opening the door just a crack, she looked into the main room where her mother had just finished undressing her Uncle Charlie and was wrapping a white sheet around him. By the time she'd helped him walk the few steps to the washroom, the sheet was turning a scarlet red around his hip and shoulder.

Just as Bea heard splashing of water in the bathtub, the front door burst open and a man wearing a badge rushed inside, followed by the local doctor.

"In here, Sheriff," Charlie said as calmly as if he was inviting him to a game of poker.

There was only enough room in the small water closet for one additional person, so the doctor went in. A moment later, he and Bea's mother assisted Charlie as he hopped on one leg to the dining room table.

"Beatrice," the doctor called, "get in here and help your mother."

Bea grabbed her robe off the back of the door and wrapped it around her as she entered the room. She quickly cleared the tabletop and moved the chairs as the deputy and doctor laid her uncle out on the table.

Her mother went into the kitchen to boil water. Bea took her uncle's hand and held it to her chest. Through the pain, Charlie smiled at his niece.

"Bea," the doctor said. "I'll need you and the sheriff to hold your uncle down while I try to remove the knife blade. It's lodged tightly in his hip bone. I don't have my medical bag, so I don't have any anesthetic. He'll just have to bite the bullet. Go get me some clean towels and soak them in boiling water."

"We don't have any clean towels, Doctor. Tomorrow's wash day."

"See if your mother has any Kotex, then."

Bea's face turned bright red.

"I'd rather die with infection from dirty towels than have you use a woman's rags on me." Charlie's chuckle caused him so much pain he put his fist on his forehead. "I'd be laughed right out of the rackets."

Bea ran into her bedroom and came back holding a cotton night gown.

"I just got this yesterday," she said.

Ten minutes later, the gown was boiled. Using a pair of regular pliers, the doctor went to work. At the first tug on the knife blade, Charlie's entire body convulsed—and a second later, he passed out.

"Can you sew, Mabel?" the doctor asked when he finally had the blade removed. "I'm afraid I don't have my glasses either."

"Not as well as Bea."

"Well, bring me a needle and thread." The doctor ordered.

Bea smelled the alcohol and saw the doctor's bloodshot eyes. She also caught a glimpse of his glasses case inside his jacket pocket. Her hands were shaking when she returned with the sewing kit.

"Just imagine you're sewing a pair of trousers while someone is wearing them," the doctor told her.

***

Three days later, Charlie took his niece out for lunch. He used the money he'd made setting up the roller rink to buy her a new nightgown and robe. Hers had become so bloodstained, Mabel took it out and burned it.

"Mama said you kilt Mr. Anderson," Bea remarked matter-of-factly as they walked out of the store to the car with the packages. Her mother had not allowed her to discuss it, but she wanted to know.

"Only after he refused to take a beatin' and stabbed me."

"Hello, Mr. Harris," Carl Shelton said, walking out of the barber shop next door. "How are you today?"

"Morning, Mr. Shelton. I suppose I'm a little leg weary."

"I don't blame you. I'm a little sore myself." Carl touched his chest, then tipped his hat. "Why, hello Beatrice. You look lovely."

"Thank you, Mr. Shelton."

Her uncle tipped his own hat as Carl walked past them. Charlie opened the car door for Bea.

"Don't you ever let me catch you talkin' to a Shelton unless I'm with you."

"Why, Uncle Charlie? Do you think they might hurt me?"

"No. In fact, I feel a might safer havin' you along. Even the Sheltons wouldn't kill a kid."

Despite those words, Black Charlie reached in the backseat, pulled his Thompson machine gun out from under a blanket, and set it in the front seat between him and his niece.

3

Bernie liked to eat T-bone steaks, mainly because he could pick them up by the bone and gnaw on them without bothering the eating utensils.

"Would you please use the knife and fork like a human being?" Carrie chastised. She'd prepared his favorite meal, complete with baked potatoes and peas.

"Why is it okay to eat fried chicken with your fingers but not other foods that have bones?" Bernie wondered aloud.

"It's not civilized, you big, dumb ox."

"Who says so?"

"Emily Post, that's who says so." Carrie just happened to have a copy of the famous socialite's book on the top of the china cabinet. She retrieved it and plopped it down on the table beside her husband. "You need to read her *Book on Eatin'quette.*"

Bernie thumbed through the pages while he bit off chunks from the steak in his left hand. "It says here you are supposed to eat peas by stabbing them with your fork." He tossed the book in the fireplace, took up his spoon, and began shoveling peas in his mouth as fast as he could.

The violent fight that evening resulted in the breaking of much furniture and most of Carrie's favorite china. The love making afterwards, though, made the husband and wife feel the material loss was worth it.

From the bushes outside Bernie's windows, Black Charlie saw and heard everything that occurred that evening, including the sadistic sex that left more lamps and coffee tables broken than the fight had.

The love making didn't interest Charlie except to spark his curiosity as to ways he could kill Bernie during the act. Since Carrie was such a wild cat, he knew he'd have to eliminate her too. After much contemplation, he decided that this was not the day for murder and mayhem.

Black Charlie stayed in the shadows as he walked back to the hard road where he'd left his car. He found it hard to believe that the Shelton brothers rarely used lookouts. He figured that was because they were so unpredictable in their whereabouts. Usually when they left a place, there would be several vehicles exiting all at the same time and heading in different directions. They rarely stayed in the same home or hotel more than two or three nights in a row.

They had plenty of reason for taking such precautions. Since they still owned most of the downstate gambling and prostitution operations, there were plenty of crime organizations that would like to step in.

Black Charlie's desire to kill the Sheltons was mostly personal. They had set him up for the paper hanging wrap. The funny money Carl gave him to buy bootleg liquor with had cost him ten years of his life behind bars in Leavenworth.

He turned on the light switch when he entered the little room he rented at a boarding house. Cockroaches scurried across the floor and walls to find darkness. The insects were no strangers to a man who had just spent ten years in prison. He often told himself that if he had to spend time in the big top, the 1930s had been the right years. In fact, he'd met many a man who had intentionally got arrested during the depression just so they would have free room and board.

When Black Charlie approached his sister's farm house the next morning, his niece, Bea, was riding the Shetland he'd stolen for her. She trotted the pony over next to his car, then raced him to the house.

"I beat you, Uncle Charlie."

Charlie got out of the car, pulled a square of sugar from his pocket, and fed it to the pony.

"Did you ride by the Shelton farm like I asked you?"

"Yes, Uncle. Bernie and Carrie were loading two horses in a trailer," Bea raised one leg up over the Shetland's neck and rested it around the saddle horn. She accepted a licorice stick that her uncle offered her and took a big bite. "That Carrie sure is a beautiful woman."

A memory of Carrie naked on top of Bernie flashed in Black Charlie's mind. He supposed she was attractive, but pretty females no longer seemed a prerogative after spending ten years in the slammer.

"Do you know where they were taking the horses?" her uncle asked.

"I think I heard them say Peoria. I do know they said something about meeting with someone named Garrison."

Charlie was elated. Clyde Garrison was the mob leader in Peoria. Some young Chicago thugs called the Forty-Two Gang had been in Leavenworth and asked him to take part in the kidnapping of Garrison's wife when they were released. The plan was to run the mob boss out of town and take over Peoria as a stepping stone into Capone's Outfit, which was now being run by Frank Nitti.

What a pleasure it would be to somehow connect the Shelton brothers to Garrison. Uncle Charlie would have kissed his niece if kissing was something he did. Instead, he handed her the entire sack of licorice.

4

"Those street punks from the Forty-Two Gang in Chicago are too stupid to live," Earl told Carl as they were rocking and reading Sunday newspapers after church.

"Yes, but the ones not getting killed are moving up through the ranks of The Outfit." Carl put down his paper and adjusted the dial on the big radio that took up most of the coffee table. "That's another reason to avoid the big cities from now on. Just don't you forget it."

Carl was enjoying his semi-retirement and wasn't interested in criminal enterprises outside of Little Egypt. Being rid of the East St. Louis connections was almost a relief. The national crime syndicate that seemed to be developing was something Carl didn't want any part of. The empire that Capone had built in Chicago was consolidating with crime organizations all across the nation.

"You think we'll get pulled into that war in Europe?" Earl asked. "It says here that eighty percent of Americans are against it."

Carl wasn't listening. He'd finally dialed his way through squelching and squawking to a radio station that came in clearly.

"We interrupt this broadcast to bring you a special report. The Japanese have attacked Pearl Harbor and all naval and military activities on the island of Oahu, principal American base in the Hawaiian Islands."

"What the hell?" Carl got Earl's attention with a wave of his hand.

"The Cabinet is convening and the leaders in Congress are meeting with the President. The State Department and Army and Navy officials have been with the President all afternoon. In fact, the Japanese ambassador was talking to the President at the very time that Japan's airships were bombing our citizens in Hawaii and the Philippines and sinking one of our transports loaded with lumber on its way to Hawaii."

"Those sneaky Japs!" Bernie shouted as he rushed into the room.

Carl shut off the radio and fell back into his chair. While his brothers excitedly talked war, he stared out the window. The news was a shock, but not a surprise. The shock was that the American military had been caught with their pants down. He felt certain the enemy had done minimal damage to the military base, probably with few lives lost.

It wasn't a surprise to Carl because no one knew better than he that bullies left unchecked would never stop taking until they were stood up to. He and his brothers had been bullies most of their lives. He often played the role of the crazy killer to intimidate his victims, and he suspected that was what Japan was up to.

Of course, Bernie was a little more like Germany's Hitler was proving himself to be. They both longed for more power than they needed. If his younger brother had his way, he would have fought Al Capone himself for a shot at being number one in the crime world.

Carl had his sights on a more reasonable goal. As much as he was enjoying his semi-retirement, the excitement of getting back into action was too enticing, especially after being ridiculed publicly over the traffic stop embarrassment. Since that day, he'd been looking for a way to rebuild his criminal empire. That opportunity presented itself six months later when the kingpin of the Peoria, Illinois, underworld paid him a visit at Bernie's Golden Rule Farm.

Clyde Garrison ran the Windsor Club, the biggest gambling house in Peoria. His wife had recently been killed when a group of Chicago mobsters botched an attempt to kidnap her. Carl recognized the moment they shook hands that Garrison was shaken by the death of his wife.

"I need muscle to protect my interests," Garrison told the Shelton brothers. "These young Chicago punks think they can weasel in on our territory. If they take Peoria, there ain't nothin' to stop them from moving in on your businesses down state."

"We have sawdust joints on the north end of the state too." Bernie said.

"What's your proposition, Clyde?" Carl quickly interjected. He didn't want Bernie to show their hand if there was a deal to be made. He guessed that his youngest brother might be overly anxious to protect his Golden Rule Farm.

"I represent most of the other businessmen in the area. Even Mayor Woodruff said he'd tolerate vice as long as it brought in revenue for the city and violence was kept to a minimum."

That didn't surprise Carl. Bernie's most frequent municipal guest to his parties was none other than eighty-one-year-old Edward Everett Woodruff, the liberal mayor of Peoria. The courtyard around his city hall was filthy with the homeless and their empty whiskey bottles. Prostitutes lined the streets in the red-light district. When newspaper men asked the mayor why he allowed this, he responded, "What the heck? You can make prostitution illegal, but you can't make it unpopular."

"The depression kept everyone down and out for over ten years," Garrison continued. "What with the war puttin' everyone back to work, there's a strong need for folks to let their hair down. I don't know about you, but gambling in my joints has gone through the roof."

Carl sat quietly, listening. Bernie was fidgeting, anxious for his big brother to make a deal, unaware that the more Garrison tried to convince the Sheltons, the higher the price that Carl would demand.

"So, what's your proposition, Clyde?" Carl asked again.

"W-well," Garrison stammered. "I was thinking a fifty-fifty split of the mob action would be fair."

"Hah!" Carl laughed. "We do all the dangerous stuff and you offer us only fifty percent? Tell me another joke, Clyde."

Beads of perspiration appeared on Garrison's forehead. He extracted a handkerchief from his pocket and dabbed at his face, unaware that the simple gesture cost him an additional fifteen percent from what Carl had originally intended to demand.

"Okay, sixty-forty." Garrison groaned. "But that's my final offer."

Carl rose from the leather chair behind his desk, walked around and put a firm hand on the Peoria boss's shoulder. "You go back and tell Mayor Woodruff and your business partners that for seventy-five percent they will never have to do anything except count their twenty-five percent. The Shelton brothers will handle everything else and no one will get hurt."

Carl turned and left the office. For just a moment when he was alone on the other side of the door, he felt Charlie Birger's ghost standing in front of him, shaking his head. *Make sure you hang up your guns and enjoy life—before the bullet sends you to bootlegger heaven.*

"Just one more run for the gold, Charlie," Carl whispered aloud. "Just one more for old time's sake."

***

Carl, Earl, and Bernie sipped coffee in a truck stop café north of Peoria when Ray Walker walked up to their table. "Three car loads of Chicago red hots are coming down the dirt road toward Chillicothe," Ray Walker reported. "They should be passin' through this area in about forty-five minutes."

Carl had plenty of reasons to be worried. The gunmen Clyde Garrison had handpicked for them were toughs in Peoria, but he wasn't sure how they would be in a gunfight with Chicago mobsters. Bernie worried him, too. His little brother was strutting around the truck stop like he was the second coming of Machine Gun Kelly. The Sheltons knew several cons who called the famous gangster "Pop Gun Kelly" because of all the bragging he did while behind bars at Leavenworth. Carl was afraid that if Bernie didn't start taking his homicides more seriously, he too would wind up reinventing his career to anyone who would listen—or worse, to hacks guarding him on death row.

The six members of the assassination squad stood around the rear end of a flatbed pickup truck, smoking marijuana. When Ray and the Sheltons walked out of the cafe into the noon sun, one of the thugs passing the joint gave the roach a sharp flick with his index finger. His baby-faced cheeks puffed as he rolled the smoke around in his mouth before blowing it out his nose.

"You boys want a hit?" The youngster held out the drug as he coughed.

Bernie was reaching when Carl slapped the joy stick out of the youngster's hand.

"You've got maybe forty minutes to either sober up or write your last will and testament," Carl said, his jaw line set. "Your choice."

The three Sheltons squeezed into the cab of the pickup truck while Ray and the six young thugs jumped into the back beside their arsenal. They checked the weapons as Carl drove to the bridge that crossed the Illinois River. If everything went as planned, the Chicago hitmen would soon be floating face down on their journey to the muddy Mississippi.

"The best-laid plans of mice and men," Carl quoted when he saw a bus loaded with elderly passengers sitting crossways in the middle of the long, narrow, steel bridge. A half dozen gray-bearded men filed off the bus to stand around and look down at their front left tire.

The tire was shredded as if the driver had tried to continue on it when he should have parked and waited for help.

"What would you do, Earl?" Carl asked. "I mean, what would you do to fix that tire if we weren't fixin' for a gunfight?"

"Well, I believe I would see if there's a jack and a good spare tire," Earl said. "That ain't a real big bus, so I imagine I could have him on his way in about twenty minutes."

"That would be cuttin' things pretty close, don't you think?" Bernie looked at his pocket watch.

"Let's you and me go ahead and try," Carl said. He and Earl removed their coat jackets and rolled up their sleeves. "The rest of you boys spread out among the trees and don't smoke. Don't smoke *nothin'*." He stared at the young thug with the attitude.

Carl and Earl walked across the bridge to where the bus was broken down.

"Who's the driver here?" Carl asked.

"I am." A small, gray-haired lady stepped forward, a well-worn cane steadying her as she walked. Her horn-rimmed glasses were prevented from falling off her head by a string of pearls wrapped around her neck.

"*You're* driving these men?" Earl asked.

"Yes, but they ain't *real* men," the lady driver snapped. "They's bankers who never did a day's hard labor their whole entire lives."

"Now that is not so, Mrs. Periwinkle," one of the graybeards rebutted. "I, for one, have trimmed my own lawn on several occasions when the servants were indisposed."

The bankers raised their chins, grasped their fingers together behind their backs, and took a slow stroll toward the opposite end of the bridge.

Mrs. Periwinkle pointed her thumb toward the bankers and shook her head. "Pitiful, ain't they? I was dancing in vaudeville before these fancy pants were born, and I sure enough know more about the world than they do, Mr. Shelton."

"How do you know my name, ma'am?" Carl asked.

"I read the papers, young man. Are your boys going to shoot it out with Scarface's boys?"

"Al Capone is in prison, Mrs. Periwinkle, and what makes you think there's gonna be trouble?"

While the old lady bus driver talked to his brother, Earl chuckled and entered the bus. Under the backseats he found the spare tire and a jack that had obviously never been used before. While he was changing the tire, Mrs. Periwinkle continued educating Carl.

"We were leaving a road café up north just as those mobsters were going in. They weren't there to eat. Just relieving their radiators and getting some more booze, I'd imagine." Mrs. Periwinkle suddenly swung her cane and struck Earl in the backside. "Raise that vehicle with the jack before you try to loosen them nuts, you ninny. You want to strip the threads?"

Grumbling, Earl rubbed his sore butt with one hand while giving the jack handle several pumps with the other.

"If your intent is to ambush, you might want to tell those youngin's hiding in those trees to lose the weed." Mrs. Periwinkle laughed. "That marijuana smell might alert Al's boys. For a big time gangster, you sure act like you're new at this."

Carl blushed and sniffed the wind. He was mad at Bernie for letting the Peoria thugs light up again but he didn't want to have an old lady tell him how to set up an ambush. "Now Mrs. Periwinkle, I doubt they'll smell it while in a moving car."

"Ha!" Mrs. Periwinkle laughed. "The way them fellas was drinking you can bet they'll stop their cars right on this bridge to take another pee. I have never known a man yet that didn't stop to take a pee off a bridge."

Carl looked around. The bridge did indeed span the Illinois River in a secluded area that was inviting to a man's basic urges. In fact, just a few hours before, while scouting the location for the ambush, he and his brothers had stood on this very bridge taking a whiz.

"That water is cold," Earl had said as they watched their streams arch into the water below.

"Yep," Bernie agreed, "and it's deep, too."

The joke never got old to his brothers even after twenty years, but was tiresome to Carl.

Earl finished changing the tire just as the sound of approaching engines could be heard.

Carl pulled a hundred-dollar bill from his coat pocket and handed it to Mrs. Periwinkle. The graybeards were anxiously reboarding.

"Stay on the bridge until the cars stop behind you. Tell them you just changed the tire and would get out of their way."

Earl left the destroyed tire and rim along the trellis and ran with Carl back to where their men were hiding. They had no sooner reached the trees than three automobiles appeared at the far end of the bridge. Carl was afraid the old lady might be right about the Chicago hoods smelling the odor of the Mary Jane. Just then, Mrs. Pennington extracted a marijuana cigarette from her hand-bag. Using the side of the bus, she lit a match and expertly waved it back and forth beneath the joint.

"What's going on here, lady?" a man yelled from the car in front.

"Just changed that damned tire!" Mrs. Periwinkle screeched back, pointing at the shred-ded tire on the bent rim. "Hold your horses! I'll be out of the way in a minute."

Limping slowly with her cane in one hand and her weed in the other, she climbed aboard the bus, got behind the big steering wheel, and pulled the vehicle to the end of the bridge. Her head could barely be seen above the dash, but her tiny hand raised in a little, fluttery wave of fingers was unmistakable.

Then the Chicago gangsters proved to Carl that Mrs. Periwinkle knew male behavior better than did he. The three cars unloaded and fifteen men spread out on either side of the bridge to do their business. Carl wanted to kick himself when he realized that the .45 caliber gats which the Peoria men were using wouldn't be effective from such a distance.

"Don't shoot until they get back in their cars and drive to our end of the bridge," Carl whispered to Earl. "Pass it on."

Earl hunched down and made his way back through the trees to Bernie. "Don't shoot until they get back in their cars and reach our end of the bridge. Pass it on."

Bernie carried the message to the young doper. "Don't shoot until they get back in their cars and reach our end."

The doper moved quickly to the next thug. "Don't shoot until they get back in their cars."

When Carl saw the gangsters moving back to the vehicles, he turned his back to the tree and checked the firing mechanism on his gat one last time. He glanced back through the wooded area just as the six Peoria thugs stepped out from behind their cover and let loose with a torrential downfall of bullets, each of which fell far short of the intended targets.

"Shoot higher, you idiots!" Carl shouted. He and Earl ran forward to the end of the bridge and elevated their fire. The bullets dropped onto the cars like rain, only a few finding windows to shatter.

The cars backed quickly off the bridge, spun around and headed back toward Chicago. Carl just hoped that Mrs. Periwinkle never learned that she'd done more to ensure a successful ambush than all the members of the Shelton gang combined.

***

"I knew Frank Nitti wouldn't like the idea of going back to the joint when they convicted him of extorting the Hollywood film companies," Carl told his brothers. They were sitting in his office at the Palace Club in Peoria when the news of Nitti's suicide was announced. "My only regret is that he probably died laughing at our failed ambush of his boys at Chillicothe."

Carl heard from men who had been in prison with the crime boss that Nitti had not minded outside work, but his claustrophobia made his many hours in the jail cell miserable.

"The ambush kept his outfit from bothering us again, didn't it?" Bernie quickly commented. The youngest brother had been thoroughly chastised by his siblings for not making sure that the Peoria thugs followed directions correctly. It wasn't Bernie's fault, but he couldn't convince them that the druggie was the one who had messed up the operation.

"Besides," Bernie added, "Nitti wasn't so competent in taking his own life neither. It took him three shots to even kill hisself. His first bullet put a hole in his fedora. So, the second attempt he put the gun under his chin and blew the front of his face off. That probably pained him enough he finally had the courage to put the gun to his temple and do the job right."

"Whatever happened," Carl said, "you can expect the Chicago Outfit to come after us again. They messed up that extortion racket down in Hollywood, so they'll fall back to Greasy Thumb's original plans to take over some of the smaller cities. You just remember that, Bernie, and be ready."

"I ain't scared of them thugs." Bernie puffed his chest. "We never had it so good. We've got control of all the rackets from in downstate Illinois. Nothin' can stop us now."

5

"Give me two suits made of that material," Buster Wortman told Leslie Pensoneau of The Toggery Clothing Store in Belleville. "One dark blue and the other dark brown."

When Pensoneau finished measuring the gangster, he took his notes into the backroom. The Toggery was a popular clothing store for gangsters since it also fronted for some high-stake poker games. Wortman sat in a luxurious chair facing a couch where Black Charlie Harris and Blackie Armes reclined.

"I want you two to get measured for suits, too," Wortman said. "Everyone around me should all wear the same suits each day."

"Why's that, boss?" Blackie asked. He was a dapper dresser, but he wasn't too keen on looking like everyone else.

"Capone's boys missed Bugsy Moran because he was mistaken for someone else dressed like him. Let's make it harder for them to know who they're killing."

"Why don't we just shoot the Sheltons and get it over with?" Charlie asked.

"Their time will come." Wortman was organizing East St. Louis but, for the most part, stayed clear of the Shelton territory in southern Illinois. He didn't have the resources or enough men yet to expand. "Until then, we want positive public opinion. No prostitution, drugs or kidnapping. We'll make plenty from slot machines and other gambling. I got some ideas from Greasy Thumb Guzik for bringin' in revenue. He did a hell of a job for Capone, so I figure he's worth listenin' to."

"What other ideas?" Charlie asked.

"A little numbers racket, for one. We sell insurance policies for a nickel a week to everyone in East St. Louis. As long as they pay, nothing happens to them or their property. If they do get hit by one of our rivals, we pay for the damages."

"So," Charlie said, "I'd imagine any folks refusing to pay, we hit 'em ourselves?"

Wortman shrugged. "That'll be up to you two fellas. Your salaries will come outta those policies."

"What else you got?" Blackie rubbed his hands together and smiled. He had never had opportunities such as this in all his years with the Shelton gang.

"We loan money."

"For high interest rates, I'd 'spect?" Blackie asked.

"Nope. At the same rates as the banks. We want the community and the newspapers behind our ventures. If they see they can make money by turning a blind eye to our other operations, we'll have clear sailin'."

"Sounds almost like we're goin' legit," Charlie said.

"That's what we want the public to think. We'll stop all petty crime in Collinsville and East St. Louis. If we have to get tough on some customers, we'll dump their bodies at Eagle Park in Madison or near the racetrack."

"Or in the Big Muddy!" Blackie added.

***

The only reason Black Charlie could think of to not kill the Shelton brothers was that he liked their Pa. He'd known Ben Shelton since he was a kid and even called him Uncle Ben, as did many members of the community. One time when the much older Carl and Earl bullied him, Uncle Ben gave both his boys a severe lashing. When their mother Agnes, found out, she sent her husband out of the house for a week and began calling Charlie Harris a spoiled brat.

The years passed. Ma Shelton never forgave Black Charlie, but her husband remained kind to him. Since Uncle Ben was eighty-two, it was a surprise to no one when he passed. What did surprise everyone was that Agnes didn't favor him with her customary eulogy of, "Goodbye, Ben." Instead, she pulled a roll of Lifesavers candy from her overcoat pocket and handed one to each of her six children present for the funeral, Roy still being in prison.

"That's from your Pa," she said before walking back to the car.

Hazel stood with the Lifesaver in her open palm. She put her head down and tears poured from her eyes.

Bernie put his arm around her shoulder and then deftly swapped his pineapple for her cherry.

Black Charlie was at the funeral but remained a hundred yards away next to the sandstone marker for his father. Though his pa had been abusive, Charlie saw his own miserable life in the headstones of both his father and Ben Shelton.

The name of John M. Harris was barely legible. Charlie's great-grandfather, Isaac Harris, had been the first white man to settle in what became Wayne County. The house Charlie's sister now lived in was on the very site where Isaac had built that log cabin. Yet, the Harris descendants had not prospered to the extent the Sheltons had.

On the other hand, Ben Shelton had a handsome marble headstone with plenty of room for his and his wife's name and platitudes, the markings that would last for centuries. His children were wealthy beyond measure.

Black Charlie knelt. With his left hand on his father's headstone and his right over his heart, he swore an oath. The Sheltons would pay for ruining his life. The years in prison would not be in vain. If he couldn't make the millions that they had, he could at least take away from them what they had stolen from others.

6

Lancelot was such a beautiful palomino stallion Bernie thought the newspaper boys would want to snap photos of him that would make even Roy Rogers envious.

"What the hell is this?" Bernie bellowed when he saw the photo in the Peoria paper. He wadded it up and threw it on the kitchen floor. The picture on the society page had been snapped while he and his wife were sitting on their horses on a hill. Carrie was on the higher ground, making her look like a princess, and Bernie seemed like her court jester sitting on a pony. Lancelot was barely in the picture.

"Well, I like it!" Carrie snatched the paper up, then kicked her husband's chair with the side of her foot. "I bought three dozen copies and am sending it to all my friends."

"Why did you buy so many then?" He pushed his plate across the table. "You don't have *that* many friends."

After cleaning up the oatmeal Carrie flung onto his shirt, Bernie got on the phone to Earl.

"We're gonna throw a high society party," he said. "Bring your best polo ponies. I'm invitin' all the media, government officials, and law enforcement I can. See if you can get Jerome Munie to come. I want everyone to know that the Sheltons are the cream of downstate Illinois."

A week later, the Golden Rule Farm teemed with four hundred guests dressed in their finest. Tents for changing clothes and canvas gazebos dotted the forty acres around the house. The weather cooperated with a warm day, the sun showing brightly against a cloudless sky. A dozen waiters served champagne and caviar on silver trays.

Bernie waited until all the guests had arrived before making his entrance by prancing Lancelot through an applauding crowd. His wife wasn't invited to participate in his grand entry.

At the moment the crowd cheered, Carrie was surrounded by reporters snapping pictures of her in her low-cut summer dress, high heels, and a wide brimmed bonnet. An instant later, she stood alone.

Lancelot delighted the crowd by raising up on his hind legs as Carrie's photographers rushed off to capture Bernie on his magnificent steed, waving his hat to his adoring audience.

Hands on hips, Carrie glared at her husband.

"Mrs. Shelton," a soft, feminine voice behind her said.

Carrie turned. The green eyes of the woman standing before her sparkled in the sunlight. Had Jerome Munie not been next to the woman, Carrie would never have guessed who she was. "Jeanene?"

The young woman nodded. Carrie took her in her arms. After a long embrace, she stepped back, still holding her shoulders. "My goodness, let me look at you. Why, you are like a beautiful China doll."

Finally, Carrie held her hand out to Jerome Munie. "I was so sorry to hear about Mary."

"She treasured that lamp you sent her right up to the day she passed." Jerome said.

"Well . . . ." Carrie blushed from the memory of her temper tantrum in the sheriff's home. "That's the least I could do for *accidently* breaking hers."

As the crowd around Bernie gave another whoop, an idea came to Carrie. She turned toward her husband's adoring fans, put two fingers to her mouth and gave a loud wolf whistle.

"Hey, boys!" Carrie hollered. "Get a load of this dish!"

She enjoyed seeing the look on Bernie's face as his camera men turned away from him and raced off to photograph the beautiful green-eyed girl.

***

310

The fox hunt that afternoon started well enough. Bernie, in his British riding breeches and red hunting jacket, received most of the attention, until Carrie and Jeanene rode up in their side saddles, their legs showing more knee than appropriate for a sporting event.

Earl's bluetick hound Hooch was to lead the pack, which was mostly made up of coon and bird dogs. Hooch was getting old. He had the heart but not the legs and lay quietly while the other dogs barked from inside a big cage. Earl shook the fox scent under their noses. The canines tilted their heads, giving him a puzzled look. When he thought he had their attention, Earl wrapped the scented tail in a towel and tucked it into his saddle bag. He mounted and motioned to the bugler to signal the hunt was to begin. The gray fox was released.

The boy on the bugle had played the trombone in high school for less than a year. The sound he made on the bugle had horses rearing and backing off. The instrument's wail also seemed to rile the dogs. Their barking was so loud the boy who was to release them from their cages let them out prematurely.

The gray fox had been trapped in southern Illinois and didn't seem to know where to go. When he saw hounds bearing down fast, the fox climbed the nearest tree. He sat on a high branch looking down as the coon dogs barked and jumped against the trunk. The bird dogs stopped and pointed. Old Hooch just lay down near Earl's mount and closed his eyes.

"I told you to get a red fox!" Bernie screamed at his brother. "Red foxes don't climb."

"Well, let's eat!" Carrie suggested, slightly delighted at another disappointment for her husband. "Polo starts in two hours."

Bernie was so upset by the fox hunt calamity, he couldn't eat. Instead, he donned his polo jersey and took Lancelot to the stables for a curry.

"You don't worry, old boy," Bernie whispered to him as he brushed his long mane. "Polo is our game."

After the meal, the crowd gathered along one side of the hundred-and-fifty-yard field, either standing or sitting in lawn chairs. The concierges had gifted a four-inch-long silver cigarette holder to each spectator. The men posed FDR-style with their smokes tilted upwards at a forty-five-degree angle for the photographers.

With Lancelot in the lead, Bernie's team of four players paced proudly onto the polo grounds and lined up facing the audience. Even Carrie cheered as Bernie put Lancelot into the racking lateral gait they had practiced. After two lengths of the field, Lancelot stopped, backed up a few steps and bowed his head.

Bernie waved his cap and turned toward the end of the field where Earl's team gathered.

"What the hell!" Carrie said, shading her eyes from the sun.

"What is it, Mrs. Shelton?" Jeanene asked, a large contingent of bachelors standing behind her.

"Them are Earl's cuttin' horses," Carrie said, then started laughing. "And they're riding western saddles."

"What does that mean?" Jeanene asked.

"You'll see. Those horses are taught to corner whatever critter is in front of them."

"Isn't that against the rules? To cut in front of the player hitting the ball?"

"Sure is. But what if they cut in front of the other players trying to *follow the ball*? These horses don't understand anymore about polo than any of the fellas playin'. And them referees barely know how to stay in the saddle. I'm not sure what's gonna happen."

Two referees struggled to ride ponies onto the field. They spurred more than needed and pulled one way, then the other on the reins. Earl and Bernie, both wearing number one on their jerseys, lined up facing one another. The other players also lined up across from their counterpart in jersey numbers two, three, and four.

The referee began the game by tossing the white ball between the two sides. Bernie beat Earl to the ball and whacked it hard toward the goal post at the other end of the field. None of the horses on the defending side ran toward the ball. With ears perked, front legs bent, and their heads inches from the ground, the horses on Earl's team cut off whatever direction the opponent's mounts tried to go, just as they had been conditioned to do with cows.

"Get the hell outta the way!" Bernie threw his riding crop at his brother.

When Earl whooped, Bernie spurred Lancelot in the opposite direction, then circled him wide around the field from where all the chaos was happening. With thundering hooves, Lancelot was just about to beat Earl's pony to where the ball had stopped, when Earl pulled a revolver and shot the ball, driving it out of bounds.

Taking offense to this violation of protocol, Bernie, with murderous intent, rammed Lancelot into the side of Earl's mount, causing his brother to be flung from the saddle. An instant later, Bernie was on top of Earl, throwing haymakers that might have been lethal had any of them connected.

"That was the only ball we had," Bernie lamented twenty minutes later as Carrie and Earline nursed their husband's swollen knuckles and faces.

"Relax, little brother. Ouch!" Earl pulled away from his wife's touch, then continued through loose teeth, "Maybe we invented a new game. Let's call it polo skeet shooting."

The door opened, and Jerome and Jeanene stepped into the room.

"We're getting ready to leave," Jerome said as his daughter kissed Carrie goodbye.

"Thank you for inviting us," Jeanene said. "It was a-uh, a very interesting day."

"I'm sorry we missed Carl," Jerome said.

"Yeah," Earl looked Bernie. "Where is Carl?"

***

The last thing nine-year-old Violet Christine Varner ever saw was the horrified eyes of a man with graying hair jerk his big steering wheel counter-clockwise.

Had she still been alive a few seconds later, she might have seen the car roll over once before bouncing back onto its tires, the man throwing the car door open and staggering toward her crumpled body, his tears and the blood from a gash on his forehead dropping into her face as he held her in his lap and wailed like a baby.

Violet Christine Varner would never know that a part of her killer died along with her. Carl Shelton would never be the same.

***

Black Charlie decided to go about the destruction of the Shelton empire with caution, patience, and ruthlessness. Soft targets appealed to him. Unlike Charlie Birger, the brothers had few gang members. Birger had liked to keep a large standing army around him at all times. Disloyalty within those ranks eventually turned out to be his downfall.

The number of Shelton confidants was small. Better yet, they were unsuspecting. Most believed that if a hit came, it would be one of the three notorious brothers getting snuffed. Therefore, when Black Charlie went after one of their roadhouse operators, there was little suspicion that his death was tied to connections with the Shelton gang.

Frank Knoebel had been standing in front of the fireplace of his large country home when a .351 caliber bullet rocketed through his plate glass window. As Black Charlie predicted, the first bullet deflected off the glass and missed Knoebel, but the double tap that immediately followed tore a hole through the man's forehead and then drilled a stuffed moose head above the fireplace mantle.

While using a rifle was practical for such long-range shooting, Black Charlie preferred the new M-1 Thompson machine gun that had been developed for the soldiers overseas. Its twenty- and thirty-round box magazines also made for quicker munition changes.

A Shelton bodyguard named Joel Norman gave Black Charlie his opportunity to try out the new weapon. When Norman shanked a golf ball into a timber off the fairway, he should've just taken the lost stroke. Instead, he went deep into the thicket looking for the lucky ball that had him two under par on the fifteenth green. He never found the ball, but did find a well dressed man crouched behind a clump of bushes.

"That's a hell of a place to take a shit, you damned freeloader," Norman remarked. It was not unusual to find an occasional hobo lurking in wooded areas.

The face of Black Charlie was familiar enough to underworld types that when a gold-toothed smile appeared on the man's face, the golfer turned and ran.

There was no warning shout of fore as the Tommy gun unleashed a torrent of .45 caliber lead. Twenty-nine bullets from the magazine would later be found in Norman's body. The thirtieth would be discovered in a sand trap several days later by a young groundskeeper who moonlighted as a caddy. He was smoothing out the pit early one morning when his rake struck something hard. Digging the spent bullet out, he blew the sand off and tossed it in his pocket.

A week later, Phillip Stump was driving his straight truck home from making his slot machine deliveries to various Shelton Roadhouses. He was congratulating himself for swindling the famous gangsters out of twenty percent of the machine's profits.

As he approached an underpass, he thought he saw a man leaning over the rail above him. The .351 caliber bullets that struck him in the chest and stomach caused him to twirl the steering wheel and flip his truck onto its side. He was lying against the passenger side window looking down at his blood-stained shirt when the face of a man appeared in the window above him.

"I thought you'd be Bernie," Stump said. The vision of the gold toothed man's face remained on his cornea for several seconds after he took his last breath.

7

Carl was wearing down. Running the rackets in Peoria was exhausting. He longed to be back in Fairfield, where waking up every morning and laboring on his Pond Creek farm was never a burden.

After living in Peoria for three years he had developed the habit of waking up as late as seven o'clock. For some reason he felt tired and cold all the time. He had a little stove put in close to his bed. Every morning, Pearl would fill the coffee pot. All he needed to do was reach over to the stove and pour himself a cup. Then he would lie there for an hour or more listening to the radio and reading the newspaper.

V-J Day was the headline on September 3. He read about the formal surrender aboard the U.S.S. Missouri in Tokyo Bay.

When he finally got out of bed, he stood in the shower with his head under the warm water until it began running cold.

"Violet!" The name came each time he turned off the water. He shivered as he toweled dry.

Wiping his head was the moment he always began counting the dead. Sometimes he lamented Helen Holbrook, the blond beauty who had stolen Charlie Birger's heart and prompted the gangster to have her poisoned when she left him. On this day he struggled to push aside the recurring dream he'd once again experienced that very night.

It always began with the black hood being raised over Charlie Birger's head. His final words grew louder with each recurrence of the dream. "It is a beautiful world!"

This time the words thundered and even echoed over and over in Carl's mind. He pulled the towel to his face, holding it there while the memory of Charlie's body swung clear of the gallows. The recollection also brought the crowd's awes as well as multiple screams from women, some who fainted into their men's arms. The coroner and doctors rushed under the structure to catch the body as it was lowered to the ground.

They treated it gingerly, as if it were a child being extracted from its mother's womb. The hangman's knot was loosened and removed and the hood partially pulled off his head. They inspected the elongated neck, nearly severed from the shoulders and the spinal column snapped into two pieces that bulged slightly beneath the skin. Then the hood was slowly removed from the face.

Carl Shelton's face.

***

By the time Carl arrived at the courthouse for his one o'clock meeting with the new Peoria mayor, the nightmares were behind him and he was feeling more confident. Daylight always brought a sense of euphoria, but with the victory in the Pacific officially announced, it was hard to not be even more gay. Everyone knew that after the A-bombs had been dropped on Hiroshima and Nagasaki, the end of the war had come. Still, the official word brought dancing in the streets— along with the expected drunkenness.

Carl's brothers were of course in the latter category. He, however, was more concerned with figuring out how to deal with an honest mayor. Carl Triebel was a farmer and laundry operator who shocked the underworld by defeating Ed Woodruff. He promised a new order of reform with an end to gambling and prostitution, the Shelton's primary source of income.

After the preliminary greeting in the mayor's office, they made small talk about the Japanese surrender. Then Carl got right to the point. "I've come about the slot machines."

"What about them?" Triebel took his seat behind the big mahogany desk, a move that let Carl know who was in charge.

Carl was caught off guard by the mayor's dominance. It reminded him of Jerome Munie. "We'll handle them for you."

"You'll what?"

"We'll take care of them." Carl extracted a wad of bills from his vest pocket that was held in place by a diamond-studded money clip. "How much do you want out of them?"

"Nothing."

"All right. Then we'll pay something into your campaign fund."

"That won't be necessary."

"No? Why?"

"Because there are not going to be any slot machines."

"Did I hear you right?" Carl stood—a gesture that often made his opponents cower.

"That's right." Triebel looked up into Carl's eyes.

"Do you mean what you say?"

Triebel nodded.

Carl sat back in his chair and closed his eyes. His eyeballs fluttered beneath their lids. Charlie Birger's body swung beneath the gallows. *"Hang up your guns and enjoy life, before the bullet sends you to bootlegger heaven."* Nightmares returned, then evolved slowly to hope. He felt Violet's small hand in his.

Triebel mistook the Shelton gangster's behavior for anger, but he was determined to stand his ground. "So what will it be, Carl?"

"Well." Carl opened his eyes and looked down at his empty hand. "I guess that'll give me more time to farm."

"Farmin' is more interestin' to me, too." Triebel took a deep breath and exhaled. He rose from his chair, came around the table and set on its edge. "What kinda yield you gettin' down south?"

The two men talked farming for thirty minutes. Finally, Carl stood, shook hands with the mayor, and left.

8

It was a moon-bright night as Black Charlie slung his rifle across his back and climbed the ladder to the roof. He remembered being on top of that building one other time. He couldn't recall the year, but he could almost smell the girl's scent. It wasn't the odor of perfume or even her soap. Her skin was clean. It smelled and tasted like spring rain.

As he knelt into a firing position facing the Farmer's Club, he forced the recollection from his mind—not just so that he could focus on the assassination, but also to rid himself of the memory of the girl's anger when he almost beat her brother to death for interrupting one of their private moments.

When he'd received word that evening that Big Earl was in a poker game at the Farmer's Club in Fairfield, Charlie prepared. The game would be in a room on the second floor. And because of his liaison with that young girl many years ago, he also knew of the fire escape ladder onto the auto dealership next to the Farmer's Club.

The alley between the buildings was so narrow, Charlie felt he was in the room with the four men playing five-card draw around a small table. The view was enhanced by an electric chandelier above them—so bright he could actually read the cards Earl held in his hand. Two eights, a five, a three, and a Jack.

Charlie slung the rifle from behind his back. He wrapped the strap around his right elbow and pointed the barrel toward the window. It would be the easiest kill he'd ever had. In fact, it was so easy, he held his fire until Earl drew his three cards. Disappointment came when the middle Shelton added a queen and a pair of deuces. Charlie had been hoping he would get a pair of aces to go with the two eights. A Bill Hickock dead-man's hand would have brought immense satisfaction to the job.

The first two bullets tore through Earl's torso, blasting him forward and out of his chair. Charlie added one more hurried shot just for fun, then slung the rifle back over his shoulder and sprinted for the fire escape. He put the arch of his shoes on the outside of the ladder and slid down fireman style.

***

Carl felt light-headed when he saw Earl lying in the hospital bed in the Fairfield Hospital. Bandages covered so much of his upper body there was no need for a gown. He and Bernie approached the bed reluctantly.

"You look like you tried to pick an apple from the top of the tree," Bernie said.

"I did," Earl whispered, then shut his eyes.

"Remember playin' king-of-the-mountain when we was kids, Earl?" Carl's lip quivered.

Earl nodded weakly.

"I was always the king." Carl forced a smile. "No one ever knocked me off. Until one day you finally figured out you was bigger and stronger than me. You took me down, by golly."

"Yes," Earl struggled with his words. "Then you changed the game to smear."

"I used to play smear." Bernie held up a hand. "Whoever had the ball, all the other boys would tackle him unless he passed it off first."

"Yep," Carl said. "And I was the fastest kid out there. But sooner or later, I'd get tired and you know what I always did, Bernie? I passed the ball off to Earl, and he'd get his butt kicked. Right, Earl?"

Earl laughed until he started coughing up blood.

"Anyway," Carl continued, "that's what I feel like I did today. I passed the ball off to you and let you get smeared."

Earl wanted to sleep. Carl wanted to reminisce.

"Remember when we worked in the coal mine, you and me, Earl?" Carl's eyes were misty. "We made moonshine to supplement our income."

"I remember." Earl's voice was getting weaker.

"I remember too," Bernie said, though he'd been a young boy at the time.

"We saved our money and bought those taxis after the first big war. That was our beginning. An empire built from moonshining."

Earl smiled. "A moonshine empire."

Carl stopped talking. He took his brother's hand.

"Kill Black Charlie for me," Earl whispered.

"I'll do it for sure, Earl," Carl said, a rare tear in his eye. "I promise."

9

"I'm gonna be the boss of Peoria County," Bernie told Carrie, "and ain't nobody's gonna stand in my way."

He was elated. With Carl retired, Peoria was his and his alone. Earl would be recovering from the multiple gunshots Black Charlie had provided him, plus he seemed to have little desire to invest much time in the northern part of the state.

To celebrate his promotion, Bernie captured and tortured one of Buster Wortman's men. After strangling him, he wrapped him in barbed wire and left his body in a ditch near Kankakee, Illinois. He hoped the murder would draw Black Charlie out so Bernie could kill him.

Instead, it provoked a visit from Buster Wortman, Greasy Thumb Guzik, and a delegation that was attempting to form a national crime syndicate. By uniting mobs in New York, Chicago, St. Louis, and Kansas City, as well as lesser cities like Peoria, the gang wars would end.

"We want Peoria to be in our organization," Guzik said when all twelve men in the room were seated around the big conference table, Bernie at the head of one end and Guzik at the other.

Every thug Bernie had been able to round up was in Peoria for the meeting. He'd met with Carl the week before and told him that if ever there was a moment to take over all organized crime in America, this was it.

"You're an idiot, Bernie," Carl had scoffed. "You'll be dead in twenty-four hours if you try something like that. Don't you know them wise guys have got their shooters all over that town? They're probably at this very minute looking for good spots to ambush you and your thugs. Hell, besides, the Hoover boys are certain to have all your phones bugged and G-men on every corner. If the United States Government is afraid to wipe out the mafia, what makes you think you can?"

Bernie didn't like hearing that, especially when it came from a condescending older brother. He'd been in Carl's shadow his entire life, and now things were finally going his way.

"I ain't playin' second fiddle to nobody," Bernie said to the crime bosses at the table. He then turned a little red when he realized he'd inadvertently done his Edward G. Robinson impersonation.

Guzik remained poker-faced. Wortman, however, raised his hand to his mouth, his cheeks puffing a little around his eyes.

"It's a free country." Guzik shrugged.

***

"Guzik promised ten thousand dollars on the head of any Shelton brother. Plus, half that for any of their lieutenants," Wortman told Blackie Armes and Black Charlie Harris the next day at The Paddock in Collinsville. "Get the word out."

"Can we have a try for the money first?" Blackie asked. "I want to get Ray Walker myself. That son-of-a-bitch got me prison time."

"Make it quick," Wortman said. Guzik had promised him free rein of downstate Illinois, so he wanted to clean out all competition as quickly and efficiently as possible. He was now in the big-time rackets. A simple mistake such as accidently insulting another crime boss or an appearance of weakness could mean his own demise.

For that dubious reason, he was constructing a fortress mansion near Collinsville with an armory containing everything from machine guns to bazookas. To make an invasion even less likely, he was having the entire grounds surrounded by a twenty-foot-deep moat.

"I'll give you boys one-month head start. Then I want every torpedo in America aimed at the Shelton gang."

***

Ray Walker had a habit of tugging on his left ear. Not the earlobe, for that had been shot off by Joe Schrader during a gunfight years ago. The blood and stinging pain from the wound had caused Ray to surrender right away. It was a decision he regretted when he discovered the blood geyser on the side of his head only resulted in the loss of a loose piece of skin he didn't even need.

To make matters worse, though, Schrader bragged he'd intentionally aimed for the earlobe because he wanted to bring the Shelton lieutenant in alive. Walker didn't like enhancing a lawman's reputation at his own expense.

Considered a pretty boy, the muscular Ray had his choice of southern Illinois belles. His only gangland rival in that department was Blackie Armes, who had run with the Sheltons in his early years. After Munie's deputies arrested Armes, along with Buster Wortman, at the moonshine cabin, Blackie made it known he would pay Ray back for his treachery.

Ray tried to convince people he'd not squealed on his fellow gangsters, but it was too late. His reputation was tarnished in the criminal under-world. Except for those closest to the Sheltons, few trusted him. Knowing this, Carl took his friend off most other duties and made him his full-time personal bodyguard.

That was the role that brought Ray to Collinsville. Carl and Pearl intended to dine at The Paddock. It was Ray's job to scout it out for escape routes inside and outside. The fact the restaurant catered to gangsters was of little consequence, since it also was a favorite establishment for high-ranking government officials and policemen.

What Ray didn't know was that the establishment had recently come under the proprietorship of Frank "Buster" Wortman with Blackie Armes in charge of its security.

"You lookin' for some eggs to suck?" Blackie said when he ran across Ray in the empty parking lot. "By your clothes, I'd say you're church mouse poor."

"God sho' don' love ugly, Blackie. Them fancy clothes will be perfect for your casket. I'll be certain not to miss your wake."

The two gangsters walked in a circle, never taking their eyes off the other.

"You'll be in hoodlum hell long before me." Using only his left hand, Blackie put a cigar in his mouth and lit it with a lighter. "How's big Carl, now that he's retired?"

"He was just as yawny as could be last I saw him. He's married to Pearl Vaughn now, you know."

"Well, sir." Blackie grabbed his crotch, "Maybe I'll just have to stop over there and give that pretty Pearl a little ride myself."

"Oh, hell, Blackie! I can't see you doin' that. Carl's mules have bigger balls than you do!"

"Did you say hello to Buster while you was in The Paddock? I don't believe he'd be none too friendly, seein' how you cost him two years in the big top."

"I seen him." Ray smiled. "I believe that when he said, 'Have a good day,' he meant it."

"So, he talked to you, did he?"

"Well, he was hankerin' for a longer conversation, so I slipped out the backway."

"Good choice." Blackie raised his arm. A derringer popped out of his sleeve. He pumped two bullets into Ray's chest.

Ray screamed with pain.

"Shutup that caterwaulin'," Blackie said as he tucked the weapon and the spring holding it back in his sleeve.

Two weeks in the hospital and three surgeries later, Ray was released. That same day, he got word that Blackie Armes was at a Herrin Nightclub owned by Ray's cousin, Thomas Propes.

The crowd scattered when a scowl-faced Ray walked in carrying a gat. The only ones who didn't rush for the door were Ray's cousin and Blackie Armes. Blackie was able to get his revolver out of his holster, but his body crumpled to the floor before he could get off more than one shot. That bullet was enough to end the life of Ray's cousin, who happened to get in the way of the flying lead. The eight holes in Blackie's body took nearly an hour before he beat Ray Walker in their race to hoodlum hell.

***

Black Charlie wasn't happy to hear that Blackie Armes had been killed. The two had been plotting the Shelton empire demise for months. He was more determined than ever to get that ten thousand dollars for the head of each Shelton. In fact, he was hoping to make much more.

Having grown up with them, he knew the five Shelton brothers as well as anyone. Buster Wortman had not specified Carl, Earl, and Bernie as the only Sheltons with money on their heads. Perhaps he didn't know about Dalta and Dalta's young sons, Little Earl and Little Carl, who had just joined the gang after returning from the war. And what about Roy, who was still in prison? Black Charlie wanted them all dead—and wouldn't be afraid to argue with Buster that the bounty should extend to all Sheltons.

Bernie was still spending most of his time up north in Peoria. Assassinating him in a city he ran would be more difficult and require a little luck.

Catching him near his Golden Rule Farm would be easier, plus Black Charlie liked the idea of *doing unto Bernie before he could do unto him.*

Little Egypt seemed the best place for a hit. Due to Carl's extensive purchasing of land throughout the downstate area, he'd come into disfavor with many of the residents. The eldest Shelton liked to buy land and then quickly sell it, but keep the mineral rights. It was a shrewd move, since oil had become a valuable commodity in the swampy downstate area.

Many who refused to sell their land to Carl found themselves missing livestock and having mysterious fires. Arson and cattle rustling were games that Black Charlie could play also.

As Shelton property came up missing or burnt, Charlie Harris found himself being hailed the local hero to many who'd been abused by Carl's strong-armed tactics.

Black Charlie was just getting started.

10

Bernie was upset by two news articles that appeared in March of 1947. He wasn't sure which bothered him more.

The first was an explosion at the Number Five Mine of the Centralia Coal Company. One-hundred-eleven men killed out of the one-hundred-forty-two underground when it happened. The Shelton brothers knew several of the dead as well as their families.

Ma Shelton organized a fund-raising drive similar to the one she implemented after the tri-state tornado of '25. She was shocked when even some from her own church chose to take part in a separate fundraiser that was ran by Black Charlie, his sister, and his niece, Beatrice.

The second bit of news that month disturbed Bernie every bit as much as the coal mine disaster. Major League Baseball was trying to allow a Negro named Jackie Robinson to play alongside White boys.

"Where's the Ku Klux Klan when we really need 'em?" Bernie lamented.

"We got rid of 'em," Earl answered as the brothers took their daily stroll around the Golden Rule farm. "Don't you remember, Bernie? You shot a few of 'em yourself."

"Ah, them were Liquor Ku Klux Klan," Bernie said, "not Nigger Ku Klux Klan. There's a difference, you know."

***

A few days later, Pearl walked into the bedroom of their Peoria home and caught Carl in bed with another woman. He thought he was in trouble. His wife was supposed to be at the Pond Creek farm.

"I brought collard greens, black-eyed peas, turnip greens, Sorghum molasses and a custard pie." Pearl glared at the young girl. "Honey, if you can cook as good as you look, I'd appreciate you goin' downstairs and findin' some meat to go with it. I've got something very important to discuss with my husband."

The girl didn't hesitate. Nearly naked, she jumped out of bed, grabbed her clothes off the floor, and hurried out of the room.

Carl sat up in bed and looked around for some protection. He didn't think his wife would shoot or stab him, but there were plenty of hard and sharp objects that could do some major damage if thrown accurately. He settled on a pillow for a shield by bringing it from where his head had been around to his front. He almost sniffed the pillow. His wife smelled of flour. His girlfriend smelled of flowers.

Pearl, though, didn't seem interested in violence. Instead, she stood watching the girl's hips swing as she descended the steps. Then she shut the door, walked to the bed and set on the edge.

"Big Earl, Ray, and Bernie took one of Buster Wortman's lieutenants to the Pere Marquette Hotel," Pearl said without any comment on Carl's girlfriend. "They rolled him up in a sheet and hung him out the hotel window. They asked him questions about Buster and Black Charlie, and every time they thought the poor fella was lying, Earl would cut a slit in the sheet."

"How high up were they?"

"Ninth floor."

"That'd make quite a bounce." Carl admired his brother's ingenuity. "What's got the boys so het up on everything?"

"Carl," Pearl slowly shook her head, "Do you not understand there's a gang war brewing? Everyone associated with your businesses are getting shot, killed, or burnt out."

"Gang war?" Carl laughed. "Hell, Charlie Birger and me, *we* had a gang war. Chasing each other in armored cars, bombing each other's joints." He lay back and admired the visions of memories that flashed across the ceiling.

"Carl, Buster Wortman is recruiting everyone who was once loyal to you. Creeks and ditches are filling up with the bodies of anyone who doesn't join him. Folks are saying you're a has-been!"

Carl turned his head and stared at his wife. "A has-been?"

"Yes, Carl. A has-been."

Despite his nakedness, Carl leapt from the bed. "I want some of that custard pie." He wrapped himself in a robe. "Then, I'm goin' back to Fairfield to show folks that *I'm* the one who runs Little Egypt."

***

Earl drove Carl back to Fairfield. They traveled the long way, since Carl had taken to avoiding the road through Decatur where young Violet died.

When Carl traveled by automobile, he always sensed nine-year-old Violet's ghost sitting next to him. He thought that getting back to Pond Creek and his trucks, tractors, and favorite Army surplus Jeep might bring fewer such hauntings.

"Carl," Earl finally said when they passed Springfield, "you know that Black Charlie has been sellin' insurance policies to some of our contacts."

"What kind of contacts?"

"Mostly sawdust's that handle gambling and girls."

"What have you been doing about it?"

"Well, not much lately. I got shot, if you don't remember, and Bernie's been havin' his hands full keepin' the Chicago Outfit outta Peoria."

Carl bit his lip. He didn't want to return to running the rackets, but his pride prevented him from letting punks like Buster Wortman and Black Charlie Harris take over his operations.

His mood didn't improve a few moments later when Earl drove the Buick down the long lane to the Shelton farmhouse. The pasture that contained their blooded black angus cattle was empty.

"What the hell!" Carl slammed both his hands on the dash.

Their brother Dalta's two sons rushed out of the house as they were parking and getting out. Little Earl Shelton didn't think any gangland gunfight could be as bad as what he'd experienced in the war. After being wounded in Sicily, the troop transport he was on got torpedoed and sank. Little Earl was badly burned in the mad rush to get off the ship.

Still, he felt lucky compared to his brother. Little Carl had the misfortune to be on the U.S.S. Indianapolis when it was torpedoed and sunk on its way back from delivering the A-bomb to Guam.

Little Carl went into the water with eight-hundred-ninety crewmen and only a few rubber life rafts. Three days later, only three-hundred-sixteen survived the vicious shark attacks that came every night.

When they returned from the war, both he and Little Carl had started at the bottom of the gang. Dealing cards, pit-bossing crap games, and, if a guest was a big enough winner, beating up and rolling him before he got the money home.

"Who stole the beef?" Carl bellowed when he stood in front of his nephews.

"Not for sure," Little Carl said. "But I heard Charlie Harris just sold a truckful of angus on the hoof to the meat market."

"He sold our full-blooded registered cattle for hamburger?" Big Earl was every bit as incensed as his big brother.

"Some of Charlie's cousins actually handled the transaction," Little Earl said.

The next night, the young Shelton nephews and Ray Walker sat at the bar in the Farmer's Club tavern in Fairfield.

Virgil Vaughn whispered sweet nothings to Eleanor Hopkins. Little Earl had always favored the young beauty for himself. This occasion offered the opportunity to kill two birds with one stone. He hated Virgil Vaughn—not just because he was Charlie Harris' nephew, but because they had been rivals all through school.

"You know they said Virgil helped Charlie rustle them angus last month," Little Earl told his brother and Ray as they munched pork rinds washed down with beers.

"Do tell." Little Carl was looking for a fight. He blamed himself for the loss of the cattle, since he'd been asleep in the house the night they disappeared.

"Don't do nothin' here," Ray Walker warned the two. "Wait until he leaves. I happen to know he's working at the winery tonight. There's a good-sized lot he'll be parking in."

Later that night, after the three gave Virgil Vaughn a good beating, Little Earl returned to the Farmer's Club and bought Eleanor Hopkins a drink. A month later, they were married.

11

The day Little Earl bought his new Buick Roadster was one of the happiest of his life. Finally, he and his wife Eleanor had moved up in the world with their own house and now a brand-new car to replace the old second-hand flivver his Uncle Carl had given him.

As he pulled into the driveway, Eleanor ran to the screen door. "Let me grab my jacket!" she squealed.

Little Earl took the moment to proudly run his hands over the big steering wheel. All the instruments on the dashboard made him feel like an airplane pilot. He gave the metal half circle that was the car horn a few short, lively taps to let his wife know he was anxious to take a spin in the marvelous machine.

So engrossed was he in enjoying the moment, he was barely aware of the automobile that pulled up behind him, followed by the squeak of a car door opening.

"You shouldn't have beat up my nephew," a voice said.

When Little Earl glanced to his left, he peered into the sinister gold-toothed smile of Black Charlie Harris. A two-second jam from the Thompson machine gun gave Little Earl just enough time to fall flat onto his back on the floorboard. Most of the first hail of bullets failed to penetrate the driver's side door, but those that did, along with a few ricochets off the dashboard, lodged in Little Earl's lower extremities.

When the twenty-round magazine in the weapon ran dry, Charlie pulled his revolver and shot as he laughed and danced around the car, firing through the windows. The mobster's second weapon clicked empty. Little Earl heard Eleanor's screams. He raised his head to see her rushing Black Charlie with a skillet raised above her head. A moment later the assassin was back in his flivver and motoring slowly away.

***

"I counted twenty-one bullet holes in Little Earl's brand-new car," Bernie announced to his brothers that evening. "Boy, is he gonna be pissed."

"That's fine, Bernie." Carl shook his head. "Did you bother counting how many holes were in Little Earl?"

"Well . . . ." Bernie missed the sarcasm. "The doctor said nine, but I figure some were in and out holes. Besides, they were all in his legs and the cheeks of his ass, so nothin' serious."

"This is a fine time for brother Roy to be comin' home, ain't it?" Earl lamented.

"Roy can handle hisself," Bernie said. "Besides, he's never ran with us. Why would they want him?"

12

When Carl picked up his brother at the train station, his first impression was that Roy seemed gaunter than ever. With half his adult life spent in prison, the most troubled of the Shelton brothers seemed incapable of doing much more than shake hands and look at Carl as if he were a stranger. He silently followed his sibling to the automobile.

Roy hadn't been in Fairfield much during his adult years. Prison had been his home. It worried him that he missed it. He just sat and silently stared at his old neighborhood as Carl drove them through town.

"People been dying awful regular these past years, Roy," Carl said to make conversation. He wanted to warn his brother to be careful, but didn't know how to phrase it.

Words often eluded Roy, as if they got lost somewhere between the speaker's mouth and his own ears. He didn't remark on the morbid comment. Rather, he continued his silent gaze at the community where so much of life had passed him by during his absence.

He would never want to admit it to anyone, but he'd been playing a game in his head for years. When he was reminded of a significant event that had happened during his youth, he imagined what it would be like to go back in time to that moment and live it all over again. He'd even taken to ranking the fantasies from one to ten. It seemed that almost all of them centered around the age he was fourteen, the year he committed his first crime.

Arriving at his parents' house for his reunion with his family was the most awkward moment in his life. Though there was genuine jubilation, no one seemed to know what to say. Ma Shelton, Hazel, and Stella mostly cried. Bernie and Lula made crude jokes about prison life. Carl and Earl just stared at him as if seeing him for the first time. Most of the stories they managed to conjure up that evening had occurred during the years of Roy's absence, reminding him of the things he'd missed during his eighteen years in prison.

Watching his son grow up was one of them. The boy shook his hand and forced a smile. Roy struggled to remember his name, calling him Bernie most of the time. That night, he and Stella just lay on their backs in the bed looking at the ceiling.

The next morning was better. He snuck out of the house before sunup, hitched a plow onto the tractor, and headed for the same south forty where he'd found Earl plowing so many years before. It had been the day he got out of prison the first time.

As he came up on Pond Creek road, Roy stopped the tractor beside the grove where he and a girl named Sally had picnicked when they were in grade school. Somehow, he thought he recognized the scent of her skin amid the fragrance of freshly plowed fields and budding trees.

For lack of practice, he grinded the gears a little as he started back up and guided the tractor through the culvert and into the field. He plowed three slow and leisurely rounds. A cool fall breeze combined with a cloudy day caused his eyelids to grow heavy. This was his first content moment in many years.

The first bullet passed so quickly through his shoulder and out his back, Roy barely noticed. Two seconds later, two of his ribs were shattered with enough impact to lift his body off the tractor seat. He was puzzled to find himself sitting straight up in a freshly plowed groove of dirt, his legs sprawled in front of him. The tractor didn't seem to notice his absence, plowing forward in the wide circle he'd set as its course.

Roy glanced into the gray sky, thinking that perhaps lightning had struck him. He'd heard of such things, though no one he'd known had ever been lightning struck.

When a third bullet slammed into his chest and knocked him onto his back, he recognized two realities at once. He was being shot *and* he was going to die. He barely managed to get his head turned toward the trees.

A short, well-dressed man emerged, carrying a rifle.

An almost electric pain swept from Roy's toes to his neck. There was a moment of satisfaction in knowing the physical pain—as well as all other problems—would be gone in just a few moments.

The fact the assassin didn't simply finish him off from the cover of the trees made Roy think the man might want to make sure his last shot was quick and merciful. Then he saw that it was Black Charlie Harris coming toward him. Roy heard himself whimper, so he clenched his teeth, closed his eyes, and tried to relax the back of his head into the dirt. For just a moment, he reveled in the smell of fertile soil from the plowing.

Feeling the presence of Charlie next to him, he opened his eyes and looked up at the famous killer. Charlie was watching the tractor pull the plow, which was still chugging its wide circle around the field. Roy had meant to grease the steering, a mistake he now regretted very much as he realized the assassin's intent.

Charlie squatted, using the stock of his .351 caliber Winchester automatic rifle in the dirt as a balance. Roy wished the man would lean his head over the barrel. If Charlie did, maybe he could make a final lunge and pull the trigger that was only three feet away.

The opportunity came and went. The sound of the tractor was getting louder. It had made the final half of the wide circle and was heading for the two men. Charlie rose, grabbed his victim's ankles and dragged him a few feet into the unplowed area.

That was when Roy realized he was paralyzed. He wouldn't have been able to reach for the rifle trigger anyway. The comprehension was almost a relief. That left one less regret for him to reflect on in his final moments.

The tractor was close now. He wished he could turn his body just a little to make certain that one of the massive tires finished him so he wouldn't get chewed to pieces by the angry steel blades of the plow. Any hope of the tires giving him a merciful death were erased when Charlie again grabbed his ankles and pulled him another foot across the ground.

The big machine was so close now, Roy could feel the ground shake under his head. He saw Charlie smile and squat again a few feet away. The killer pulled a cigarette from his breast pocket and lit it. The doomed man shut his eyes and braced himself. Then the machine's engine sputtered---and stopped.

Roy opened his eyes.

Charlie's smile turned to a frown.

But hope only lasted for a fleeting sixty seconds for the troubled Shelton brother. During that time, Black Charlie walked to the tractor, adjusted its choke and throttle, gave the crank on the front a hard, quarter spin, then flipped the gear shift forward.

Out of the corner of his eye, Roy caught a glimpse of Charlie jumping backwards, then he sensed the two smaller front tires crush his chest into the ground. Blood came up through his throat and out his mouth. Though he felt nothing, he knew his feet were next, being smashed by one of the big tires. At the same time, Roy felt the other big tire brushing past the top of his head.

If the blades that tore into his body brought a geyser of blood, Roy didn't know. But somehow, his head and thoughts survived the plowing. The rest of his body was a gnarled mess. The last thing he ever saw on Earth were the insane eyes and evil gold-toothed smile of Charlie Harris just inches from his face. Then he was no more.

***

Roy was laid to rest next to his father in the Fairfield Cemetery.

"Goodbye, Roy!" Ma Shelton said.

13

Bernie was mad! It was one thing for his brother Roy to get shot, but for him to be ground up into dog meat was a downright embarrassment.

A week later, he overheard a Navy vet in a Peoria bar laughing and describing Roy's murder. Bernie went off on him. The vet held his own for a half-dozen blows and even got in a few of his own. Then Ray Walker showed up, and the two gangsters were able to quickly pummel the man. They might have killed him if the police hadn't arrived and arrested them both.

"Why you slobber-knockered the teeth right outta that fella!" Ray told Bernie for the umpteenth time.

Carrie bailed them out of jail later that night. When they were far enough away from the police station, Carrie swung what would have been a blistering slobber-knocker of her own, had Bernie not been expecting it and ducked.

"The bastard was badmouthing my murdered brother, Carrie! What did you expect me to do?"

"Well, you coulda sucker-punched him. At least then you wouldn't have needed Ray's help. I could afford bail for you, but for both of you I had to go borrow money."

"What's so bad about that? We got money in the bank."

"It's Memorial Day, you buffoon. The banks are closed."

Bernie brooded the rest of the way home. Matters got even worse when he saw one of his henchmen standing on his porch smoking. The man was supposed to be in Springfield making the monthly payoff to government officials.

"Not good," the man said. "Adlai Stevenson has decided he's too good to take our money."

"He wasn't too good these past few months since he took office." Bernie slammed his fist into the porch column. "What changed?"

"I heard he wants to run for President."

That was the last thing Bernie wanted to hear. He already had the national crime syndicate breathing down his throat. Then there was Black Charlie Harris stalking around looking for his next Shelton to kill.

"What you fixin' to do about it, boss?"

"I'm fixin' to get ring-tailed drunk," Bernie said on his way inside. "I don't trust my own judgment when I'm sober."

***

Black Charlie was disappointed. He wanted to try out his new machine gun on a tripod. Finding out that Bernie was traveling to Iowa to sell a palomino pony seemed like the perfect scenario for using the big gun for the ambush. He sat on the hill in the thick brush until mid-afternoon waiting. Finally, so that his effort was not totally wasted, he unloaded a round into a family of coyotes that had gotten too used to leisurely crossing the nearly abandoned country road.

To make the day even worse, he burned his hand on the hot barrel because he was in too big a hurry to load it back in his pickup before it cooled.

Over the next three days, he cussed Bernie Shelton each time he lanced and peeled the blister on his palm. In typical Shelton fashion, Bernie had let it be known he would take one route to Iowa, then at the last minute took the longest and most unlikely roads to get there. Such caution was the reason Charlie's former childhood friends had lived as long as they had. Still, it was vexing to lose such a good opportunity to kill someone with his new machine gun and tripod.

Then one day when Charlie least expected it, he found the opportunity that only came once in a great while. Bernie turned a corner in front of him at a stop sign, obviously on his way to his Parkway Tavern in Peoria.

Charlie followed a few blocks at a safe distance, then turned up a hill into a cemetery that overlooked the tavern. Exiting the car, Charlie opened his trunk and retrieved his .351 caliber Winchester automatic rifle. He was dressed in a fine three-piece suit and tie, appropriate for a mourner in a cemetery on a Monday afternoon.

Sliding more than walking down the side of the hill, Charlie watched Bernie sit in his Ford in the empty parking lot, probably listening to the previous day's baseball scores. By the time he turned off his car and exited the vehicle, Charlie was set up behind some shrubs, his Winchester propped in the nook of two tree branches.

His target had taken only two steps toward the back door of the tavern when Charlie put a well-placed bullet right between his shoulder blades—a sure if not instantaneous kill. Since there was no one at the scene, Charlie decided to enjoy his success. He walked down and stood over Bernie.

"I always wanted to ask you," Bernie gasped when Charlie was over him. "I knocked out that one eyetooth when we was kids. Who knocked out the other?"

"No one. I had the dentist do it 'cause I like the way it looks, being gold and all."

"Well, I'd 'spect you've done for me." Struggling for a breath, Bernie rolled to his side, spit a mouthful of blood, and attempted to stand. "I think I'll have a final drink before I go."

"You'll never make it inside."

"I might fool you," Bernie panted. A gush of blood from the exit wound on his chest turned his shirt crimson. "Bet you fifty I make it."

"I got a hundred says you'll never even make it to the door. You're bleedin' out."

Bernie crawled.

"You're a lot talkier than your brother Roy was." Charlie squatted and watched the trail of blood behind his victim. It reminded him of slug slime.

"Well," Bernie grunted, his voice growing weaker. "I'd 'spect he lost some of his sand, bein' in prison most of his life."

A moment later, Bernie reached the door. He stretched up, grabbed the knob, and tried to pull himself up.

His heart stopped.

Charlie removed a hundred-dollar bill from his trousers, placed it in Bernie's breast pocket, then turned and walked back up the hill to his car.

14

"If some night club operator wants to give me a present because he likes the color of my eyes, well, why shouldn't he?"

"Because you're the Peoria County Sheriff!" one of the dozen newspaper reporters yelled at the back of the lawman as he entered the courthouse.

"What the hell is wrong with these people?" the sheriff asked no one in particular after he escaped the journalists' screaming questions. The main foyer was filled with deputies, FBI agents, and state policemen.

His fellow lawmen knew better than respond, but Mayor Triebel didn't. "This town and this country are sick and tired of the graft and corruption of their government officials. I should think you'd see that by now."

"But it was only a Shelton that got killed."

"Yes, and probably by the Chicago Outfit." Triebel was at his wits end. "Keeping the mob out of Peoria should be your number one priority."

"Bernie kept the mob out," the sheriff grumbled.

"So, with him gone, you're going to have to start *earning* your money," Triebel spoke slowly so every lawman in the foyer heard him. "And I don't mean the cash you get paid for looking the other way."

***

"Who did it?" Ma Shelton demanded as she rode in Earl's car to the cemetery. "Was it that same dirty dog that killed Roy?"

Earl was half out of his head from the drugs he was still taking for his own wounds. "I talked my head off to the state's attorney and even the governor, but what's the use? We'll get no protection from the law."

"Don't do anything rash, Earl," Ma said. "I can't bear to lose another child."

"I fear it's too late for your warnin', Ma. I was so mad when I saw Bernie's body, I squealed on everyone."

The Fairfield Cemetery was filling up with Sheltons faster than Ma Shelton wanted. Besides the family and friends attending the burial, the grounds were filled with hundreds of curious spectators, as well as dozens of reporters. The clicking sound of photographers snapping pictures didn't even slow during the Methodist minister's eulogy and prayer.

Carrie, slump shouldered and silent, stood between Lula and Hazel. When the service was finished Carl and Earl held their mother's elbow as she placed her hand on her youngest son's coffin then bent down to kiss it.

"Goodbye, Bernie."

***

Little Earl woke up happy on the worst day of his life. The drugs he was taking for pain had one added advantage—they gave him the wildest dreams he'd ever had. Most of them were just strange, but the one that night had been prompted by news that a wave of morality was sweeping through Illinois. His Uncle Bernie's murder was the beginning of an epidemic of underworld assassinations as rival gangs battled for control of Peoria and its surrounding towns. Irate citizens had had enough. They were demanding that politicians and law enforcement end the violence.

In Little Earl's dream, he'd given up the rackets and gone legit. He and Eleanor lived in a big mansion, only Eleanor didn't look like Eleanor. She had the face and body of a model he'd become so obsessed with he'd bought a half-dozen magazines she was in and hid her pictures all over the farm. In his dream, he could feel the curves of Bettie

Page's body but was still able to enjoy Eleanor's fine cooking.

"Wake up, Little Earl," Bettie/Eleanor whispered in his ear. "I hear Big Earl downstairs hollerin' to you that it's time to go fishing."

The sun wasn't fully up twenty minutes later as the uncle and nephew Earls rode the Army surplus Jeep along Pond Creek road, but it was a warm morning. The half-dozen fishing poles tied down to the rear roll bar rattled each time Little Earl drove over a rough spot in the road, a common occurrence that had his uncle firmly grasping the front roll bar.

Little Earl liked to sing, a fact that irritated his uncle to no end. Still, on such a happy and beautiful morning, he risked being chastised.

You get a line, I'll get a pole, honey
You get a line, I'll get a pole, babe
You get a line, I'll get a pole
We'll go down to the crawdad hole
Honey, baby, mine

Big Earl's right hand that was grasping the roll bar jerked downward and toward his nephew. At the same time, the Jeep bounced hard on a pothole, causing the older man to nearly tumble out of the vehicle.

Little Earl thought he was in for it until he saw blood staining his uncle's forearm.

"I've been shot!" Big Earl shouted. "Keep driving."

They were about to cross the hard road, so Little Earl accelerated, then jerked the steering wheel and skidded the Jeep sideways in the direction of Herrin.

When he got his uncle admitted into the hospital, he immediately telephoned his friend Delos Wylie and woke him out of bed.

"Big Earl's been shot again. Phone Ray and get over to the Herrin hospital as fast as you can. Bring all the backup you can."

When Delos pulled up in front of the hospital five minutes later, he was alone. His revolver in hand, Little Earl rushed out from the door of the emergency room and jumped into the flivver.

"Ray and a half dozen boys will be here in a minute." Delos handed his friend a cigarette.

The two had just lit up when the car they were sitting in also lit up, except with bullets penetrating and ricocheting throughout the car. Little Earl used the same strategy that had kept him alive during the last ambush and fell down on the floorboard.

Delos used his own tactic. He opened the car door and ran for the hospital. Adrenalin kept his legs moving, but the dance he did as a half dozen bullets hit his body made him look like a puppet in a marionette.

At least, that's what Black Charlie thought as he emptied the clip on his gat and then slipped away into a back alley.

***

An hour later, Big Earl was released from the hospital, his arm in a sling. They gave Delos the same room Big Earl had been in. He was expected to survive.

"The bullet passed right through Big Earl's arm," Ray Walker told the four men standing in the lobby.

"How many bullet holes that make you now, Uncle Earl?" Little Earl joked nervously.

"I count an even half dozen, if you count those that went in and back out," Big Earl said. He kept his shaking hands in his lap. Making light of the dire situation was a way to hide fear.

"I'm not sure it's within the rules to count the same bullet twice, Uncle Earl," Little Earl pondered.

"Well," Ray said, "why don't you go check the Marquess of Canterbury rule book and let us know."

"I've heard of the Marquess of Queensberry Rules on bare knuckle fighting," Little Earl said, "but never that Canterbury fella. Wasn't he a ghost or something?"

"Let's rendezvous at Hill Top farm," Big Earl told the men. The conversation was getting forced and ridiculous. "We've got some revenge plannin' to do."

Ten minutes later, cigarettes drooped straight down from the gangsters' mouths toward the ground. The sedan had just come over Hill Top Ridge when they spotted the smoldering ashes of the Sheltons' biggest horse stables. Several men holding Tommy guns were watching the last of the flames eat away at lumber and horse flesh.

Eleanor ran into her husband's arms. "Black Charlie was one of the ones did it," she said. "He stood back there by his car, laughing. He even tipped his hat at me as he got in and drove away."

Three bodyguards escorted Little Earl and his wife home that evening. Eleanor went straight for the kitchen to make coffee. Her husband watched and tried to again envision her with Bettie Page's body. He couldn't.

"We'll have men on each side of the house all night," one of the guards told the couple. He was just a scared-looking youngster.

Little Earl nodded. He went upstairs, got dressed in his pajamas, and was lying on the bed when Eleanor came up.

"I gave the boys the coffee pot," Eleanor said. She snuggled next to her husband.

Little Earl didn't care at that moment that his wife didn't have Bettie Page's body. He was almost asleep when he heard glass break. Eleanor jumped up, sat on the side of the bed, and was calling the sheriff when her husband got to the top step. Flipping the light switch on, he looked down the stairwell. A sealed tin lying on the next-to-last step rolled slowly toward the edge.

He dove back into the bedroom just as the can fell. The explosion of nitroglycerine blasted Little Earl into the air. When he landed next to his wife, he looked back. The entire front side of the house was missing. The young man assigned to guard them stood at the end of the driveway with his mouth open.

Eleanor was the first to get up. She took her husband's hand, pulling him to his feet. Flames danced all around them, but the ones where the wall was missing burned from the first floor up.

"Jump through the flames and we'll land in the bushes!" Eleanor screamed.

"But I can't jump with my bum leg," Little Earl replied.

The last thing he felt on the worst day of his life was his wife behind him, pushing him into the bushes below. When he awoke the next day, he was in the same hospital bed he'd been in after being shot by Black Charlie, his Bettie Page wife named Eleanor gently stroking his bandaged forehead.

15

Eunice Hendricks was determined to live until her ninety-first birthday, which was in two months. For that reason, she ate nothing but fruits and vegetables, and exercised by walking to the end of the block and back every day. Her goal was to outlive her sister, Ima, who had died two years ago. Ima died just one day before her ninety-first birthday.

Outliving her older sister was important. All their lives, Ima had rubbed victories in Eunice's face. The eldest sister had ten children, thirty-six grandchildren, and twelve great-grandchildren, compared to Eunice's piddly three children, four grandchildren, and one great-grandchild. Ima's house was bigger with hot and cold running water in both the kitchen and bathroom. She had more horses and then a motor car, although neither of the sisters ever learned to drive.

That day, Eunice carried a paper sack full of groceries on her walk back from the Fairfield general store. She felt something wet on her hand. The bottom of the sack was soaked. When she held it up to look at it, the entire contents of the sack fell through and scattered across the sidewalk.

Eunice was so upset she started crying. She tried to kneel to pick up some of the produce, but her trick knee gave out. She began falling and would have hit the pavement face first, had not a strong arm wrapped itself around her midsection and brought her back into a standing position. She looked up into the friendly, smiling face of a handsome gentleman with two gold teeth.

"May I be of assistance, kind lady?" Black Charlie Harris asked.

To be spoken to in such a gallant manner made Eunice feel she were a young girl again. She, of course, remembered Charlie Harris, the bright young child who had played hopscotch with his friends on the sidewalk outside her house.

This day, though, Mr. Harris walked with a limp. His long overcoat trailing down to his ankles seemed a little unusual to Eunice since it was a mild fall day. Never-the-less, she was grateful to have him pick up her groceries and carry them to her doorstep. When she opened the front door, he nodded for her to enter first. She'd rarely met such a gentleman in the crude little town. He set her groceries gently on the table inside her door, then, with a tip of his hat, returned to the street.

Eunice stood for a moment in the open door admiring the way Mr. Harris was so immaculately dressed. She felt so sorry to see a man only in his middle years limping. He held his hand against his bulky overcoat. Perhaps it was arthritis in his hip that was giving him such great pain.

When he reached the road, Lula and Guy Pennington stepped out of the hardware store across the street. Eunice had always liked the youngest of the Shelton children. When she saw Lula look up and recognize Mr. Harris, Eunice thought, *how nice, they are probably friends since her older brothers are about Mr. Harris's age.*

Then Black Charlie Harris pulled a Thompson machine gun from beneath his topcoat and bloodied the Pennington couple with bullets.

***

Lula knew they were in trouble the minute she saw Black Charlie wearing a top coat in the middle of the afternoon. What surprised her even more was that she was still standing after being hit by several bullets. If the breath had not for some reason been knocked out of her, she might not have even dropped slowly to her knees.

People on the street were screaming and running. Her husband lay on the ground groaning. Black Charlie cussed as he walked across the road toward them, trying to clear a jam in his gat.

Lula moved more quickly than she imagined possible, leaving a trail of blood as she crawled toward the only cover nearby, a yard full of tall prairie grass. She looked back. Charlie dropped his big gun and pulled a revolver from beneath his sports coat. He aimed it right at her head. But the gun didn't even click when he pulled the trigger.

"It must be your lucky day, Lula." Black Charlie sneered. He turned and walked back across the street toward his car. As he passed Guy, he gave him a hard kick in the ribs. Then the handsome, well-dressed gangster got into his flivver and drove slowly away.

"I saw the whole thing," shouted a man Lula knew. He ran toward the bloody sidewalk. "It was Black Charlie Harris shot them."

Lula never saw that man again. A day later he was shot dead and his body burnt along with his house. Other witnesses received phone calls or messages warning them to keep their mouths shut.

The Penningtons convalesced in the hospital for a week.

16

Edward Hillary O'Connor liked to be called "Big Hill" because he was bigger than his father, who was nicknamed "Little Hill." In grade school, he had to live down being called "Hillary," which was too much a woman's name. Luckily, he hit a growth spurt at an early age and got so big he was able to start bullying the other boys himself.

Big Hill liked working for the Sheltons because they had such nice farm equipment. He also thought it special that he was riding the tractor Roy Shelton had been on when he was killed. He was thinking about the killing as he spread cow manure on the same field where Roy had been shot.

The tractor had been spared because it wasn't parked in the Hill Top barn when it was burnt to the ground a few weeks before. He was glad, because he always imagined buying the machine one day to keep as a souvenir.

As he entered the clearing where Roy had been shot, he flipped the release on the manure spreader. An iron axle with big chains connected to it began whipping around in a circle behind him, kicking the cow poop out of the trailer and into the field. Big Hill was careful to not look back, and he pulled his coat collar up over his head so when a clod of shit was flung in his direction his hair would be protected. Clean hair was important to a boy his age.

The first thing Big Hill thought about when he awoke hours later in the hospital was his hair. That was because his head hurt so bad, he immediately reached to his forehead and felt a bandage. The second thing he noticed was the smell of cigar smoke.

"Glad you're awake."

"What happened?" Big Hill said, then winced when the effort of making those words brought additional pain to his throbbing head.

"I shot you."

Big Hill turned his head to the side.

A well-dressed man sat in a chair, smoking. The man had his legs crossed in the elegant style of a movie star. He looked very handsome sitting there. Kind of like Cary Grant. Then he gave a gold-toothed smile. The man stood and leaned over the bed until his face was inches from the wounded boy. "We don't want the Sheltons to make any more money off their land," Black Charlie said. He put his hand on Big Hill's head, making him moan.

"My hair!" the boy screamed. The pain caused him to shut his eyes.

"You may need to change the part of your hair over to the other side," Black Charlie said.

When Big Hill awoke the next time, he knew right away he didn't ever want to see the Sheltons' tractor again.

***

That same afternoon, Ray Walker had Sheriff Hal Bradshaw shoved up against a wall in his own courthouse office.

"You'd better do as you're told or you and your entire family are dead," Ray bellowed. He was friends with Little Hill O'Connor and didn't like it that his son had been shot. The Sheltons could fend for themselves, but an innocent young boy being shot drove Roy over the edge.

"You and the Sheltons ain't givin' the orders in Little Egypt anymore," Buster Wortman said from the doorway.

His words were a shock to Ray, since no one had been in the office when he entered. There were a number of reporters in the hallway, though. One of the three thugs accompanying Buster slammed the door shut behind them.

"You gonna help us kill Black Charlie, Buster?" Ray asked. His blood was still boiling. The fact that he was alone in the room with an unscrupulous sheriff, Wortman, and three burly gunmen didn't diminish his anger.

"I suppose if I did kill Black Charlie," Wortman said, "I could recoup the twenty Gs I just paid him for knockin' off Roy and Bernie."

"You did it!" Ray lunged for the crime boss. The bodyguards easily stopped him. Ray was muscular, but not scrappy enough to overcome three men.

"Well," Wortman chuckled, "technically it was Greasy Thumb's money. But I was the middle man. Tell Carl and Earl if they don't sell out and get out of Little Egypt by the end of the year, the mob is gonna invade Wayne County and kill every Shelton and every gang member we can find."

Ray's face was a bloody and bruised mess an hour later when he reported to Carl's house. Pearl and Earline cleaned his facial cuts. Carl and Earl joined him. They put their elbows on the table, since Ma Shelton wasn't around. Each lowered his head into his hands.

For once, the Sheltons were miles away when the next explosion rocked Fairfield, but they heard it. Wobbly, Ray staggered to his feet and followed Carl and Earl out the kitchen door.

Hundreds of people stood in the streets of Fairfield when they arrived at the site where the Shelton's Farmer's Club roadhouse had once stood. It seemed that windows in every building on main street were shattered from the nitroglycerine explosion. Flames from the burning building reached toward the dark clouds, lighting the entire community and the faces of angry citizens. Faces that glared angrily at the last remnants of the Shelton gang.

17

"It's me Black Charlie wants next," Carl told Earl the next evening after dinner. "I'm going into town in the morning to make out my will."

"That's fine." Earl laughed. "Long as you leave everything to me."

"I'll bet you a thousand dollars you don't outlive me." Carl opened his wallet.

"You're on." Earl retrieved his money clip that was wadded like a head of cabbage and started counting. "I'm planning on making at least ninety."

"If anything happens, get Ma out of the state, Earl." Carl handed ten one hundred-dollar bills over to Lula to hold. "Get everybody out of state."

***

The next morning, Carl asked Ray Walker and Little Earl to follow him in a truck to the farm so he could leave his Army surplus Jeep. They would then take him in the truck back to town in time for his scheduled meeting with the lawyer to draw up his will.

Carl enjoyed driving his Jeep, especially on a beautiful fall day. The trees had just hit their peak of brilliant autumn colors. Since it was a warm morning, he left the top and the doors off the vehicle. Though he knew it would be filled with falling leaves by the time he arrived, he wanted to feel the morning sunshine on his face.

When he reached Pond Creek Road, he pulled his .44 caliber revolver from beneath his belt and set it on the passenger seat beside him. He felt safe in the wooded area he and his brothers had grown up in. They had explored those hills since they were young children. They had hunted many a squirrel, rabbit, turkey, coon, and deer in these back woods. He knew every path, tree, and creek.

As he came up on a bridge overlooking one of those creeks, he shifted into a lower gear in anticipation of a bump that caused many a stranger's speeding vehicle to slide sideways.

A bang like a backfire made him glance over his shoulder to see if the truck Ray was following him in might have had a tire blow. A second and third bang brought sharp pains to his shoulder and right side. Carl flung himself out of the Jeep and headfirst into the deep ditch. The Jeep, still in gear, careened past him and into a nearby tree. A half dozen more shots kicked up divots in the ground around him, and one bullet found his thigh just above his left knee.

For the first time in over twenty years, Carl did a full somersault so as to get to his vehicle. He found his pistol still in the car seat. When he grabbed for it, more bullets ricocheted off the dash. He returned two quick shots in the direction he thought the ambushers were hidden. For some reason, he was reminded of a similar ambush over ten years ago when the law finally caught up with the famous outlaws, Bonnie and Clyde.

Carl had two bodyguards, though he worried that since he'd not heard return fire from them, Ray and Little Earl might have been shot. Then again, they *were* both nearly invalids, Ray from his recent beating and Little Earl from Black Charlie's bullets. They may not be of much help. The thought of anymore of his friends and kin being killed got his dander up. He hopped on one foot; then he tried weight on his wounded leg. Finding it functional, he fired three rapid shots toward the thickets where bluish gun smoke rose, and charged across the road toward the hitmen.

A heavy thud on his chest told him he'd made a major error. With great effort, he dove back into the ditch feet first and rolled over on his back. Sunlight glared in his eyes. He felt his pistol poking into his back, but when he tried to reach for it, his arms refused to move.

"I got him square in the chest," a man shouted from the thicket.

Carl heard the rustling of footsteps running across the leaves, the slamming of at least three car doors, and an engine roaring to life. A moment later, the car sound faded into the distance.

***

That morning, Bea Riley had awoken excited. Her Uncle Charlie was driving her to St. Louis, where she would board a bus for her home in Phoenix, Arizona. She'd enjoyed her time with her Uncle Charlie, but his frequent and long absences from the house made for some lonely times. It would be good to get home.

As Uncle Charlie drove along Pond Creek Road, he rattled on about how proud he was of Bea for graduating high school that past spring in Phoenix. He'd given her two hundred dollars as a token of that pride.

Gunshots suddenly echoed from the woods. They weren't those of hunters or practice shots, but of a battle between multiple types of weapons.

"Get out and run toward that house up yonder," Charlie instructed Bea. He'd been coaching her for years on how to behave in this very situation. "Stay low through the bean field."

Bea darted out the door, glad the situation happened near a field that was being harvested late.

When she reached the house, she looked back. Uncle Charlie stopped the car near the Pond Creek bridge. When he got out, he was carrying his Thompson machine gun.

***

The first human Carl saw after being shot was the silhouette of a head against the morning sun. He hoped it would be Ray or Little Earl. The face appeared dark and fuzzy, but then two gold teeth caught a reflection and glittered.

"Don't shoot me no more, Charlie. It's me, Carl Shelton. You've kilt me enough."

"Ain't you gonna say what a beautiful world it is, Carl?"

Charlie emptied the twenty-round box-clip into Carl Shelton, then pulled his .45 caliber revolver and gave him one more bullet.

Bea sighed with relief when she saw her uncle driving his flivver toward the farmhouse she'd fled to. When she got in, she immediately asked him what all the shooting had been about.

"I was just givin' a twenty-one-gun salute to an old friend."

***

The attendance at Carl Shelton's funeral was even greater than at Bernie's. The difference was that Earl and Ray Walker had prepared better. They stationed dozens of gang members around the burial plot to keep reporters and curious onlookers away.

"Goodbye, Carl," Ma Shelton said. She dropped a handful of dirt on top of his casket in the grave.

"Ma," Lula, limping and with her arm in a sling, took her mother's hand as they left the graveside. "Why is it that you only say goodbye when some-one dies?"

"I don't want to show impartiality," Ma said. "The dead know what's in my heart."

After placing her mother in the backseat of the car, Lula limped over to Earl and handed him the ten one-hundred-dollar bills Carl had given her to hold.

"You just make sure--" Lula took a deep breath. With tears in her eyes, she patted her brother's chest. "You make sure that you reach ninety years old like you promised."

THE FINAL CHAPTER

The car radio played *The Death of Carl Shelton,* written by Earl Shelton and performed by Fairfield's Fred Henson.

No one in the automobile, except the driver, Dalta Shelton, heard or paid attention to the song. He only half heard it, since it had been played on every radio station every thirty minutes since they left Fairfield. In the front seat next to him sat Guy, his leg bandaged and propped atop Little Earl's legs. They were both sound asleep, as were Big Earl and Lula in the backseat, resting their heads on either of their mother's shoulders.

Ma Shelton's eyes, though, were wide open, staring straight ahead. Each white center line on the road seemed to mark a minute of her long life. In her mind, she imagined her five sons youthfully frolicking in the backyard, angels that, in her eyes, could do no wrong.

Just as a WELCOME TO FLORIDA sign appeared alongside the road, the two dogs riding in a cage tied to the car roof howled into the wind. To Agnes Shelton, they were singing a tribute to her three murdered sons.

EPILOGUE

To this day, many of the descendants of the Shelton family live in Jacksonville, Florida.

Earl Shelton died in 1986 at the age of ninety-six.

Black Charlie Harris was convicted in 1967 for the 1963 murder of a young woman he lusted for and her (even younger) lover. He was released in 1981 after a little more than 15 years in prison. He lived with his niece, Bea Riley, in Kansas, until his death in 1988, just shy of his 92nd birthday.

END

THE SHELTONS
from left to right:
Back row: Roy, Carl, Earl, Dalta, Bernie
Front row: Lula, Ben, Agnes, Hazel

CHRONOLGY OF EVENTS

The following are the true events that are covered in this novel although often reorganized for dramatic purposes.

1924

9/27 Sheltons attempted robbery Kincaid bank

Black Charlie in Yuma jail

1926

Detroit card game murders

Aug. Egan Rats and Dipisa in Detroit car battle

12/25 Johnny Reid murdered by Frankie Wright

Egan Rats shoot up Papa Leo's restaurant

Egan Rats slay two thugs, Dipisa offers for peace

1927

5/13 Charlie Harris enters Leavenworth Prison

8/29 Shelton's tried for Kincaid robbery

1928

Sheltons and Capone make deal for territory

3/28 Fred Burke and Detroit Massacre

4/19 Charlie Birger hanged Benton. Illinois

7/1 Burke and Winkler murder Frankie Yale

1929

2/14 St. Valentine's Day Massacre

6/20 Carl Panzram kills Leavenworth officer

8/1 Leavenworth food riot

1930

9/5 Carl Panzram's Leavenworth hanging

10/2 Tommy Hayes kills Cuckoos

10/19 Frank Nash escapes Leavenworth

12/1 Jerome Munie becomes St. Clair County sheriff

1931

Search for Jeanene Munie in church

Roy Shelton paroled from prison

Bernie meets Carrie Stevenson

Carrie's car wreck on ice covered bridge

2/2 Carl and Bernie kill three Cuckoo gang

12/11 Leavenworth 7 escape and gunfights

1932

Al Capone sent to Atlanta Prison

Earl arrested. gets prison for Florida rum running

Bernie saves fed agent from druggie

Carl in Danville jail and saves deputy.

Joe Schrader and Bill Miskell join Sheriff Munie

James Hickey killed: wife interrogated.

Invasion of Bernie's Happy Hollow dude ranch.

Carl's second wife, Margaret dies

Oliver Moore, union leader Tommy gunned

Bernie's gun battle on East St. Louis streets

1933

Schrader and Miskell hired to chase down Shelton's

Schrader and Miskell kill James Hickey

Schrader and Miskell raids on Shelton Roadhouses

1934

Wortman, Armes & Walker arrested

Carl marries Pearl Vaughn

Carrie tears up Sheriff Munie's jail

1935

Lula kidnaps own son, Jimmy Zuber

Roy Shelton back in prison

Carl arrested in the company of a Negro

1937

12/27 Charlie Harris released from Leavenworth

1940

Wortman and Armes released from prison

Carl tosses Black Charlie gun during fight

1941

Peoria crime boss asks Shelton's help

1943

11/16 – Carl accidently kills little girl with car

1944

Pa Shelton dies

Peoria Mayor Triebel pushes Carl into retiring

Wortman puts a hit on Shelton's

12/14 - Blackie Armes killed

1945

Bernie takes over as boss of Peoria

Wortman gang member killed by Bernie

1946

Frank Kramer killed while in his house

Joel Nyberg killed on golf course

Phillip Stumpf killed while driving

1947

10/23 Carl Shelton killed

1948

7/26 Bernie Shelton killed

1949

5/24 Earl Shelton survives being shot

9/9 Little Earl Shelton survives shots

1950

May Big Earl shot in the arm

6/5 Little Earl friend Delos Wylie shot

6/7 Roy Shelton killed

Dec. Big Earl's house bombed

Wortman's thugs protect Black Charlie.

Most all the Shelton lands get auctioned off

1951

6/6 Black Charlie shoots farmer and threatens

6/7 Big Earl's barn burnt to ground.

6/28 Lula& Guy Black Charlie shooting

Ray Walker threatens Sheriff Hal Bradshaw

LAST MONTHS – Every Shelton building burnt

1952

3/27 Earl pleads with Governor Stevenson

7/15 Sheltons FARMER'S CLUB blown up

Surviving Shelton's flee to Jacksonville, Florida

ABOUT THE AUTHOR

After retiring from a career as an educator, Kevin Corley turned to his love of writing as a way to retell the stories he had shared with history students in his classroom. He recognized that the coal mining communities of Illinois were center-stage in the development of unions in the first half of the 20th century. From the Virden and Pana massacres of 1898-99 to the migration of miners after the Cherry mine disaster of 1909, Christian County became the rallying place for unionization.

Teaching history to many of the descendants of the coal mine wars, Corley developed a bond with the working man, a bond that was strengthened in 1986 when he was selected to research, through oral history interviews, the men and women who lived through these powerful and often terrifying events. His research was used by the late Carl Oblinger to write his book, *Divided Kingdom*, which was published in 1991.

Bootlegger Heaven is Corley's fifth published novel and a sequel to *13 Steps for Charlie Birger*.

Corley retired to his hometown in Shelbyville, Illinois, in 2017. E-mail him at charliebirger@yahoo.com

Franklin County Historic Jail Museum

Styled in "Georgian Revival" and listed on the National Register as a rare surviving design of renowned architect Joseph W. Royer, the 1905 Franklin County Jail would most likely not have been preserved, if not for its historical significance as the site where the notorious gangster Charlie Birger dropped into history in 1928 as the last public hanging in Illinois.

In addition to having a spectacular collection of related weapons and artifacts relating to the Southern Illinois gang era, the museum explores the rich historical inventory of Franklin County Illinois. Displays feature Benton's Civil War Major General John A. Logan, Benton's historic 1963 "before he was fab" visit by Beatle George Harrison, as well as tributes to Benton native's actor John Malkovich and NBA basketball star Doug Collins. The museum is located at 209 West Main Street Benton, Illinois with hours Tuesday-Saturday 10:00am until 3:00pm. Call 618 435 5777 or visit our website at Historicjail.com

Other books by Kevin Corley:

Based on actual events from 1898-99 Pana, Illinois. Big Henry Stevens leads hundreds of African-American coal miners and their families from Alabama to Illinois. When they arrive, they find instead of good pay for honest work, they are strikebreakers crossing picket lines.

The incredible, violent story of central Illinois coal mining from 1898-1933 *Sixteen Tons* carries the reader down into the dark, dirty and dangerous coal mines of the early 1900s, as Italian immigrant Antonio Vacca and his sons encounter cave-ins and the deadly black damp deep below the earth's surface.

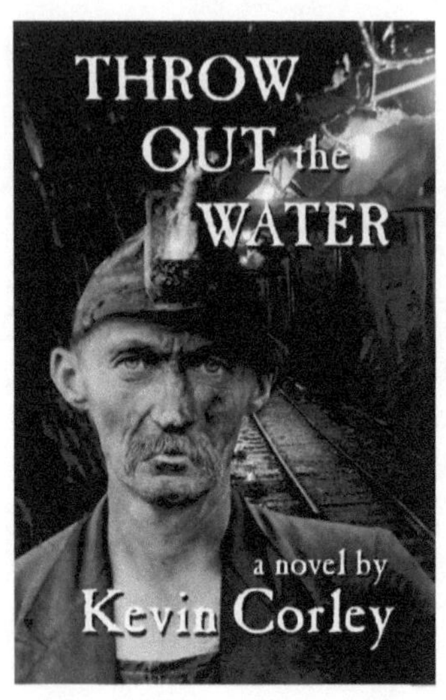

The exciting and highly anticipated sequel to Sixteen Tons. Throw Out the Water continues the saga of the Vacca, Eng, Harrison and Hiler families as they choose sides in the bloody Christian County Coal Mine War that that took place in Illinois from 1933 to 1937.

Before the Shelton brothers could build their crime empire, they first had to join Charlie Birger's gang to fight a violent and bloody war against Glenn Young and his three thousand Ku Klux Klan members.

Check out these books from IllinoisHistory.com

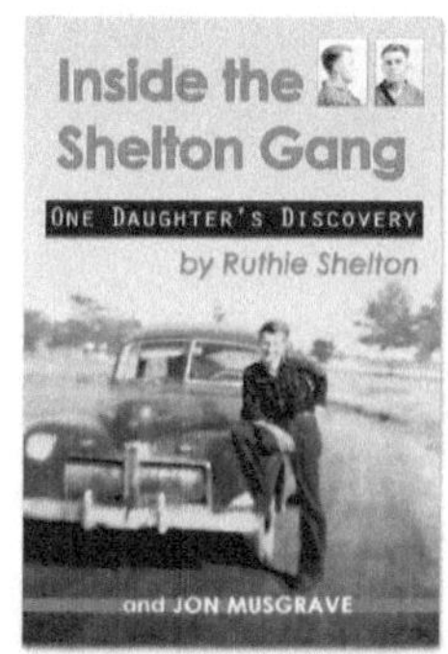
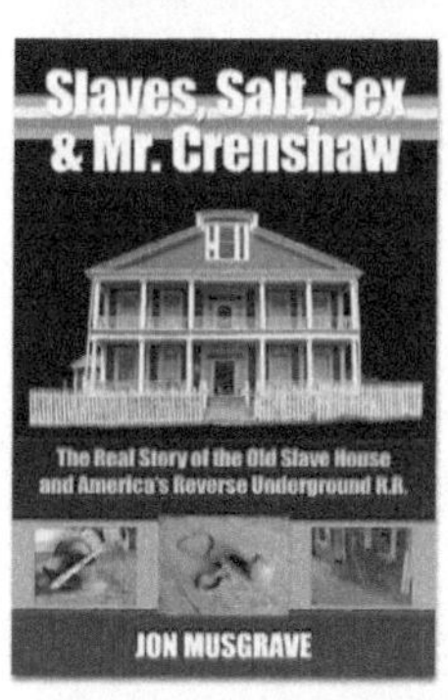

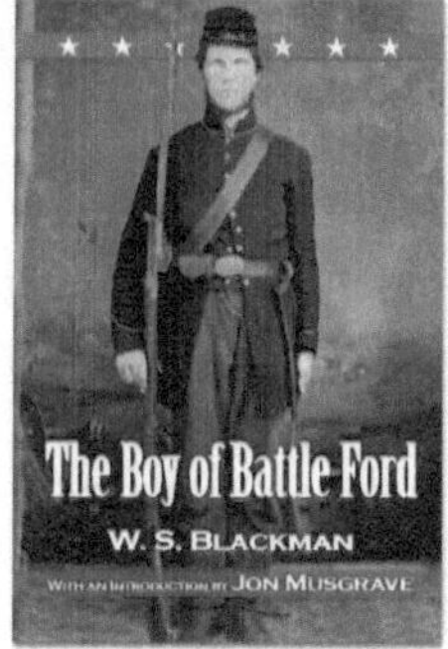

www.ingramcontent.com/pod-product-compliance
Lightning Source LLC
Chambersburg PA
CBHW030827110726
47900CB00006B/1782